LISA LOGAN

Delia was leaning forward, almost bending in two, only the top of her head showing. Going forward in a little rush, Lisa knelt down on the carpet, trying to face her.

'Mother? Where is he? He'd gone off to work when I went out. Has he had an accident or something?' She tried to grasp one of Delia's hands. 'Oh, please don't cry like that! Try to tell me. *Please!*'

Slowly raising her head, Delia looked upon her daughter. A feeling of blind rage roused her from the stupor she had wallowed in all that long, dark day. There was love and a desperate concern in Lisa's face, superimposed on a creeping fear.

But it wasn't for her. Oh, dear God, no, it wasn't for her mother. It was all for *him,* the way it had always been. The two of them, banded together, against her. And now she was able to wipe that look from Lisa's blindly trusting face for ever.

Lisa Logan

MARIE JOSEPH

ARROW BOOKS

For Daniel Stevenson

Arrow Books Limited
62-65 Chandos Place, London WC2N 4NW

An imprint of Century Hutchinson Limited

London Melbourne Sydney Auckland
Johannesburg and agencies throughout
the world

First published by Hutchinson 1984
Arrow edition 1985
Reprinted 1985, 1987, 1988 (twice) and 1989

Printed and bound in Great Britain by
Courier International Limited, Tiptree, Essex

ISBN 0 09 940710 8

Prologue

'I always loved you, but I love you this minute more than I have ever done before.'

Even in the midst of his genuine distress, Angus was fully aware that his words had a grand poetical ring about them.

Captain Angus James Logan, as straight and tall as in the days of his soldiering in France when he had passionately believed he was fighting a war to end all wars, stood by the bedside of his daughter Lisa. All he could see in the diffused light filtering from the landing was a tangle of dark hair on the pillow. It hid Lisa's face completely. A sob rose in Angus's throat. She had always slept like that, disappearing behind her long hair, drawing it round her like an extra sheet.

The enormity of what he was about to do filled him with a despair so profound he shuddered violently. A tear crept slowly down his cheek. Lifting a finger, he wiped it away.

Would she ever understand, this child of his heart? Might it not have been wiser, kinder, to have sat down with her and explained? Angus slowly shook his head from side to side, seeing, in his imagination, Lisa's huge grey-blue eyes fixed on his face as he stumbled through the words.

'There are times,' he might have said, 'when the only thing left for a man to do is to run away.'

He stiffened, as if to attention. Now the dramatic side of his nature, the frustrated actor in him, was taking over, setting the scene as if in a play. With Angus Logan taking the leading part. Naturally.

'You'll be well rid of me, my bonny wee lass. Aye, I mean what I say.'

5

The voice in his head deepened. 'I am like I am because of what happened to me out there in the mud at Ypres, nineteen years ago.' He raised a suffering face. 'Out there with my men, drowning in a sea of stinking filth, I was too much of a coward to run away. But now . . . ah, now. . . .'

Moving with the unsteady gait of a man who, in the course of a long evening, had drunk an amount of gin which would have left a lesser man prostrate, Angus walked over to a pink velvet chair and sat down.

In that year, 1935, Angus Logan was still suffering, like so many of his contemporaries, from a prolonged state of shell shock. He had endured four hellish years of trench warfare, been awarded a medal for outstanding bravery in the face of enemy action, and had returned home apparently unscathed.

The name of Captain Angus James Logan was not entered in any medical records. His nervous legacy took the form of a feverish pursuit of pleasure. Adrenalin still pulsed through his veins, but any sudden noise, such as a clap of thunder or a whoosh of a rocket on Bonfire Night, was enough to send his mind, if not his body, screaming for the safety of the nearest bolthole.

Now, on that dark night, with the winds from the Lanca-shire moors battering the trees, bending them into nebulous shapes, Angus sat very still in the darkened bedroom. Burying his face in his hands, he groaned softly.

His financial ruin had been slow but inevitable. The inher-ited wealth from his father and grandfather, thrifty Scottish ship owners, had been frittered away by his inept handling of financial affairs. On the Manchester Exchange he was known as a likeable rogue, a fool to himself, even by those who accepted his generosity. Now that he was finished, men he had always considered to be his friends watched him slyly, raising their glasses to each other as if gloating over his downfall. For the space of a few terrible minutes Angus Logan stopped play-acting and faced the truth.

And oh, dear God, the sensation was as if the earth had suddenly lost its speed, to whirl unfettered into infinity.

'Lisa . . . Lisa . . . I have no choice. Believe me.' The

whispered words were torn from his heart. 'There is no other way. Maybe some day you'll understand.'

His drooping shoulders were bone-thin, as angular as the rest of his tall frame. In his fuddled state his thoughts fought the gin, his fingers plucked at his knees like spiders scampering up a wall. His head jerked sideways in the direction of the closed door to his wife's bedroom. He pictured her asleep, her mouth slightly open, her face shiny from its application of Pond's cream, her hands in the white cotton gloves she wore to preserve her skin's whiteness. Delia had always taken the preservation of her looks very seriously.

Angus tightened his lips. It had been a long time since he found the nightly procedure amusing. . . .

'She doesn't need me, Lisa,' he whispered. 'Your mother hasn't needed me for a long time.'

His moustache quivered. 'Aye, and the truth is I've no' needed her, either.'

Angus stood up and walked slowly back to the bed. Stretching out a hand, he gently lifted a strand of his daughter's hair. It was much darker than the red-gold of the Logan hair, but in sunlight the auburn lights could be seen clearly.

Swaying where he stood, Angus swallowed the ache of tears in his throat. All at once he remembered Lisa running towards him across the sands in Brittany on their last year's holiday, her young breasts outlined in her wet woollen bathing costume. How beautiful she was. How beautiful she was going to be. . . .

The tears ran down his cheeks, into his military moustache, over his weak chin. His bonny lass would grow into womanhood, and he would not be there to see.

'Forgive me. If you can. And always remember me with love.'

The drama of the softly spoken words comforted him. As he backed slowly from the room he fancied he could hear them lingering like an echo, repeating and fading until they were no more.

Angus was still wearing what he had always called his penguin trappings, but a packed suitcase was down there in the hall, his raincoat folded over the top.

He buttoned the coat, taking his time. Then, without a backward glance, he turned the key in its lock and stepped into the wide black-and-white tiled vestibule. Closing the door behind him, he opened the heavy front door.

It was a night without stars, a night as cold and damp as if the sky itself was clouding the topmost branches of the tall trees. An exit like that called for a long slogging walk, with a man's head bent against the sighing wind and the driving rain.

But Angus had always managed somehow to suffer comfortably, ever since his four-year sojourn in France, so now he wrenched open the door of his car, a bull-nosed Morris, and slipped behind the wheel to switch on the ignition.

Captain Angus James Logan, late of the Scottish Highlanders, twice mentioned in dispatches for outstanding bravery in the face of enemy action, was running away at last.

PART ONE

One

In the previous summer of 1934 Hindenburg had died in Germany; a man called Hitler had become Führer of his people; and the Logans had sailed for Brittany on their annual holiday.

In the West End of London Noël Coward's *Conversation Piece* was playing to a packed audience, and errand boys pedalling down English country lanes were whistling a song called 'Smoke Gets in Your Eyes'.

The Logans lived pleasantly in a charming red-brick house called The Laurels on the outskirts of an East Lancashire cotton town, but on street corners the unemployed gathered, hands in pockets, and Woodbine stubs of cigarettes were passed from mouth to mouth.

Their houses, terraced and as uniform as strings of cheap beads, straggled up the steep streets without a touch of green anywhere to gladden the drabness or soothe the eyes of those who lived there.

In that year many of the men had been out of work for four years or more. The hardship of their hand-to-mouth existence showed in the grey resignation of lined faces and the slump of thin shoulders. There was a recognizable leaning in the way they walked, as if their faith in the brave new world promised to them after the war to end all wars had long since evaporated.

Clever boys and girls won scholarships to the grammar schools and their mothers went without food to provide blazers and decent shoes. Or, at times, sadly explained that the scholarship would have to be sacrificed.

But away from it all, totally impervious to the grinding

ache of poverty, families like the Logans took their middle-class status for granted.

Angus and his wife Delia kept up a hectic round of dinner parties, refused to see that the dizzy twenties had gone for ever, danced into the early hours on well-sprung dance floors, drove like maniacs round the lush Lancashire countryside, followed the cricket scores on the wireless, and took their annual holiday as a matter of course.

On a windswept beach in Brittany Lisa glanced down at the scooped-out neckline of her bathing costume.

Horrified, because *they* were showing, she pulled it up, tugging angrily at the sodden woollen material.

Angus saw her and sighed. Fourteen and a half was a terrible age to be, neither one thing nor the other, not child nor yet woman. Patting the sand around him into a more comfortable hollow, he groped in the pocket of his khaki shorts for matches, bent his head and struggled to get his pipe going.

'Where's Mother?' Lisa ran up to him, flopped down and snatched off her white rubber bathing cap. She shook her head, releasing two thick plaits. 'Don't tell me she's gone off round the headland again with Uncle Patrick? There's nothing there but rocks and little pools with slimy grey crabs in them. Honestly! You'd think they'd seen enough crabs to last them a lifetime.'

'You haven't enjoyed this holiday much, have you, love?' Angus, contented for the moment because his pipe was going nicely, teased her with his smile. He was rewarded by a look of scathing disgust.

'Why Uncle Patrick and his hateful son Jonathan had to come with us I don't know.' She hitched the front of her wet costume up again. 'I mean, it might not have been so bad if Jonathan's mother had come with us instead of her horrible son. It would have done her chest as much good here as in Switzerland. At least you could have talked to her whilst the other two went off crabbing or wasted hours trying to go brown.' She frowned, glancing sideways at her father. 'It's been beastly for you, too. I can tell that. I hope they don't jolly well want to come with us next year.'

'I've been OK, love.' Angus flipped a small pebble towards the sea. 'What about Jonathan? Didn't he feel like a swim before dinner?'

'Him?' Lisa snorted. 'He's just a great big show-off, if you must know. Well, of course he's a boy, so he's bound to be, isn't he? He's *juvenile* really.'

'At nearly nineteen? Not all that juvenile, surely?'

Liza gloomed at the horizon. 'All he wants to talk about is his car. It's a 3–litre Bentley, I'd have you know, dark green to match England's racing team. It has a Union Jack on the side and a leather strap round the bonnet. You'd think he was Malcolm Campbell to hear him talk.' She pulled one of her plaits round and chewed on it for a while. 'Jonathan Grey has always been conceited. That day we went to Lannion on the bus – you know, that cold day when he wore plus-fours – I told him he looked like Ronald Colman, and guess what? He believed me!'

'How do you know he believed you?'

'I could tell by the way he stroked his silly five-a-side moustache.'

Lisa's tone was lofty, but Angus sensed the overwhelming insecurity. He patted her knee. There were freckles marching like a battalion of ants across the bridge of her nose and over her cheekbones. Two weeks of sun and wind had tinged her fair skin to a pale milk-chocolate shade and brought out the auburn tints in her dark hair. Her expression was sullen, her short upper lip quivered with indignation. She looked at war with the world.

'I'll go up to the hotel now.' Leaping up quickly, she wrapped herself around in a voluminous towelling tent-like garment, tying the cord at the neck into a fierce double bow. 'Are you coming with me?'

'I'll stay and smoke my pipe out.' Angus turned back to the sea, his profile averted. Lisa stared at him for a moment, biting her lips. She slip-slapped her way over the sands in her yellow bathing shoes with the pink rubber flowers on the toes. The multi-coloured wrap clashed with the red and

13

green of her costume; she was all colour, but her thoughts
were as grey and brooding as the winter moors in her native
Lancashire.

This year's holiday had been truly awful. It was all the
fault of Uncle Patrick and his boring son, of course, and yet
somehow there was something else. Lisa shook her head.
Normally she was so proud of her father. He was always so
smartly dressed in his go-to-business suits, or his speckled
tweeds, but beachwear didn't show him off to advantage at
all.

He was quieter. Nothing like his normally ebullient self.
Lisa whispered the word aloud. Ebullient. Yes, it was the
right one for her father. His high spirits did have an aggres-
sive bullying force about them. She nodded.

Lisa liked words. To her they were as expressive as music.
For a moment she cheered up, remembering a picture she'd
seen just before they'd come away. Robert Donat in *The
Thirty Nine Steps*. He'd been magnificent. His husky voice
had thrilled her right to her marrow.

Leaving the beach, she began the long climb to the hotel.

Her father wasn't even trying to be pleasant. The August
sun had reddened his face to a bright lobster shade. His
nose was beginning to peel, not that he cared, Lisa was sure.
And what was worse, Uncle Patrick's face was a lovely shade
of walnut, not a sliver of hanging skin in sight. Lisa trudged
on, hating the sun for its unfair discrimination.

It was an awful thing to admit, even to herself, but
somehow her father had really let himself down these past
two weeks. For one thing, his shorts were too long, especially
for 'abroad'. The Frenchmen wore their shorts well above
their knees, and so did Uncle Patrick. Which went without
saying. Lisa gave an unladylike snort.

Her father looked much too British sitting on the beach
smoking his pipe and reading the *Financial Times* – a three
days' old *Financial Times* at that. She stopped for a moment
to catch her breath.

It was also a bit much him going to that crummy little
casino every night on his own. You couldn't even call it a
real casino. More of a gambling den really. Lisa nodded in

a smug puritanical way. The croupiers reminded her of Hollywood gangsters in their white shirts and black bow ties, with cigarettes stuck in their faces. No wonder her mother was reduced to having to put up with Uncle Patrick's company such a lot.

It wasn't as if Uncle Patrick was her real uncle, or that the hateful Jonathan was her real cousin. Lisa shuddered. At least she'd been spared that.

Monsieur Dubois, the proprietor of the small hotel perched on the cliff side overlooking the bay, was in his tiny office cubicle by the entrance to the black-and-white tiled reception area. A swarthy man with a bushy moustache which swamped his face, he looked up from his ledgers, nodding a smile at Lisa.

Answering the smile in an absent-minded fashion, she crossed the hall and ran up the wide staircase. The floors of the landing were highly waxed and her rubber shoes made no sound as she padded along to her room at the far end.

'Lisa! I thought you'd gone for a swim.'

The woman coming out of a bedroom – Uncle Patrick's bedroom – put a hand to her throat. 'You told me you were going for a swim.'

'I've been for one. The sea's too cold to stay in.' Lisa opened the door of her own room wide as her mother followed her inside.

Delia Logan's cat-like eyes had a wary look about them. Her face was flushed as if she too had just come in out of the sun. She moved over to Lisa's bed and sat down, her usual jerky movements stilled for a moment as she pondered what to say.

Delia Logan was so fashionably thin that her bones seemed to move skeletal-like beneath the folds of her dresses. Three times a year she suffered the indignity of having her raven-black hair strung up to an electric contraption in Lewis's beauty salon in Manchester. The result was that it clung to her head in corrugated waves, ending in three rows of tiny sausage curls. A slavish follower of fashion, she had discarded the twenties' pencil-slim silhouette, her long cigarette holder and her Eton-cropped hairstyle, long before any

15

of her contemporaries. Her calf-length dress on that late summer's day was in green marocain with a bib front of silk organdie.

She took a leather case from her purse and lit a Park Drive cigarette with a nervous flick of a gold lighter. 'I started my packing then found I'd lost the keys to my case.' Narrowing her eyes, she watched her daughter carefully. 'So I went into Uncle Patrick's room to see if he had one that fitted.'

'Oh, yes?' Lisa snatched up a toss of clothes from a chair and walked through the open archway into the bathroom, the set of her back daring her mother to follow.

Delia couldn't remember the last time she had seen her daughter's nude body. Lisa guarded any intrusion on her privacy with an almost fiendish determination. In Delia's present state of nerves the situation was both irritating and ridiculous; but all the same she stayed where she was.

'Uncle Patrick hasn't got any keys to his case so I needn't have bothered,' she called out.

'Oh?' Stepping out of the wet bathing costume, Lisa hurled it into the bath. She wished her mother would go away. It was a boring conversation anyway, and she'd left her knickers in the dressing-table drawer. Now she'd have to drape herself in a towel to go and fetch them. She jerked her chin up in a gesture of exasperation.

'Father's down on the beach, smoking his pipe. On his own,' she added, stepping round Delia's legs and clutching feverishly at the slipping towel.

Through a curl of smoke Delia narrowed her eyes. Had that last remark been merely an innocent criticism, or did Lisa suspect? With a bounce of her long plaits Lisa flounced back into the bathroom, leaving her mother puffing jerkily at the cigarette. Delia let out a breath on a sigh of relief. No, Lisa was just willing her mother to go, making it quite clear that in her daughter's bedroom she was an intruder.

Delia relaxed a little. All the same, it had been a stupid risk going to Patrick's room in the afternoon. She felt the heat rise to her face with the recollection of their love-making. The risk they had taken seemed to have added an

16

extra dimension to his passion. He had been like a man possessed, clinging, moaning, telling her she was the only reason he could tolerate his present existence.

What he really meant was that his invalid wife was too ill to be made love to. Sometimes, in the early hours, lying wide awake, Delia admitted this to herself. But now, sitting on Lisa's bed and smoking, she closed her eyes and felt again the smoothness of his back, tanned like her own to a satisfying copper shade.

'We must be mad,' he'd whispered, and she'd agreed. But oh, dear God, it was a madness worth every moment of heart-stopping fear. Loving someone the way she loved Patrick wasn't wrong. Love was never wicked. How could it be? Alice Grey had incurable TB. The doctors knew it and so did Patrick. He couldn't be expected to live his life like a monk, he wasn't made that way. And if it wasn't her then it would have been someone else.

Delia felt a stab of pain at the thought, then immediately blanked her mind against its implications.

'We're dressing up as it's the last night.'

Getting up from the bed, she stubbed out her cigarette in a round glass bowl on Lisa's dressing-table, hoping vaguely that it was an ashtray. She raised her voice. 'I wouldn't mention to your father that I lost my keys. They're bound to turn up, and you know how cross he gets when I lose things.'

In the tiny bathroom Lisa was buttoning herself into a liberty bodice. She knew that any day now she would have to bring up the subject of a brassière to her mother. Most of the girls in her form wore them, dividing their fronts into two. Lisa poked a covered button through its buttonhole, grateful that for the time being the bodice flattened her bosoms nicely into a shape far from rude.

'I won't tell him,' she promised. 'Do I *have* to wear my pink dress? It's a bit tight. Underneath the arms,' she added quickly.

The men wore their dark suits that evening. Jonathan Grey had slicked his black hair back with brilliantine. Lisa could smell violets whenever he inclined his head towards

17

her. The points of the collar on his white shirt were fastened beneath the knot of his tie with a narrow gold pin. His tiny sideburns reminded Lisa of smears of gas-tar imprinted with his thumb. Tonight he's decided he's Ivor Novello, she thought uncharitably, the pink dress making her mean-minded.

The first course was oysters, served in a huge blue bowl. Lisa watched Uncle Patrick's Adam's apple move beneath the skin of his neck as he swallowed. Catching her eye he winked, but she turned her head away. Not for anything would she have winked back. Not for all the tea in China, she told herself fiercely.

The French holidaymakers were eating as if every mouthful was to be their last. They gnawed at chicken legs, snapped off lobster legs with small silver pincers taken from their top pockets. Lisa didn't eat oysters, so was free to stare around her. The French children were drinking red wine, watered down for the youngest it was true, but drinking it all the same. Lisa glowered into her glass of still lemonade, unaware of the fact that Jonathan Grey was looking at her with an expression akin to distaste.

Usually, whenever he saw Lisa Logan, she wore school uniform, a gym slip with box pleats descending from a yoke, a white blouse and a tie striped in her school colours, navy and a paler blue. Her plaits stuck out from a hat shaped like a pudding basin, and her legs were encased in black woollen stockings. Now, sitting there in the pink dress with its large Peter Pan collar, she looked strangely top heavy.

'Did you go in the sea this afternoon?' he asked suddenly, feeling sorry for her without having any notion why.

Lisa turned startled eyes in his direction, and Jonathan blinked. Just for a fraction of a second he saw the promise of beauty in the small, oval face, the depths of the enormous grey-blue eyes. Give her a year or so, he thought compla-cently, and little Lisa Logan might be worth a second glance.

'I did go in, but only for a few minutes. Too cold.'

'Yes, the sea always is on this coastline,' Jonathan said, then gave up.

'Coming to the casino later?' Angus smiled at Jonathan

over the rim of his wine glass. 'Last jolly old night and everything. You never know, we could recover the cost of these past two weeks.' He turned to Jonathan's father. 'How about you, Patrick?'

'Might as well.'

Jonathan intercepted the swift interchange of glances between his father and Delia which seemed to say, 'Oh, God, what a sell! Still, we mustn't rock the boat too much.' Jonathan read their thoughts easily. How transparent they were. How boringly obvious. It was truly pathetic.

'I think I'll go for a stroll along the beach.' He raised his glass to Lisa in a mocking gesture. 'Care to come with me, *Miss* Logan?'

To his amusement Lisa blushed so scarlet that her freckles almost disappeared. 'Yes, please,' she said, without thinking, the blush deepening at such an idiotic reply.

'That leaves little me to amuse myself,' Delia said, pouting in a vivacious way.

The two men laughed. At what Jonathan didn't quite know.

When the long meal was over they excused themselves. Delia jumped up, obviously a bit miffed, Jonathan was pleased to see.

'I'll go up and finish my packing,' she said.

Lisa picked in a half-hearted way at a bunch of grapes in a basket. The black ones were juicy and sweet, but the green had a sharper taste. Leaning across the table, Jonathan filled her glass with the remains of the carafe of red wine.

'What the eye doesn't see,' he said heartily, and sighed. Already he was regretting his impulsive invitation. Lisa Logan was only a kid in spite of her sprouting chest. He bit morosely into a grape. The whole holiday had been a disaster from start to finish. He had only agreed to come because his mother had asked him to take her place.

'My mother is very ill,' he said suddenly.

Lisa looked acutely embarrassed. 'Do you think the doctors in Switzerland will be able to help?'

Jonathan took a cigarette from a slim silver case. 'Nope. I doubt it.'

'How awful.' Lisa took a grape, then put it straight back, feeling now was not the time to chew.

'She's like D. H. Lawrence. Her mind is burning up her body. She writes poetry. Unpublished, but very good.'

Lisa wished she could think of something to say that would be appropriate. She had read D. H. Lawrence, of course, and thought some of the passages in his books very rude. She coughed in a self-conscious way. 'Lawrence is a bit too consciously analytical for my taste,' she said, remembering having read that somewhere. She was rewarded by the sight of Jonathan's dark eyebrows ascending almost to his hair-line.

'Don't tell me you read him at school?'

'Not in the fourth form, but I read him in bed. I keep him underneath the mattress. Mother would have one of her pink fits.'

'I doubt it.' Jonathan's voice was starchy with contempt. 'Middle-aged people surprise one sometimes.' He got up from the table, the cigarette held loosely between his fingers. 'Shall we go then? If you want to go up for a cardigan I'll be waiting outside. OK?'

Walking self-consciously in order not to wiggle her bottom, Lisa preceded him out of the dining-room. Reaching the stairs, she bounded up, dignity already forgotten.

Jonathan went outside into the clear warm dusk. He sat down on a low stone wall, smoking and staring at the speckle of lights from the other hotels scattered at intervals round the wooded slopes overlooking the bay.

There were times, like now, when he wondered if he'd been right to chuck up his scholarship after only two terms? He'd enjoyed Oxford at first, but the pressures to be either a Marxist or a Fascist had irritated, then angered.

'All I ever wanted to do was to come into the business,' he had told his father. 'Maybe bum it for a while round Yugoslavia or Greece with a haversack, then come home and work my way up from the bottom. Lugging a hod of bricks up ladders might help me to forget some of those effete types I met at Oxford. Mass ideology isn't for me.'

Amazingly Patrick Grey had agreed at once. 'Oxford was

always more your mother's idea than mine. Lot of pansies at Oxford, anyroad.'

And yet there were times when Jonathan wondered if he hadn't been too hasty, too intolerant. Tonight was one of those times.

'Here I am.'

He looked round, startled for a moment, as if Lisa Logan was the last person on earth he expected to see. She had fastened a blue cardigan over the pink dress, with such obvious haste that there was a left-over piece at the bottom with a button doing nothing at the top. She had changed her shoes too, replacing her evening pumps with what looked like school sandals, flat brown monstrosities with T-bar straps.

Jonathan threw his cigarette away. Getting up from the wall, he thrust his hands deep into his pockets. 'Off we go, then,' he said morosely.

It was a warm night, filled with the scents of late summer, mingled with the tang of seaweed from the rocky headland at the far end of the small beach.

'Not much night life round here, apart from the bloody casino.' Jonathan swore because it suited his mood. 'Your father's lost a packet over the last two weeks.' He glanced sideways at the small girl trotting stolidly by his side. At least the ugly sandals meant he didn't have to monitor his stride. She too had pushed her hands deep into the pockets of the woollen cardigan, stretching it out of shape. There was a vulnerability about this girl which caught him unawares at times; as though for all her cheek – and she had plenty of that – Lisa Logan was in reality almost pathologically shy.

'What's your mother doing? Packing, like she said?'

Lisa shrugged her shoulders. 'I don't know. She went straight to her room. To look for her keys, I expect.' Slithering down the grassy slope leading to the beach, scorning the offer of a helping hand, Lisa turned her head. 'My father has a thing about locking cases. You'd think we had the Crown Jewels in them the way he goes on.' She took the last bit at a run, the two thick plaits swinging out then flopping back into place. 'Mother was so upset, she went into your father's room this afternoon to see if he had any keys that might fit. You've no idea how stroppy my father can get at times. He seems to be in a bad mood most of the time these days.'

Jonathan widened his eyes. 'How do you know your mother went in my old man's room? Did she tell you?'

'I saw her coming out.' Lisa's tone was faintly patronizing. 'I saw for myself how worried she was. My father makes big fusses about little things. I've *told* you. She almost burst into tears when she saw me.'

'I'll bet she did.' Jonathan mumbled the words to himself. He shook his head slowly from side to side. Surely Lisa must suspect something? Surely she had some inkling? Nobody could be that innocent, even at fourteen.

Over by the rocky headland the waves were lapping. The night was so still they lapped then receded silently, as smoothly as if they were of oil and not water. There were dark purple patches on the sea where seaweed moved blistered tentacles to and fro. There was no sound, nothing but the soft rhythmic lapping.

Sighing, Jonathan took off his jacket and laid it down on the sand. 'The sand'll brush off. Come on, Lisa. Sit down. We can rest our backs against this rock. We should have kept to the cliff road if we'd wanted a long walk.'

With an awkward, ungainly flop, Lisa sat down at the very edge of the silk-lined jacket. She hugged her knees up to her chin, first tucking her dress down carefully between her legs.

In case the sea saw her knickers, Jonathan guessed.

For a while they were silent, both of them staring straight ahead at the darkly blurred smudge of horizon. Once or twice Jonathan turned to look at her, and once, conscious of his gaze, Lisa smiled a wide touching smile.

'You don't have to talk to me. Just get on with your thinking. I'm OK.'

Jonathan took out a cigarette and lit it, holding the match in a cupped hand against a non-existent wind. He heard himself being pleasant, although in his present mood it went against the grain. 'Are you working towards university, Lisa?'

'I suppose so.'

Now that he was really listening to her for the first time, he realized her voice was husky and lower than he might have expected coming from such a small girl.

'But I don't want to teach,' she was saying. 'I'd be awful at it. I'm too bossy as it is.'

'What would you like to do?'

'Travel,' she said at once. 'If I was a boy I'd just take off. Riding a bike with a tent strapped on to the back.'

Jonathan hid a smile. 'Your parents would never allow that.'

'Gosh, no. They'd have a pink fit. Especially my mother. She's stricter with me than my father.'

Without warning a great weight of boredom settled itself on Jonathan's shoulders.

What the hell was he doing sitting with this strange little kid on a beach in Brittany in the dark? And, more to the point, what was his mother doing lying out on some sana-torium balcony in Switzerland, staring at the mountains? Spending two whole weeks on her own. He shifted his posi-tion on the jacket. Why hadn't his father gone with her? His mother had travelled with a nurse, but if you were ill it was a familiar face you wanted to see.

She was going to die, his mother. Not this year, maybe not next year, but her coming death was written on her face. Jonathan had seen it there. It was a kind of dignified loneliness, as if she was trying to tell you that she knew and couldn't bear hurting you with her knowing.

'Life can be pretty bloody for some people,' he said.

Lisa didn't know what to say, so to cover her shyness she said the wrong thing. 'Can it?'

'Oh, well. Not for you.' Jonathan refused to look at her. 'You think life's just a bed of roses, as they say. Don't you?'

'Now you're cross.' Complacently Lisa pulled one of her plaits round and began to chew the end. 'Why don't you go back to the hotel? I don't care. I can always tell when people are in moods.'

Jonathan stared at her placidly chewing the end of her plait. God, how insufferable she was! What on earth had ever made him think she was even remotely pretty? Exasperation rose thick in his throat.

'You're a little snob,' he said clearly. 'Paid for to the High School. A pony of your own in the paddock at the back of your house. Holidays abroad every year. Dancing and piano lessons. Don't you ever stop to think what it's like for some people?' Savagely he threw the cigarette stub into the sea. Why had he said all that? He didn't mean it, not really. He really was in a lousy foul mood.

'Are you a Bolshie?' Lisa sounded fascinated. 'Is that why you work on one of your father's building sites? Do you think I should leave school to work in a cotton mill? Standing at my looms in clogs and talking like Gracie Fields?'

'*You* standing at three looms?' Jonathan gave a short laugh. 'That would be the day.'

Lisa was in no way perturbed. She picked up a pebble and flicked it towards the sea. 'I suppose you don't realize what a hypocrite you are? My father talks to me sometimes about your sort of person.'

'Carry on.' Jonathan's voice was deceptively soft.

'Well . . . you *might* be working as a navvy at the moment, but you're not going to end up as a navvy, are you? Oh, no. What you're going to end up, Jonathan Grey, is as a director of your father's firm. But the men you are working with will still be heaving bricks and digging holes, won't they?' She nodded her head up and down twice, infuriating him. 'Then, of course, they'll respect you, because you were once one of the lads. "Mr Jonathan doesn't ask us to do owt he wouldn't do 'imself," they'll say.'

Before he could speak she smiled her strangely disarming smile. 'I love arguing, don't you? My father and I have jolly good arguments. I don't mind what you say to me, honestly.'

Her sudden sweetness was too much for Jonathan to take at that moment. Almost despairingly he pulled her towards him, bent his head and kissed her.

It was a hard, closed-lips kiss, utterly devoid of passion,

but the push Lisa gave him sent him sprawling backwards on to the sand.

For a split second he lay where he was, too surprised to move. The sand had got into his hair. It was stuck to the brilliantine he had used earlier in the evening. He didn't use much, just a bead in the palm of one hand rubbed into the other then smoothed over his hair. But now the blasted sand was sticking as if he'd used glue.

His temper flared so quickly he could actually feel the heat of it burning his face. Lisa was walking away, and if she'd been a boy he would have rushed after her, knocked her down and rubbed her own face in the wet sand.

She wasn't running, merely plodding along with her graceless tomboy slouch, her shoulders hunched as she trotted bumpily over the ridged beach. Jonathan closed his eyes and saw red.

As he caught her up, swinging his jacket over his arm, his cigarette case fell out of his pocket. The catch had needed mending for a long time, and as the case bounced against a rock it sprang open, spilling his cigarettes into a tiny pool. Jonathan swore.

Grabbing Lisa by the elbows, he swung her round to face him. 'What's wrong with you, for Pete's sake? Have you never been kissed before?'

'Not by a boy!' His anger was mirrored in her eyes. 'And not like that. Not on the lips!'

Jonathan stared at her in amazement. If she wasn't so obviously in deadly earnest it would be funny. She *looked* funny, squaring up to him like that, with both hands clenched and her chin thrust forward. Her top teeth stuck out as well, not too much but enough to give her a marked resemblance to a skinned rabbit. She was actually doing a little dance on the sand, shuffling her feet as if they were in a boxing ring sparring up for the first exchange of blows.

'If you could just see yourself with your hair all mucky with sand. If only you could see. . . .'

There was a break in her voice. She was close to tears, but Jonathan was past caring. All his bottled-up worry about his mother rose to choke him, just as if a hand had suddenly squeezed his throat. Bending down, he picked the cigarette case out of the shallow pool. His mother had given him the silver case for his eighteenth birthday, and as he shook the sea water out of it he saw her face, pointed and thin, and her blue eyes with that awful bruised look around them. She was going to die, and Lisa Logan's mother would go on living.

'Your mother doesn't have the screaming ab-dabs when my father kisses her. I would say she enjoys it no end,' he said deliberately.

For a long moment they stared at each other, Lisa's eyes wide with shock, before she turned to run from him, not looking where she was going, slipping on the wet sand, tripping once, then stumbling on.

'Come back, stupid!'

Jonathan's voice spiralled after her, but Lisa ran on. Her mind was in a turmoil, thoughts whirling round and round. It was as if Jonathan's words had lifted the lid off a cauldron filled with unspeakable truths, only half understood up to now.

Her mother going off for long walks with Uncle Patrick round the headland, disappearing for hours at a time, coming back with her curly hair like a nimbus round her brown face. Appearing like that on the landing with guilt in her eyes, following Lisa into her room and going on and on about the lost keys. Lisa caught her toe on a loose pebble, winced with the pain of it, and kept on running.

Her mother wouldn't do *that*. Not with Uncle Patrick. There was a stitch in her side but Lisa ignored it. Kissing maybe, but not *that*?

Reaching the hotel, she stopped by the low stone wall. It was damp and mossy, but she sat down, crossing her arms over her bolstered breasts, rocking herself to and fro.

It was awful. She blinked back the tears pricking behind her eyelids. Tomorrow they would be going home. They would climb into the rickety local bus and be driven at speed through leafy lanes, past grey stone houses shuttered against the sun. Maybe there would be the same old woman in a blue sun bonnet, out in the middle of a field, calmly milking a cow. At St Malo they would take a taxi cab to the quayside, perhaps see the same old man sitting there smoking a clay pipe, his creased face folded into lines of contentment.

They would sail back to England, and before the new term began she would go with her mother down to the town to buy a new navy-blue gaberdine coat and a pair of indoor shoes for school. Everything would be normal and ordinary, and yet how could anything ever be normal and ordinary again? Her mother was a whore. . . . Lisa said the word quietly inside her head. Words like that were not for speaking out loud. She was a whore, and her father was a cuckold.

Sensing that someone was standing in front of her Lisa looked up and saw Jonathan.

'Aren't you cold, kiddo?' His voice was ragged with shame. There was an apology in the way he stood. 'It wasn't true what I said.'

'No, I'm not cold, thank you.' Lisa stood up and moved round him. She was not cold, not her body, anyway. The cold was deep inside her, gripping her stomach with an icy hand. At the door of the hotel she faced him, her head held high. 'It's quite true what you told me. I knew it myself, as a matter of fact.'

She turned to go inside, leaving the impression of her shocked and tearless face imprinted on Jonathan's mind. Wheeling round, he ran with his loping stride down to the beach again. From over the sea sheet lightning flashed in a white flame. With the approach of the storm the waves began to curl in fury.

'Oh, hell! Oh, flamin' hell!' Jonathan raised his face and felt the first drops of rain. 'Oh, God, why does my mother have to die? Why?' Then he turned to walk slowly back to the hotel, his black hair sleeked to his head as if he were a seal coming out of the sea.

Two

'Honestly, Lisa, I wish you'd stop turning round. You've been doing it ever since we came in.'

Rachael Levy, a small plump Jewish girl, the only Jewish girl at the High School in 1935, brushed the sleeve of her coat with the tips of her fingers. 'The big picture's coming on, and besides, you keep marking my coat with your choc-ice. Honestly, you are a fidget.'

Reluctantly, Lisa faced forward. 'It's just that there's a boy I know sitting behind us, with a girl,' she whispered. 'And I don't want him to see me.'

'Why not?' Immediately Rachael twisted round in her seat. 'Is he in the back row? On one of the double seats?'

'Of course not. He's about twenty, for heaven's sake.'

'Have you been out with him?' Rachael was not one to give up easily. 'I thought you told me you wouldn't go out with a boy even if one asked you.'

Lisa thought she detected a note of sarcasm in her friend's voice, but decided to give Rachael the benefit of the doubt. The newsreel preceding the big picture had shown Jews in Berlin being made to scrub the pavements outside their shops, and she knew for a fact that Rachael had relatives in Germany.

'He's a family friend,' she hissed from behind her choc-ice. 'He came with us on holiday last summer to Brittany. With his father,' she added. 'He's horrible. Honestly!'

'Sh . . . sh.' A woman in the row behind tapped Lisa's shoulder. 'Some folks have come to see the picture. *If* you don't mind.'

It took a few minutes for Lisa to blot from her mind the

sight of Jonathan Grey sitting in one of the red plush seats with his arm laid nonchalantly across the seat on his right, his hand resting on the shoulder of a girl with a floss of fair hair. What was he doing in the pictures in the afternoon, anyway? Surely he should be slapping cement on bricks somewhere, or had he been rained off? Not that she cared, of course.

Since the holiday in Brittany Uncle Patrick's visits to the house had been much less frequent, but Lisa was sure her mother was meeting him somewhere. There were days when Delia came in after Lisa had got back from school, flushed and anxious, making excuses when excuses were not necessary, rushing upstairs to change out of her smart costume, saying she didn't want to seat the skirt.

Back from an assignation with her lover, Lisa would tell herself bitterly.

Up on the screen Leslie Howard waved a long kerchief in front of his aristocratic nose: 'They seek him here, they seek him there. Those Frenchies seek him everywhere.' His voice, as English as buttered toast for tea, lulled Lisa into a state of mind at first relaxed then more and more excitable as the tale of *The Scarlet Pimpernel* began to unfold. Merle Oberon was so beautiful, with her high cheekbones and her luxurious dark hair, but why didn't she guess the identity of the Pimpernel? Lisa's eyes glowed in the warm gloom as, identifying thoroughly with the characters, she rode the streets in the tumbrels, laid her head on the block, knitted round the guillotine, and then, as Merle Oberon, raised her exquisite face for the dashing hero's kiss.

As usual when a story held her, she wasn't reading or watching. She was there, breathing, living every moment, so that when the lights came on at the end and she followed Rachael out to the foyer it was as though Leslie Howard walked by her side, his hand on her arm, his eyes filled with love, his honeyed voice telling her to watch her step.

'Hello there, Lisa!'

With a tremendous effort Lisa tore herself away from Leslie Howard's side. Her big grey-blue eyes were red-rimmed from the tears she had shed on Merle Oberon's behalf, a sodden handkerchief was still held tightly in her clenched hand, and it was obvious to Jonathan Grey that she was finding the transition from make-believe to reality almost impossible.

'Won't be a minute,' he told the girl clinging on to his arm. Pinching the crown of his brown trilby, he placed it on his head, remembered he was still indoors, and took it off again. He smiled at Lisa, hoping the fat girl she was with would take the hint and step away, but Rachael stood her ground, scowling at him from beneath fierce black eyebrows. *Now* what had Lisa Logan been saying about him, Jonathan wondered.

'Enjoy the picture?' He spoke directly to Lisa, and as she blinked he saw she was still in some far-away place.

'Not bad,' she said. 'But when you've read the book it's all a bit tame somehow.'

Jonathan sighed. God, but she hadn't improved. Still the same kid he'd always known, saying one thing while obviously thinking another. And what the hell was her fat friend giggling about? Forgetting all about manners, Jonathan placed his hat on his head, nodded and touched the brim with a finger.

'See you at the dance tonight, then.'

As he walked away Rachael gripped Lisa's arm tightly. 'What did he say? *What* dance? Oh, isn't he like Ronald Colman!'

'The Conservative Ball in the Public Halls.' Lisa looked martyred.

'I'm going with my parents, worse luck. Jonathan Grey will be there with his father. My Uncle Patrick,' she added bitterly. 'Not that he's my real uncle, thank God.'

Then, remembering what Rachael's real uncle might be doing at that very moment in the troubled streets of Berlin, she was overcome with fervent compassion. Tucking her arm into Rachael's, she gave it a squeeze against her side so that they walked out entwined into the street crowded with shoppers.

Lisa heard her mother speaking on the telephone as she let herself into the big detached house on the outskirts of the town. The hall, like the rest of the house, was thickly carpeted and when Lisa stopped by the sitting-room door, she hesitated, one hand on the round brass knob.

'Oh, please,' Delia was saying. 'Please, darling. It's been so long. I know we shouldn't, but if you only knew. . . .'

Lisa leaned closer to the slight gap in the not quite closed door. Eavesdropping was a despicable thing to do, but it wouldn't be the first time. Anyway, she owed it to her father, surely? She gripped the cold brass knob hard, straining to hear the softly spoken words.

'We aren't hurting Alice, darling. She doesn't know. How can she even begin to guess when we've always been so careful? All I want is just a little time alone with you to talk. Just that. I can drive out to the same place. Please. I think I'm going mad. There'll be no chance to talk tonight.' There was a pause. 'Please?'

At that moment the expression on Lisa Logan's face was one of pure loathing for the woman sobbing into the telephone. She opened the door.

Through the books she read, the films she saw, Lisa was capable of identifying with heartbreak. She could suffer anguish over fictional characters, yet there in the hall, darkened with the gloom of a rainy late afternoon, she failed utterly to recognize the desperation in her mother's voice. The women in the tumbrels, rolling their way through the streets of Paris to the guillotine, had been more real to Lisa than her mother who was moaning now, the telephone receiver held close to her chest.

As if it were a stethoscope sounding out her heart, Lisa thought, totally immune to the sight of her mother's ravaged face.

'That was Uncle Patrick you were talking to!'

Bursting into the room, the wet, bedraggled beret she wore slipping down over her forehead, her eyes narrowed into slits of adolescent accusation, Lisa faced Delia. 'You don't care tuppence for how you are deceiving my father! You don't deserve to be married to a man like him, and if I didn't care about hurting him I would tell him. Yes, I would!' With the violent nodding of her head, the beret

31

slipped even further down her forehead. There was rain on her nose, and in her fury the freckles on her cheekbones stood out against the whiteness of her skin.

Delia stared at her daughter as if she couldn't believe the evidence of her eyes. Replacing the receiver with a hand that shook, she sagged into a chair and covered her face with her hands. She was shivering uncontrollably. First Patrick's evasive mumblings at the other end of the wires, then this. . . . Oh, God! It was too much!

'Go away,' she whispered. 'Just go away. That's all.'

Dripping rain on to the Chinese carpet, Lisa stayed where she was. One half of her, the half that on most days genuinely loved her mother, wanted to kneel down by the chair and pull Delia's hands away from her face and tell her she understood. Angus had been very difficult lately, staying away in Manchester for days on end, prowling round the house in a bad mood, flaring into a temper when spoken to. No wonder her mother had been flattered by Uncle Patrick's attentions. Jonathan's father could charm the birds off the trees, even Lisa had to admit that. It was the Irish in him, she supposed.

But her mother *loved* him. Had lain with him. The pedantic phrase culled from the love stories Lisa was in the habit of reading rose to torment her.

'You're too old!' Her voice dripped scorn. 'It's disgusting! Do you ever stop to think you're having an affair with a man whose wife is slowly dying?' The beret fell over her nose and she pushed it back with a trembling finger. 'It would kill my father if he found out. Can't you see?'

To Lisa's horror, Delia threw back her head and laughed. It was a terrible kind of laugh, high-pitched, staccato, interspersed with hiccuping sobs.

'Oh, dear God! Kill your father, did you say? Oh, dear, dear God! That's rich, that is.' The laughter stopped as suddenly as it had begun. Delia's dark eyes were like black coals pricked out in the pallor of her face. 'It's always him, isn't it? Your paragon of a father. Upright, noble Angus Logan, virtue personified.' Delia's mouth tightened into a

32

thin line. 'Before you carry on condemning me, standing there like the Day of Judgement, let me tell you. . . .'

The big front door opened, then closed with a resounding crash. As the two faces swivelled round, Angus came into the room, hurling his briefcase into a corner of the massive chesterfield, before making straight for the drinks' cupboard over by the window.

'What a day!' He poured a glass of gin with a lavish hand, then slopped tonic into it more modestly. 'The bloody train from Manchester was crowded, then I couldn't start the car.' He turned round. 'What are you two doing? I thought you'd both be upstairs titivating yourselves up for tonight. We'll have to leave in less than an hour if we're to be in time to partake of cocktails with the Mayor and his good lady.'

When Delia rushed frantically from the room, he took a long drink. '*Now* what have I said?'

Lisa felt her very heart would melt with love as she stared at her father. He was so obviously overtired, so bowed down with worry, she had an urge to hurl herself at him as she'd done as a child, burying her head deep in his chest, hugging him until he pretended to plead for mercy.

'You haven't said anything, Father,' she said, wrenching off the beret and unbuttoning her coat. 'I don't think Mother realized how late it was.' She forced a smile. 'You know how long she takes to get ready.'

Angus drained the glass and went straight to the cupboard for a refill. He guessed something had been going on but let it go. He had accepted many years ago that his loveless marriage was in no way unique. There weren't enough fingers on his two hands to count the number of his friends and colleagues locked together in similar bleak circumstances. This was a house where any attempt at what was lately being described by fashionable psychiatrists as 'communication' had ceased to exist a long, long time ago.

'Has it been a bad day, Father?'

Angus smiled wearily. That remark must surely be the understatement of the year. Sitting down in a winged armchair, he closed his eyes, resting the cold rim of the glass against his forehead. What a funny child she was, his little Lisa. So fierce, so loving.

'Would you like me to massage your neck?'

'That would be lovely.'

Slowly, gently, Lisa began to move her thumbs, rotating them over the hard knot of tension at the back of her father's neck. He needed a haircut. The thick, red-gold hair straggled down over the top of his white collar, and yet on the crown it was beginning to thin.

An overwhelming sensation of tenderness and love stilled Lisa's hands for a moment. He wasn't old, this beloved father of hers, but he was a long, long way from being young. Much too old, anyway, to have a wife who sobbed into the telephone over another man. Lisa shivered.

How could she? How could anyone of her mother's age? Perhaps Delia was going through the 'change'? Lisa had listened to Mrs Parker in the kitchen talking about the awful things in store for women of a certain age. Mrs Parker had gone through torture with her hot flushes, and had told Lisa about a friend who had gone off her husband. . . .

Which was surely worse, Lisa decided. Now her fingers were moving automatically. Angus was so relaxed Lisa guessed he was probably half asleep. She changed the kneading motion to a soft stroking. Above the bowed head her own face was so impassive she might have been asleep, but her thoughts were wandering free. Delia was forty-two. Lisa pondered. If it wasn't an early 'change' then it could be because her mother had been brought up in India. They did say that hot countries brought that sort of thing out in people.

'Father?' she said suddenly, jolting Angus awake. 'I saw Jonathan Grey at the pictures this afternoon.' She stared down at her father's head for any sign of agitation. There was none. Lisa took the experiment one step further. 'Jonathan will be at the dance tonight. Will his father be going too?'

'I expect so.'

'With his wife?'

'Auntie Alice's dancing days are over, I'm afraid, love.'

34

Lisa peered round the side of the chair at Angus's face. It was immobile, but closed, giving nothing away. The poor love, she thought, he doesn't even begin to guess what's going on. He's so bowed down with worries about his stocks and shares he has no idea his own wife is deceiving him so horribly.

'I think there's something very cruel about a man who can go to a dance leaving his wife at home on her bed of pain.'

Angus tilted his head back, looking up into the upside-down face of his daughter. For a moment he hoped, almost prayed, that Lisa might be speaking lightly, but no, she was perfectly serious. He sighed.

'Hadn't you better go and get ready, love? I'll be up in a minute.' He stared down into his empty glass. 'And wear your hair unplaited, eh? For me? I like it loose.'

Now why had he said that? Angus rubbed the frown line between his eyes. All the spirit ebbed slowly out of him. Unplaiting her hair wasn't going to make Lisa grow up overnight. Sometimes he wanted to grab her and shake her, *yelling* at her to grow up. He shook his head from side to side, fighting the desire to pour himself another drink. To Lisa, black was black and white was white, no grey truths in between. Her pragmatic brain accepted only what she heard and saw, never for one moment tolerated the sins of the weak.

Angus groaned. From where had he and Delia spawned a child like Lisa? He got up slowly from the chair. And they *were* weak. Giving in to temptation, he poured a third drink and carried it up the wide winding staircase. Lack of money bred weakness. Mounting debts made a man vulnerable to the whole world. Shortage of cash took away the power that made a man feel safe. Passing his wife's bedroom, Angus turned into his own at the far end of the landing.

His evening dress suit, plus his white shirt and black tie were laid out neatly on the bed. Tossing the drink back, Angus surveyed them with distaste. His penguin trappings he had always called them. Now they mocked him, laughing at him as if they were some sort of fancy dress.

Immediately, his spirits lifted. The actor in him rose to the surface. He could almost hear drums roll and smell the grease paint as he strode out from the wings.

'All the world's a stage.' Fuddled with too much drink on an empty stomach, Angus slurred the whispered words. Tomorrow the curtain would come down. Come tomorrow the world would know that Captain Angus Logan was a ruined man.

But tonight. . . . Wrenching off his jacket, tearing at the buttons on his shirt, Angus made his way unsteadily into the bathroom. Tonight was for forgetting, for dancing the hours away. For doing what he'd been doing for a long time now. Making believe. . . . The actor in him sharpening his features to a kind of nobility, Angus ran his bath, turning on the taps with a flamboyant gesture that he felt would have sent an audience wild with appreciation.

'May I have this dance, Miss Logan?'

Alderman Tomkins, flushed with cocktails, heavy with his chain of office, bowed from the waist, extending a podgy hand. As he held her close, revolving slowly through a waltz, Lisa could feel the heat emanating from his body. If she turned her head she could see the sweat beading his forehead, and through the crêpe de Chine of her long blue dress his hand on her back guided her through steps at total variance to the dance being played by the band specially hired from Manchester.

Her dark hair, brushed out from its plaits, fell in crinkly waves, almost to her waist. She had tied a blue ribbon round it, holding it back from her rounded forehead, and but for the soft cushion of her breasts pressing pleasurably against his chest, the Mayor would have guessed her age at about twelve.

'Your mother's looking bonny tonight.' The Mayor spoke into Lisa's right ear. 'She dances like a professional, doesn't she?'

Lisa's eyes narrowed as she watched Delia and her partner gliding effortlessly through the correct dance routine. Her mother's dress was a sheath of purple satin. Delia's small tight bottom wiggled as she dipped and swayed, pirouetted and revolved. Her face was alight with animation and enjoyment, and Lisa found it hard to believe that it could be the same face so wrenched out of shape with tearing emotion not two hours before.

Automatically she looked for her father. He was there, where she had guessed he might be, standing by the bar, a lone figure with a glass in his hand, sipping from it morosely, and looking so lost and alone her heart ached for him.

Alderman Tomkins gave a sideways glance at Lisa's small set face. He knew and accepted that God had left him out when a sense of rhythm was being dispensed, but this strange silent child was making no attempt to follow him.

'Go and ask the Logan girl to dance,' his wife had whispered. 'Just look at her sitting alone pretending not to be a wallflower. She reminds me of how I used to feel when I was young. She must be dying a thousand deaths.'

It was exactly like taking a walk backwards, Lisa was telling herself, as the music changed tempo and the lights dimmed, throwing the central spotlight into a whirling glory.

'I'll follow my secret heart,' a man with patent-leather hair crooned into the microphone, and over the Mayor's padded shoulder Lisa stared straight into Jonathan Grey's mocking eyes. He closed one eye in a deliberate wink at the exact moment the Mayor trod heavily on to Lisa's foot. She blushed, tried to get back into step and failed, catching Jonathan's wide grin as he guided his partner expertly out of range.

Lisa felt sick. She could have been sick right there. She knew she looked awful. The ribbon band was slipping down her forehead, and her dress with its long sleeves and tight bodice was all wrong. Suddenly she found difficulty in breathing. If this dance didn't end soon she would faint, she knew she would.

The Mayor's beer-belly was pressing obscenely against her. It was a nightmare there on the crowded floor with couples going round and round and the moving spots from the central light illuminating first one vivacious face then another. Lisa closed her eyes.

Jonathan's partner was the same girl he had been with at the pictures that afternoon. She was very pretty and her dress of sea-green velveteen, cut on the cross, clung to her like a second skin. When the dance ended at last Lisa saw that the front dipped to a cleavage so low she could hardly believe her eyes. Even Delia's dress was chaste by comparison.

'That was lovely,' the Mayor said insincerely, before mopping his brow and going mercifully away to rejoin his wife.

'You were honoured, love,' Angus said, swaying on his heels, gazing bleary-eyed over the rim of his glass at Lisa.

To his surprise Lisa looked as if she might be going to burst into tears.

'You've had too much to drink, Father,' she told him, her eyes flashing. 'Why aren't you dancing with Mother, anyway? Look at her now, going on the floor with Uncle Patrick. That's the third time she's danced with him. People will be saying things.'

'Oh, don't be such a little prig, Lisa.' It was the drink talking and immediately Angus realized his mistake. His daughter had turned quite pale. There *were* tears glistening on the ends of her long eyelashes, and people *were* staring at them. He drained his glass in one quick swallow.

'I'm not a prig, and you know it. If you knew how broad-minded I am you wouldn't be saying that.' Lisa glared at him, biting her lip and holding her head high.

Angus smiled for the benefit of a woman in a red cloque dress pointing them out to her partner. He said in the suavest of voices, 'Of course you're not a prig, lovey.' His voice came out twice as loud as he'd intended. 'But some-times – well, sometimes you do give the impression that your sense of humour is lacking.' Shaking off his daughter's restraining hand on his arm, Angus turned for the bar. 'I need a bloody drink,' he stated loudly.

Lisa looked down at her silver shoes and frowned. She had seen her father the worse for drink before, but never like this. One more drink and heaven knew what might happen. The Dorothy bag, trimmed with pearl sequins, over her arm had a metal clasp, and in her agitation Lisa snapped it open and shut, open and shut. She could hear her father's voice arguing with the man behind the bar.

'Just do as you're told and give me a bloody drink,' he was saying, while out on the floor Lisa's mother danced with Uncle Patrick, one hand on his shoulder, the fingers openly caressing. Her eyes were searching his face, and they were moving as though they were welded together. Lisa glowered at them, her small face set into lines of distaste.

Once again the lights were dimmed and the spotlight was turned on to the centre mirrored bowl. Pale oval shapes drifted like snowflakes over the dancers. The small crowd of dedicated drinkers round the bar stood lifting their elbows as if they were in a pub, as if what was going on behind them was none of their concern.

The music, the clink of glasses, the sporadic laughter, ebbed and flowed in Lisa's ears. A man pushed past her, a drink in each hand. Bending his head he kissed her lightly on the cheek. Lisa jerked away so violently that a rivulet of whisky and dry ginger flowed down the front of her dress.

'Whoops! Sorry, love.' The man, a golfing friend of her father's, stared at her in dismay. 'God, I'm sorry! Will it stain?'

'It doesn't matter. Honestly.' Clenching her hands, Lisa turned back in time to see Angus slumped on a high seat at the far end of the bar. As she stared at him in consternation, he laid his head gently down, his red-gold hair mopping up the spills on the semi-circular counter.

Lisa felt her mind swim in confusion. People were pointing, laughing. Her beloved father was showing himself up properly. She should have been ashamed of him, and yet in that moment the oddest sensation took over. It was if her heart were melting, leaving her body hollow and empty.

When she went to him, laying a hand on his arm, Angus lifted his head. From one of the glass marbles which seemed to have replaced his eyes a tear leaked. It ran slowly down his cheek to mingle with his moustache.

'My bonny wee lass,' Angus whispered, before laying his head down again.

'You with him, chuck?'

The bartender, a dark man with his black hair parted in the middle, came over to speak quietly to Lisa. 'I think he ought to go home.' Making jerky dabs at the counter with a cloth, he whispered out of the side of his mouth, 'It's not what he's had here. I reckon he'd had a skinful before he set foot in here.'

'He's my father.' Lisa looked round feverishly. 'I'll just go and tell my mother.' Her eyes widened as Angus gave a loud, vulgar groan. 'She's dancing,' she added wildly. 'I won't be a minute.'

Desperately Lisa pushed her way through the couples waltzing slowly round the big ballroom. They were like figures in a nightmare, the floating spots illuminating first one, then another.

'Someday I'll find you,' the crooner wailed into the microphone. 'Moonlight behind you,' a little man sang into his partner's ear.

Lisa side-stepped, turned and bumped straight into Jonathan. Ignoring the girl staring at her in astonishment, she said, 'I'm looking for my mother. She was dancing with Uncle . . . with your father.'

Immediately Jonathan's eyes slewed towards the balcony, in total darkness now, with couples sitting close together on the velvet seats.

'My father is dead drunk,' Lisa said straight out. 'I must get him out of here.'

Afterwards, when they were squashed in Jonathan's car, speeding up the Preston Road on their way home, Lisa wondered how it had all happened so quickly.

'The girl you were with?' She glanced sideways at Jonathan's set face. 'What will she think?'

'What she chooses to think.' Jonathan jerked his head backwards. 'I'll see your father into your house then I'll get back.' His lips twisted. 'I just hope your mother's looking for the pair of you.'

'Serves her right,' his expression said, before he turned a corner on two wheels. 'She should have seen what he was like before you came out,' he said aloud.

40

'She was upset,' Lisa whispered, remembering the way her parents had sat side by side in the taxi, Delia hugging her white fur wrap underneath her chin, and Angus with his head on his chest as if he was snatching forty winks.

The car turned into the unmade road leading to The Laurels. Angus moaned.

'If he's sick in my car there'll be hell to pay.' Jerking to a halt in a flurry of gravel, Jonathan nodded to Lisa. 'OK kid? Think you can give me a hand to get him inside?'

Twice Lisa trod on the long blue dress as they awkwardly negotiated, with Angus lolling between them, the three steps leading to the front door.

'We'll put him on the chesterfield.' Jonathan dropped Angus on to the moquette cushions, before stopping to pull the black patent dancing shoes from the apparently boneless feet. He tweaked at Lisa's blue ribbon, pushing it even further down over her forehead. Poor little devil, he thought. He doesn't deserve her. With a jerk he unloosened Angus's bow tie before unfastening the stiff collar.

'I'd better get back,' he said. 'Sure you'll be all right?' He glanced upwards. 'Mrs Parker out for the night?'

'Gone to see her sister.' Lisa knelt down on the thick carpet. 'I'll make him some black coffee when you've gone.' She raised an anxious face. 'That's what they have, isn't it?'

'Strong and black.'

Jonathan backed towards the door. His last sight of Lisa was her long dark hair falling almost to her waist as she bent over her father. When she turned and thanked him, he was gone.

'Imagine how I felt,' Delia said, coming into the house an hour later, the white fur wrap dangling from her hand. '"Your husband has been taken home dead drunk," they said. I was dancing with the Mayor at the time, but I wasn't spared. Oh, no!' She twirled the wrap on to a chair with a sweeping flourish that would have done a bullfighter proud. 'Jonathan Grey's voice could be heard over the band. He did it on purpose! And I wasn't amused!'

'I couldn't find you!' Lisa nodded towards Angus, sitting

41

up now, head bowed, hands hanging loosely between his knees. 'I tried to find you, but you weren't dancing.' Her voice rose. 'Where were you, Mother? Where?'

For a long moment mother and daughter glared at each other with mutual dislike. Delia was the first to look away. 'I must have been in the cloakroom,' she said. 'Surely you could have looked for me there?'

'I did! When I went to fetch my cloak I asked the lady and she said you hadn't been in. I *described* you.' Lisa's voice was sharp. 'Father was ill. He might have died, and you weren't there.'

'Oh, my God!' Delia's dark eyes flashed fire. 'Ill? Did you say ill?' Her laugh was a mockery. 'Sodden with gin, you mean.' Her voice rose almost to a scream. 'Look at him! Take a good look. From what I was told, your father had almost to be scraped off the floor of the bar.' With nervous fingers she plucked at the tight skirt of her long dress. 'The whole town will be talking about us. From now on the Logan name will be a dirty word. No wonder I. . . .

'No wonder you what, Mother?' Lisa began to tremble. The shame of what had happened, the awful disgrace, the humiliation of seeing her father's head resting on the bar counter as his so-called friends laughed behind their hands, rose in her throat to choke her. 'It's all your fault,' she burst out. 'Can't you see?'

She had thought her father was beyond speech, but he raised his head and she saw the grey pallor of his face. He looked dreadful, his eyes sunk deep into dark hollows, his red-gold hair flopping over his forehead. Even his military moustache had a forlorn droop to it.

'Go to bed, Lisa,' he whispered. 'That's a good girl.' He moved his head slowly from side to side. 'It's late and we're all tired. Away to bed with you, lass.'

Uncertainly Lisa stared from one to the other. Angus was looking down at the carpet again, shoulders hunched over, the round balding place on the crown of his head showing. Delia's small face resembled a mask, all pinched as if her features had sharpened, especially her nose. The veil of

42

middle age seemed to have fallen over them both, hiding the gaiety they showed to their friends.

They were growing old, Lisa realized. They played at being young, but really it was just a game. She walked towards the door. In that moment of revelation she knew that she loved them both equally. In that moment she felt older than either of them.

The shouting began as she climbed into bed, and not even the heavy weight of blankets pulled over her head prevented the sound of angry voices spiralling upstairs.

'Right then. You asked for it!' Delia felt her heart pound like a drum. She knew she was burning her boats with a vengeance, but nothing could stop the torrent of words now.

'I love Patrick Grey, and he loves me. I was with him tonight, in his car, out on the arterial road in a lay-by. That's why Lisa couldn't find me. We were making love while you were disgracing yourself in front of the Mayor and our friends.' The hammering of her heart was threatening to choke her. 'What were you doing, anyway? Drowning your sorrows because you couldn't be in Manchester with your fancy piece?'

Angus stared at his wife with a distaste more wounding than pure hatred. The purple lipstick exactly matching her nail varnish was almost chewed away so that her mouth seemed thinner than usual. Her breasts were too small to do justice to the low-necked dress, and the colour did nothing for a skin turned sallow without the touch of the sun to deepen it to the brown tan she strove for so assiduously during the summer.

'Will Patrick Grey marry you when his wife dies?' His tone was weary.

'Yes! Yes! And yes! He'd marry me tomorrow if he could!' Delia spoke too loudly and with too much vehemence, but Angus was too shattered to notice.

The blood was pounding in his head. The intense throbbing pain was making him feel dizzy. And yet what his wife had just said brought the kind of peace that comes to a man who hears what he has long been wanting to hear. It was strange how his thoughts were suddenly crystal clear, not fuddled with drink. To tell the truth he was surprised. Knowing Patrick Grey as he had thought he did, he would have imagined that booze and women were mere pastimes in a life saddened by the long illness of his wife.

'So you'll be wanting to divorce me?' Angus closed his eyes. He wished his wife would stop answering his questions as loudly as if he was out in the fields. Now that the pounding in his head was easing up he was beginning to get himself under some sort of control again. He could hear himself consciously modifying his voice as he slipped into the role of injured husband. 'Or shall I divorce you?'

'You bloody hypocrite!'

His eyes snapped open as Delia leaped from her chair to stand over him, shaking with anger. 'You're not feeling anything, are you? You're going to walk out on me, aren't you?' She made a choking sound in her throat. 'You've been wanting to go for a long time, and now I've given you the excuse you were looking for. You can walk out of this house any time now because of what I've just told you. You would leave actually feeling you were doing the right thing. Actually hearing applause in your head, wouldn't you?'

'Do you want me to stay?' Angus looked away from the creased skirt not an inch from his eyes. 'Go. Stay. Stay. Go. It's all the same to me.'

When Delia knelt down, gripping his chin and forcing him to look at her, the expression in her eyes made him flinch. So intense was her loathing that he could feel the violence of it radiating from her tensed body. She was beyond herself with a frustration and rage which went far beyond the terrible things they were saying to each other.

'You're in a mess again with the bank, aren't you?' She pounded clenched fists on his knees. 'You haven't been to the Stock Exchange for weeks, have you? You've been borrowing from your colleagues again, then gambling away what they've lent you. Mrs Parker told me this morning she hasn't been paid for weeks. And you promised her you'd see to her wages yourself.'

Her next words were gabbled. 'I went down to Booths yesterday for coffee, and the man sent for the manager. He

44

asked politely if we'd forgotten to settle our account for the past three months. Three months, Angus! How long do you think they'll let us have things on credit? There's a slump in this town, Angus! Even shopkeepers can't live on air.'

'You'd be better off without me.' Angus passed a long hand wearily across his forehead. 'I'm a born loser.' He drew his thick eyebrows together as if in sudden pain. 'It was the war. You know it was the war. I reckon I'd have been better off if I'd stopped a bullet. As it is . . . .'

At once Delia jumped up. 'Oh, no you don't!' She began to shriek hysterically. 'That old sob story leaves me stone cold, Angus Logan. This time you get yourself out of whatever mess you've got yourself into.' She walked to the door, straight-backed, not a hair out of place.

As cold and hard as a bloody statue, Angus told himself.

'And Patrick Grey's lousy with money, isn't he?' he shouted.

'Yes!' Delia turned. 'Because he knows how to handle it, that's why!' There were two hectic red spots on her cheekbones. 'The building trade might not be what you call a gentleman's profession, but at least he knows how to keep solvent. He thinks you're a fool, if you must know.'

'Then go to him!' Angus yelled, making no more attempts at latching on to his slipping control. 'Either go to him, or sit tight till his wife dies. It won't be long from what I've heard.'

When the door banged, he groaned aloud. Oh, God, but he felt rough. The pounding in his head was beginning again. It was one o'clock in the morning, and in six hours' time he would have to be up, dressed, shaved and on his way to Manchester to an interview he dreaded with every fibre of his being.

And when he walked out into the street again he would be a ruined man.

Pushing himself up from the cushions of the massive chesterfield, he walked unsteadily into the hall and through to the small room he used as a study. He stretched out a hand to the roll-top desk, then drew it back. No need to look for solace there. He knew what lay behind the wooden slats. He could actually see them, pile upon pile of unpaid bills. Gambling debts most of them. Borrowing from Peter to pay Paul. Promising Paul to gain time to placate Peter. It was all too much. Far too much for a man who had suffered as he had in the stinking mud of Flanders Field.

Sinking into a chair, he buried his head in his hands.

There was a way out. His mouth twisted in a sudden moment of self-revelation. For Angus there had always been a way out. For a long time he sat there, pressing his fingers against his closed eyelids as if he would shut out reality.

Delia knew there was someone. He corrected himself. She knew there had always been someone. He sighed. But this time it was different.

Margaret was a widow, eight years older than Angus, a woman who wanted a presentable man by her side. And rich. Rich beyond the dreams of avarice. Soft of flesh and of eye, as cuddly as a plush rabbit, with a ruthless mind at total variance to her appearance.

With Margaret there would be no more jiggling with money, no more responsibility. She had made that clear. Her own plump fingers would hold the purse strings, but her generosity towards him would be unbounded. Angus wriggled in his chair. She *loved* him, was obsessed by him, had told him so, over and over again.

They would go abroad. Australia. As far away as possible from this grey northern town where tall mill chimneys pointed satanic fingers to a rain-filled cloudy sky. It would be a new beginning, like being born again.

Almost imperceptibly Angus's shoulders lifted. Whatever passed for his conscience was stilled. Delia, in telling him Patrick Grey would marry her when his wife died, had thrown the key to Angus's freedom right at his feet. Now all he had to do was to pick it up.

In his bedroom he threw things carelessly into a suitcase. He had seen actors in plays and films packing like that. Just grabbing shirts and socks from drawers, ramming a jacket down on top, then clicking the locks before taking a last lingering look round the room. Down in the hall he snatched his raincoat from the hallstand and laid it over the top of the case.

Then, still in what he called his penguin trappings, he walked slowly back up the wide staircase, one hand trailing the banister rail. The curtain was not ready to come down, not quite yet.

In his daughter's room he stood by her bed, as straight and tall as in the days of his soldiering in France.

Would she ever understand, this child of his heart, that what her father was doing had been written in his stars a long time ago?

In the diffused light filtering from the landing, all he could see was a tangle of dark hair on the pillow. Lisa had always slept like that, disappearing behind her long hair, drawing it around her as if it were an extra sheet.

The enormity of what he was about to do filled Angus with a despair so profound he shuddered. But it was the only way. . . the only way.

'Remember me with love.'

The drama of the softly spoken words comforted him. As he backed slowly from the room he fancied he could hear them lingering like an echo, repeating and fading until they were no more.

Captain Angus James Logan, late of the Scottish Highlanders, twice mentioned in dispatches for outstanding bravery in the face of enemy action, was running away at last.

Three

Miss Adams, MA, headmistress of the town's Girls' High School, gave a sideways sniff. From her position on the platform during Assembly she had a clear view of Lisa Logan being taken out on the arm of a prefect.

Lisa Logan was not one of the regular fainters. Miss Adams could have named every one of the half dozen of her girls who slumped at monthly intervals over their hymn books. There was very little the strict disciplinarian did not know about her 'gels'.

Coming from the south, initially as the school's geography mistress, she was possessed of a highly developed social conscience. The present state of the Depression in the cotton town saddened and appalled her.

For the girls with white gym blouses washed to a sketchy shade of grey, and black woollen stockings darned over darns, she showed understanding and tolerance. Sleeping as some of them did, two and even three to a bed, what more natural than at times they found the standing in Assembly too much? Breakfast for some of her scholarship girls, she guessed, was nothing more than a mug of weak tea and a slice of bread and margarine, smeared with jam if they were lucky.

But for the Lisa Logans in her school a faint meant, more often than not, a too-late night spent dancing at one of the town's many functions in the Public Halls.

That same afternoon she called Lisa to her study.

'Come!' she called, answering Lisa's timid knock.

'Feeling better?' She looked at Lisa over the top of her reading glasses, taking in the white face, the shadowed eyes, then moving down to the spotless white blouse, the neatly pressed box pleats of the navy-blue serge gym slip. Every item of Lisa's uniform was bought without counting the cost, Miss Adams knew from the school outfitters round the corner from the Market Place.

'You went with your parents to the Conservative Ball last night. I am right, am I not?' Miss Adams took off her glasses and laid them down on her blotter.

'Yes, Miss Adams.'

'And the dance finished at two o'clock this morning?'

'Yes, Miss Adams.'

Lisa stared at the headmistress's hands. They were lying neatly folded together on the pink blotter, but they might just have easily been drumming with impatience. Lisa could sense the disapproval coming at her from the other side of the wide desk.

For a wild moment she wanted to blurt out the truth. That long before the dance ended she had taken her drunken father home in a sports car, had watched him slump, grey-faced, as her mother had followed, shouting her shame aloud in the sitting-room. That she had cowered in bed hearing their voices raised in anger, and that this morning, with her mother asleep in her room and her father apparently on his way to his office in Manchester, she had come to school without breakfast.

With an effort she tried to take in what her headmistress was saying.

'There are gels in this school, Lisa, who will be leaving before they take their Matriculation examinations. Bright gels in your form, one in particular who would, I know, win an open scholarship to Oxford or Cambridge. Not for them the advantage of staying on until they are eighteen to take Higher School Certificate. And why? Can you even begin to tell me why, Lisa?'

'Because their parents can't afford to keep them on. Because they have to go out to work to earn money,' Lisa mumbled.

'Exactly. And yet you. . . .' The normally quiet voice hardened with exasperation. 'With all the opportunities available, you neglect your education by staying out all night and indulging in quite unnecessary extras such as piano, dancing and riding lessons.' The hands took up the glasses and began to twirl them round. 'There are private schools in the town for gels like you, Lisa Logan. But my school has a reputation of which I am justly proud. My gels are here to learn, to acquire academic status, to collect diplomas and go on to degree standard, not fritter their young lives away in pursuits that will still be waiting for them should they be that way inclined in later years.'

The voice softened. There was something in Lisa's air of dejection that touched the older woman's tender heart, a heart hidden by a dark grey spotted blouse with a gold fob-watch pinned to the stiff shiny cotton.

She sighed, turning the watch over to check the time. 'What do you want to make of your life, Lisa? I know your English is good. Miss Shaw tells me you have a certain flair with words. But your maths are deplorable. Miss Entwistle says if the letters are changed from ABC to XYZ on her geometry theorems you flounder. Geometry is a subject to understand and qualify, not learn off by heart without knowing why. You will fail your Matriculation Certificate if you can't get at least a Pass in maths. You know that, don't you?'

'Yes, Miss Adams.' Lisa's head drooped. 'I was hoping to go to University. Or maybe a Teachers' Training College,' she added in desperation. 'Although I'm not all that keen on teaching. Perhaps I might find something to do with horses. Or work as a dental assistant,' she went on, searching feverishly in her mind for the right thing to say, sensing her headmistress's growing impatience.

'You may go, Lisa.' Miss Adams waved an imperious hand. 'And try to get some extra sleep over the weekend. Remember there are many, many gels who would give anything for your advantages.'

'Yes, Miss Adams. Thank you, Miss Adams.'

Outside in the hall, Lisa pulled a face at the closed door. For all her intelligence and precocious perception, she had missed completely the genuine concern in Miss Adams's manner.

'She talks Bolshie, just like Jonathan Grey,' she muttered to herself, as she walked back to her form-room. 'Maybe if my mother had *made* my blouse, and I smelled because I didn't wear linings in my navy knickers, she'd like me better. Silly old pace-egg.'

'What did she want you for?' Rachael Levy, from her desk behind Lisa's, leaned forward and tugged at a plait. 'Are you being expelled?'

'No such luck.' Lisa opened a geography textbook and stared down at a contour map, her eyes as bleak as the darkening skies outside the tall windows.

It was raining hard when she walked from the tram down the short lane leading to The Laurels. The leaves on the dark green bushes looked like shiny lozenges, and the whole house had a strangely shuttered look. The leather case with Lisa's books for the weekend homework banged against her legs. A lace in her school shoes had come undone, and as she climbed the three steps to the big front door she tripped.

'Hell's bells!' she said aloud, and felt better for it. 'I'm home!' she shouted, dumping her case on the floor and hanging her coat on the hallstand without bothering with the loop stitched into the back of the collar. 'It's me!'

She was halfway upstairs, her mind already ridding herself of the hated school uniform, when a noise from the sitting-room made her stand still, her face wearing its listening expression.

Her mother was crying, and the terrifying thing was that Delia wasn't crying softly. It was like the wail of a child finding itself abandoned in a crowded place. An ice-cold finger of fear trailed down Lisa's spine.

It was a shocking way for an adult to cry. Lisa stood on the threshold of the sitting-room for a moment, frozen into immobility.

Delia was crouched over the padded arm of the chesterfield, a glass in one hand and a screwed-up lace handkerchief in the other. Her features were blurred into a mask of despair, and her eyes were red slits in the sallowness of her face.

'Ah, you!' She stared at Lisa, her mouth wide open. 'Now let's see what you can find to say in your father's defence. See if you'll be sticking up for him when you hear what's happened.'

Lisa moved slowly forward. There was a feeling of dread inside her, tightening her chest as if someone had pulled a rope round her, slipping the knot so that she couldn't breathe.

'Father? What's wrong? There was more than just his drinking wrong with him last night, wasn't there? I've been thinking all day about how awful he looked. He's in some sort of trouble, I just know!'

Delia was leaning forward, almost bending in two, only the top of her head showing. Going forward in a little rush, Lisa knelt down on the carpet, trying to see her face.

'Mother? Where is he? He'd gone off to work when I went out. Has he had an accident or something?' She tried to grasp one of Delia's hands. 'Oh, please don't cry like that! Try to tell me. *Please!*'

Slowly raising her head, Delia looked upon her daughter. A feeling of blind rage roused her from the stupor she had wallowed in all that long, dark day. There was love and a desperate concern in Lisa's face, superimposed on a creeping fear.

But it wasn't for her. Oh, dear God, no, it wasn't for her mother. It was all for *him,* the way it had always been. The two of them, banded together, against her. And now she was able to wipe that look from Lisa's blindly trusting face for ever.

Spitting the words out with cold, calculated venom, Delia trampled on that childish devotion as surely as if she had walked in heavy boots over her daughter's body.

'Your father has left us. He never went to bed at all. Early this morning he packed a case, wrote me a letter.' She nodded towards a sheet of writing paper screwed into a ball in the far corner of the chesterfield. 'Would you like to know what he said?'

Holding her breath, Lisa gave a slight nod.

'The letter said that as your father has decided in his great and kindly wisdom that we will be better off without him, he has made up his mind to go abroad and live in Australia. With his mistress.' Her lips twisted into a mockery of a smile. 'Oh, yes! He's been staying with a woman in Manchester on and off for years. A stinking rich widow from all accounts. So as far as you and I are concerned he has written us off. Finished. QED.'

Lisa held herself quiet for a long moment. It was like something she had read in one of Mrs Parker's *News of the World*. But it was untrue. It *had* to be. Hurling herself at Delia, she pounded with her fists.

'Daddy wouldn't do that!' In her terror she used the name she had always used as a small child. 'He wouldn't just go away. Not without telling me. Not abroad.'

'For ever,' Delia amended. Wildly she glanced round the room. 'He thinks that leaving me the house compensates.' Pushing Lisa away from her, she stood up to begin pacing up and down. 'The telephone hasn't stopped ringing all day. The vultures are swooping down already.' She turned on her heel swiftly, pointing a finger, stabbing at the air. 'When they found his office closed this morning they began ringing here. Bookies, Lisa. Common men with common voices, issuing threats, promising writs. To me!' Suddenly she gripped a half-moon table as if for support. 'Over the last six months everything he's touched at the Stock Exchange has failed. He's bankrupt! Finished! So he's run away.' She turned on her daughter a cold, piercing gaze. 'Now what have you to say in defence of your father?'

'He wouldn't have done it without telling me!'

Running from the room, head bowed, legs turned to water, Lisa scrabbled her way upstairs. In her room she glanced round, at her dressing-table, at her pillow, anywhere a letter might be. Then, finding nothing, she went along the landing to Angus's room.

Half-open drawers, coat hangers hanging empty on the rail of the huge mahogany wardrobe, the tortoiseshell brushes missing from the dressing-table. All told their tale.

She stumbled back to her own room, feeling dead inside. The only thing alive in her at the moment was terror. It was all adding up. Her father's terrible dejection when he came home from Manchester the evening before. His drinking himself paralytic at the dance. The shouting anger spiralling up the stairs after Delia had come home. The nights Angus didn't come home at all.

And the woman he'd gone with. . . . Lisa threw herself down on the bed, beating with clenched fists at the padded day pillow.

It was her mother who had driven him to that. Her mother and Uncle Patrick, Jonathan Grey's father. If it hadn't been for that Angus would never have found consolation elsewhere. Even in the midst of her grief Lisa's mind spoke the dramatic phrases automatically. Her father had had a brainstorm. His mind had suddenly gone. He was ill. In spite of what Delia said about him, he was mentally sick.

He would come back. When he was better he would come back. Or he would send for her. She was his bonny wee lass. He loved her, and loving her meant he could never leave. Not for ever.

Downstairs the telephone rang, and went on ringing. Then stopped.

With a childish wail Lisa buried her face in the pillow, all anger spent. And as the dam of her emotions broke down, the tears came, hot and scalding, running over her cheeks into her open mouth, tasting of salt, and the bitterness of loss that was never to leave her.

Patrick Grey was a frightened man.

It was one thing to have a clandestine affair with a woman passionately eager for what he had to offer; it was another thing entirely to have her sobbing hysterically over the telephone, saying her husband had left her and threatening to kill herself if he didn't go round and see her that night.

'That will be all,' he told his secretary. 'Thank you, Betty.'

By the way Betty had taken her time gathering note-pad and pencil together, Patrick knew she suspected something.

He could almost see her ears flapping beneath the coiled whirls of her old-fashioned hairstyle.

'Now then,' he said, taking his hand off the telephone receiver. 'Steady on. I told you last night not to ring me at work again.'

'He's gone!' Delia's voice was high with hysteria. 'When I got back last night we had a row, a terrible row.'

'Mentioning me?' Patrick's handsome features sharpened.

'He knew, for God's sake. He's known for a long time. He left a letter saying you would take care of me.'

'He what?' Forgetting to be circumspect, Patrick bellowed the two words. 'I told you last night it had to finish. God damn it, I only took you out of the dance to stop you crying. I spelled it out. Didn't you tell him that?'

'I told him you would marry me.'

Patrick's temper shot upwards like a lick of flame, flushing his face to an angry red. 'You what?' He ran a finger round his stiffened white collar. 'I'm already married! What the hell are you talking about, woman?'

Suddenly, as the meaning of what Delia had just said struck home, he felt the bile rise in his throat. 'When his wife died', that was what the crazy woman at the other end of the wires was saying without putting it into words. He took the receiver away from his ear, hesitated on the verge of slamming it down, then said in a grim tight whisper, 'Look here, Delia. What was between us was for fun. You knew it and I knew it. You were paying Angus back for his little wanderings, and I . . . well, you knew the score between Alice and me.' His hand tightened on the black bakelite receiver until the knuckles shone white. 'If you make any move to tell her, I won't be responsible. I'd swing for you first. D'you hear me?'

Delia closed her eyes and swayed where she stood. Angus had always said that Patrick Grey was working-class, in spite of his money and status in the town. Angus could do a devastating impersonation of George Raft in a gangster film, and now, this very minute, Patrick was playing him for real. How Angus would have laughed!

The laughter coming over the wires froze Patrick's blood

in his veins. Oh, God, what a mess! What a stupid unnecessary mess. He'd always known that it was madness for a man to spit on his own doorstep, and Delia Logan was as unstable as a badly roped load on the back of a lorry. He should have known that, right from the beginning when she'd interpreted his heavy-handed flirting with the single-mindedness of a bitch on heat.

Through the glass-fronted panel of his office he could see his son Jonathan making his way through the piles of builder's clutter on his way to the office.

'I'll come some time after eight,' he said quickly, putting the receiver down.

At somewhere around half-past eight that evening Jonathan Grey found himself sitting in the passenger seat of his father's car on his way to The Laurels.

The rain of the past few days had stopped and the sky was a clear washed blue. Patrick's big hands were steady on the wheel, but his profile showed a nerve jumping jerkily in his jaw.

'Delia Logan is a temperamental sort of woman. God knows what she's likely to say or do. It's good of you to agree to come along, son. It's a messy business. Angus Logan allus had it in for me for not being in the war, but by God I can't see me doing a bunk like he's done.' Patrick risked a sideways glance. 'Whatever else I might be I'm not the sort of bloke who would walk out on his wife. Nay, the thought of leaving your mother to fend for herself makes me sick to my stomach, and I don't mean because she's an invalid. She comes first with me, lad, and allus will do. You understand?'

The words had a double meaning which Jonathan understood at once. He felt sorry for the man driving with grim concentration through the town and out to the Preston road. In spite of everything, Patrick's devotion to his wife had always been beyond doubt. It was only during the past year that he had agreed to sleep in a separate room, and even now when Alice had a coughing spell during the night

Patrick was there with soothing drinks, sitting by her side till she got off to sleep again.

Jonathan spoke quickly: 'You must have guessed that Angus Logan was getting in deep with his gambling. It was obvious in Brittany that it had become an obsession with him. Will the police be brought into it? Won't Delia want him brought back to face the music? There wasn't much love lost there, was there?'

Patrick turned away from the main shopping centre into the long, straight road following the tram route. The tick in his face jerked feverishly.

'She's a lost unhappy woman.' He seemed to hesitate. 'But I don't think she wants a scandal. Even though, from what she told me on the phone, Angus's creditors are closing in already. That woman who cooks and does for them has gone already. Seems her wages haven't been paid for months.'

'And the kid? Lisa?' Jonathan turned his head as the car drove past the Girls' High School, an austere building set back on the left. 'She's an awkward young devil, but she thought the world of her father. You should have see her last night when he was drunk. I felt she was pretending to herself that he was ill. Him going off like this must have shattered her.'

'Aye.' Patrick sighed deeply. 'There's nowt so queer as folk.' He slapped the wheel with the flat of his hand. 'Stick with me when we get there, lad.' He swallowed hard. 'As a friend of the family I want to do what I can, of course. But I'm making no promises. There's nobody making me responsible for what's happened. Your mother's not to be upset, not for love nor money. Delia Logan knows where she stands, an' that's a truth she's got to accept. Right starting from now.'

Jonathan's dark, perceptive eyes contemplated his father thoughtfully. He was torn between a kind of ragged shame at Patrick's persuasive, and what was to his son, cowardly way of reasoning. And yet . . . and yet the old man wasn't a bad stick. Delia Logan had egged him on, Jonathan was youthfully convinced of that. She reminded him of a witch with those brooding eyes and slightly jutting chin. And as for keeping the whole sorry mess secret from his mother, well, he would go every inch of the way with his father down that road. It was just that the kid, Lisa, bothered his conscience somehow.

Still, men had to stick together at a time like this. As the car drew up in the drive of The Laurels, Jonathan punched his father on the shoulder in an affectionate gesture which said it all.

If Lisa was surprised to see Jonathan she didn't show it. They sat in the sitting-room like characters in a stage play, Patrick advising on solicitors, urging Delia to hand over the money side to a good man he knew who would sort things out in no time.

Delia, in the space of one day, had stepped over the boundary into middle age. She was small, cowed, and very, very angry. Lisa looked plainer than ever, Jonathan thought, her nose pink-tipped and her eyes swollen with weeping. And yet his heart ached for her.

When Patrick asked in a pointed way if any other family friends had called to sympathize, Delia shot him a glance spiced with disgust.

'Angus has been borrowing from all our so-called friends. There's a drawer in his desk full of IOUs. How much did he touch you for, Patrick?' Her voice dripped icicles. 'Because the first thing I'm going to do when things get sorted out is to pay you back. Every penny.'

Jonathan saw his father flinch. 'Angus never approached me,' he answered stiffly, 'and if he had I wouldn't dream of . . . .'

'Oh, but I would insist,' Delia told him in a high, bright tone, and it was in that moment that Jonathan knew his presence as an unwilling chaperone had done the trick. Maybe his father had underestimated her. There was pride in the way she narrowed her eyes, staring at Patrick from beneath those strangely hooded lids.

'Anyway, my father will be coming back.' Lisa spoke for the first time. 'Things had just got on top of him, that's all.' She glanced towards the door as if expecting to see Angus's red head appearing round it. 'He'd got mixed up with money worries, that's all. My father would never leave us.'

'Would you like to see the letter he left?' Delia spoke directly to Patrick. 'If you come with me through to the study I'll show it to you.'

Immediately Patrick waved her back to her seat. 'Nay, no need for that. What Angus wrote was private. He wouldn't want one of his friends to read it, I'll stake my life on that.'

He was making sure Delia didn't get him on his own, Jonathan knew. His father was making it clear once and for all that if Delia Logan imagined she could rely on him, then she'd better change her mind. Fast. Sitting quietly in a corner of the big room, observing all and saying nothing, Jonathan was experiencing a reluctant yet unstinting admiration for his father.

He glanced round the room at the distempered walls, with their ziggurat frieze, the lampshades shaped like an artist's impression of a lightning flash, the orange curtains and cushions, their shiny material stippled with black cubes. He compared the ugly modernity of it with his mother's taste for Regency elegance. And he compared Delia's hard, brooding looks with his mother's fair, fragile prettiness. For a moment Patrick's resolution not to be involved made simple and unerring sense. Callous it might be, cruel even, but Alice Grey, gentle and uncomplaining in her tenuous hold on life, must never, never hear a whisper of her husband's affair with the deserted wife of Angus Logan.

'That poor woman,' she had said, as they left the house. 'Yes, of course you must go, dear, and offer any help we can give.' She had smiled at them from her high-piled pillows, her thin face alight with pride in her husband and son. 'How *like* you, Patrick,' her expression had said, 'to hurry round at once like this.'

'You're a good man,' she had whispered, as her husband bent to kiss her goodbye.

All at once Jonathan felt nauseated. 'I think we ought to go, Father,' he said in a loud voice. 'Mother wasn't feeling well. I think we ought to get back.'

They stood in the hall, the men uneasy and embarrassed, the women with blank faces. Unbelievably, to Jonathan, they all shook hands.

'Thank you for coming.' Delia's voice was pitched on the verge of hysteria.

'My father will be back soon.' Lisa stared Jonathan out, smiling a tight little smile as he dropped his eyes. 'Sometimes people have to run off, just for a while.'

They walked back to the car. Patrick rammed a trilby hat low on his head, his handsome face blotched red beneath the casually tilted brim. 'Now I know how a rat feels as it swims away from a sinking ship,' he said, as he switched on the engine. At the traffic lights he turned to his son.

'Let's stop off at the White Bull and have a bloody drink,' he said.

Four

On the day Patrick Grey saw in the *Weekly Times* that The Laurels was up for auction to the highest bidder, along with its entire contents, he picked up the telephone, and spoke briefly to Delia.

'Seems like Angus Logan, the bloody fool, had gambled his house away,' he told his son later that day. 'So I've offered Mrs Logan one of the houses in Mill Street. At a peppercorn rent.' Patrick shuffled a sheaf of invoices on his desk into a neater pile. 'The least I could do.'

Jonathan bit back what he had been going to say. So it was *Mrs Logan* now? He waited for more.

Without looking up, Patrick said: 'I'd like you to take one of the vans and help with the flitting. Better I keep in the background.' He swallowed. 'Aye, better all round.'

'It wouldn't do for Mrs Logan to get any wrong ideas.' Jonathan saw his father look up at that, his expression betraying his feelings.

Patrick's voice was strong and cold as he said, 'You know what that woman's like. An' she's not latching on to me. No, by God, she's not. Anyroad, the house in Mill Street is empty. It's no skin off my nose.'

'A bit of a come-down, though.' Jonathan shook his head from side to side.'What about the kid? Lisa. She's paid for to the High School, isn't she? Will there be some sort of grant available to keep her on?'

'She's left,' Patrick said. 'She's been stopping at home to look after The Laurels. And her mother.' He unscrewed the top of his fountain pen and started to write. 'That's it, then.

Oh, and I haven't mentioned this, any of it, to your mother. I'm not having her bothered, and that's final.'

'How *is* your mother, Jonathan?'

'Not very well at all.'

Jonathan looked past Lisa, down the long hall at The Laurels to where Delia was emerging from the dining-room at the back of the house. He knew that his mouth had dropped open, but he couldn't help it. Lisa looked much the same as before, a bit scruffier maybe in a jumper at least two sizes too big for her; but Delia, since he had seen her last, had deteriorated to the point of being hardly recognizable.

Surely this wasn't the elegant woman with fashionable short, curly hair, her thin legs sheathed in silk stockings in her favourite gipsy-tan shade, her make-up carefully applied. Now she shuffled towards him in flat shoes, her dark hair frizzed at the ends and flat on top, her nose as pointed as if the flesh had fallen away on either side.

To Jonathan's horror she advanced, hands outstretched, her mouth widening in what had once been her hostess smile.

'How very good of you, Jonathan!' Her laugh was superior and crushing at the same time. 'There isn't much to load on the van.' She waved a hand. 'All the rest is to be auctioned tomorrow. Just a few bits and pieces, that's all. Lisa knows.' She drew on the cigarette held loosely in one hand. 'Now, if you'll excuse me.'

From the patch pocket at the front of her tweed skirt Lisa produced a typed list. Gravely she studied it, her head on one side. 'I've put down here what we're taking. The rest will be sold later on. I've packed our clothes in four cases, and the kitchen things are in a carton. The carpets we're leaving, of course. Your father said the previous tenants left floor coverings and curtains behind. So it should be straightforward.' She smiled. 'It's awfully good of you to come like this, Jonathan. My mother does appreciate it.' Lowering her voice, she glanced down the hall. 'She hasn't been well, but she'll perk up when we get settled. Then perhaps she'll be able to take up her life again.'

From Mill Street? Oh, my God! Jonathan followed Lisa upstairs. The so-called previous tenants of Number 14 Mill Street had done a moonlight flit, leaving the house, according to his father, smelling of bugs and worse. Floor coverings and curtains? He glanced down at the thick pile of the Wilton carpet and sighed. More like paper blinds at the windows and worn oilcloth on the flag floors in the house they were going to.

'I've rolled up the mattress, but I couldn't undo these bolt things on the frame.' Lisa was leaning over a bed, her plaits swinging round her flushed face. 'I suppose you really need a spanner?'

Jonathan produced one from the pocket of his blue overalls.

'What it is to have a man about the house,' Lisa said gaily.

'Stop it!' Jonathan looked as if he was about to hit her. 'Stop play-acting!' He winced as he saw the tears gather in her eyes. 'It gets on my nerves,' he added, bending down and starting to dismantle the bed. 'You've known me too long to need to put on an act with me. And wipe your nose, it's running.'

With grim determination he went on with what he was doing, ignoring the snuffling sounds behind him. When he turned round at last Lisa was white-faced, composed and silent, but as if she had spoken Jonathan rounded on her.

'And don't you dare say how good it is of my father to do what he's doing! Your mother's been at the bottle, hasn't she? So let's have a bit of truth coming out in this whole rotten mess!' Anger took over from distress as Jonathan freed the bedpost from the base, which fell with a clatter to the floor. 'It was your father who began all this with his pretending to live like a lord when all the time he wasn't worth a brass farthing.' He ran his fingers through his dark hair, leaving a dirty mark on his forehead. Oh, God, what was he saying? Why didn't he keep his mouth shut? That was what his father had told him to do. Merely to help with the removal, then scarper.

He began to dismantle the second bed-end, twisting the

spanner with angry jerks, banging when the nut wouldn't shift, releasing his fury at what he couldn't bear to accept, hearing Lisa snivelling behind him, whimpering like some small animal in pain.

'You don't still believe your father might come back?' Jonathan struggled with the rusty bolt, feeling the sweat break out on his dirty forehead. 'You don't, do you? You wouldn't be *that* daft.'

With a final twist the spanner did its job. As he straightened up Lisa came round the opposite side of the bed, ready to lift and guide the unwieldy frame through the door.

'My father is dead,' she said in a light conversational tone. 'He died about a month ago. Abroad.'

Jonathan stared through the wire mesh at a tear-stained face framed by two long, thick plaits, a face at that moment as plain as the back of a fishcart.

'When we've got settled in, Jonathan Grey, I'll find a job. My mother hasn't been eating properly, so I must see she has good, nourishing food. There are lots of ways to make money if you put your mind to it. We won't be living in Mill Street for long, you'll see.' She gave a small smile. 'Now, do you want me to lift or push? I'm stronger than I look, so don't worry.'

Jonathan gave up. Suddenly all his anger was spent. 'I've got a bloke outside in the van.' He walked over to the window, throwing up the sash. 'I'll give him a shout. I'd have brought him in at first but I thought we might've had a sensible talk.' He leaned out. 'Bill? Up here!'

He nodded at Lisa. 'Just give me that list and we'll get on with it. OK?'

As she passed over the slip of paper their fingers touched, and immediately the sadness he had felt ever since stepping into the big house came up in his throat. Gripping Lisa's hand tightly he whispered, 'Your father. What did he die of, Lisa Logan? C'mon now. The truth!'

Pulling her hand away, she met his eyes and said, lying through her small white teeth, 'Of a fever.' Then, turning on her heel, she walked out on to the landing, throwing her plaits over her shoulders as she went.

'In there,' he heard her tell the tall, shock-haired youth bounding up the stairs. 'Mr Grey knows what to do.'

Jonathan balled a hand into a fist and beat his forehead. What was the use? In all the sorry, stupid mess, what was the use?

'Beds first,' he told the boy entering the room. 'And if the other one is anything like this to dismantle, then it's a bugger.'

The house in Mill Street, two up and two down, had a front door which opened directly into a front room smelling of the possibility of mice. The room at the back overlooked a tiny yard with a lean-to coal shed and a lavatory with a stained wooden seat.

Beneath the window of the back room was a slopstone with a cold tap, and in the grate of an old-fashioned black fireplace a tiny fire burned. The oilcloth covering the floor was so thin and worn that the nicks of the flags underneath showed clearly, making a separate pattern of their own.

At seven o'clock that same evening Delia sat in a chair, smoking and flicking ash into the hearth. They had eaten a snatched meal of bread and jam, and now Lisa was standing at the gas cooker waiting for the kettle to boil.

'We were lucky there was some coal in the shed, weren't we?' She picked up a dishcloth and poured a stream of boiling water into a teapot. 'You'll feel better when you've had a cup of tea.'

Delia said nothing. Lisa bit her lips tightly together to hide her exasperation. She kept on reminding herself of how her mother had looked just a few short months ago. Then, to get her own way, Delia had only needed to flutter her eyelashes and pout. Now there was no one to flutter her eyelashes at, the friends they had danced their nights away with having disappeared like snow in the sun.

'When the sale of the house goes through things will be different.' Lisa passed Delia a cup of tea. 'This is only for the time being.' She sat down across the fireplace from her mother. 'You know what they say about the darkest hour always coming before the dawn.'

'There won't be a dawn.' Delia stared morosely into the tiny fire. 'I've given instructions to that fool of a solicitor that the money has to go to pay off your father's debts. From what he says there'll still be some owing even when we're totally destitute.'

'People would wait.' Lisa felt the ache in her back spread to her legs. 'People aren't that unkind.'

Delia clattered her cup back on to her saucer. '*Aren't* they? Bookies have hearts of gold then, have they? Patrick Grey has let us have this hovel out of the goodness of his heart, has he?' She threw the cigarette stub into the fire. 'He's the one we're going to pay back first. We're going to get a rent book and we're going to pay him every penny, week by week.'

'Seven shillings.' Lisa nodded. 'That's what the rent is. I asked Jonathan and he told me.' Leaning forward, she picked up the poker and stirred the fire into sluggish life. 'In the morning I'm going to sign on at the Labour Exchange. They might have a job for me. I'm not trained for anything, but I'm going to go to Night School to learn shorthand and typing. It's free, and if I work at – well, anything during the day, then get good speeds at Night School, leaving school won't have mattered.' She smiled hopefully at Delia. 'You never know, maybe you'll decide to find a job, when you're feeling better. In a dress shop or something.' She glanced round the bleak little room. 'It would be better than staying in here all day.'

With fingers that shook, Delia scrabbled for another cigarette, lighting it with a feverish intensity as if she couldn't trust herself to speak before she had drawn smoke deep into her lungs. Always quick to lose her temper, since Angus had gone her cold and terrible rages had increased to a point where it seemed every vestige of control had been abandoned.

'You sit there,' she told her daughter through tight lips, 'calmly suggesting that I go out to work? In a dress shop serving women who used to be my friends? God, but you take the biscuit!' She puffed frantically. 'I've done nothing to deserve this! Do you hear me? That bastard you call your father may have driven us to live in surroundings not fit for pigs, but he's not forcing me out to earn my living. You're like him. Do you know that?' She tilted her small head away from the upcurl of smoke, looking at Lisa from beneath hooded lids. 'And just who do you think is going to employ *you*? Have you taken a good look at yourself lately? Look at your hands! And your hair! You look like a skivvy and you talk like one. You disgust me!'

The hurt deep inside Lisa was like a grinding pain. It was true that since taking on the housework back at The Laurels her hands had roughened and reddened. It was also true that at times her hair stayed plaited for days. But it wasn't her fault. None of the whole rotten mess they were in was her fault. She was tired to the point of exhaustion; she was hungry and unhappy; and there were moments when she accepted in her heart that her father would never be coming back. Suddenly he was there, in her imagination, striding into the dreadful little room, blue eyes dancing, tweaking her plaits and calling her his bonny wee lass. The pain of his going stabbed her afresh.

'I can do something about my hair!' She jumped up and walked over to the kitchen dresser which filled the whole of one wall. 'That's if I remembered to bring the scissors.'

Opening a drawer, she pounced on them, waving them aloft.

She was all her father as she hacked first at one plait then the other. With a dramatic flourish she flung them into the fire, hearing them sizzle as the flames took and consumed them, seeing the sparks fly against the sooty chimney back.

'There!' she shouted in triumph. 'That's one problem solved! Now do you think I look fit to sign on at the Labour Exchange? Well?'

'You young devil!' Jumping up from her chair Delia was white with shock. 'You knew I didn't mean you to do that! How dare you take me up, just for spite?' Hysteria sharpened her high voice as she reached for the scissors. 'Here, give them to me! Let me have a go at mine, then we can both look the part!'

She was shouting so loudly that neither of them heard the

knock on the door. Whipping round, their faces blank with astonishment, mother and daughter stared in disbelief at the stout bulk of the woman standing in the doorway, holding a basin in her hands.

'I'm Mrs Ellis.' Two chins wobbled into a smile. 'Next door. Yon side.' A head waved into ridges by steel kirby-grips jerked towards the dresser. 'I saw you come at dinner time, but I thowt I'd let you settle first before I come round to see if there was owt I could do.'

'Without knocking!' Delia was beside herself. 'You come straight into my house, walking into my drawing-room without even being announced?' Her eyes flicked up and down over the stout little body, from the tortuously pinned hair to the broad feet encased in down-at-heel bedroom slippers. Frustration and despair now unleashed Delia's ungovernable temper into a fury. She sat down again, speaking fretfully to Lisa. 'Do you know this person, Lisa? Because she's a stranger to me.'

Florence Ellis had lost a husband on the Somme. She had struggled to bring up two children by going out daily, cleaning in the big houses up by the park. She had known humiliation, hunger at times; she had worked for women who treated her as less than the dust beneath their feet. But never in the whole of her life had she been spoken to like that.

'Eh on now!' She drew herself up to her full height of four feet eleven inches. 'There's no call to talk like that. I did knock, if you must know, but you was yelling that loud it was no wonder you didn't hear.' Her voice softened. 'C'mon now, luv. I know what it's like when you've just flitted, and as we're to be next-door neighbours we don't want to start off wrong.' She winked at Delia's strained face. 'I've got two lasses a bit older than what your lass is, so I know what it's like. Think they know everything when they know nowt.' She placed the covered basin on the table. 'I don't suppose either of you's had more than a jam butty all day, so there's a drop of stew there. It only needs warming up.'

'Thank you, Mrs Ellis.' Lisa was so ashamed of her

68

mother that she could hardly bear to look at her. 'You're very kind.'

To Lisa's dismay Delia waved an imperious hand at the basin. 'You can take that . . . that dish away with you. And you can go. Now!' Ignoring the stricken look on Lisa's face, she turned a shoulder and stared into the fire. 'Show this person out, Lisa. When I need charity I will ask for it. But not until.'

Lisa looked as if she were about to cry, but Mrs Ellis picked up the basin and advanced on Delia as if she were about to pour the contents over her head. Her body seemed to swell. 'Right, Mrs Fancy-pants. You've picked the wrong one to talk to like that! You think you're better than what I am, don't you? Well, let me tell thee summat. I do what's right, like most of the folks down this street, and that makes me thy equal.' She advanced a step nearer to where Delia sat, apparently unhearing. 'I wasn't going to say, but I know who you are, aye, and I know what's brought you low, an' so does everybody else round abouts. An' folks was sorry for you. Right heart sorry. There's more kindness in this street than I reckon tha's known in a month of Sundays. Want for owt in this street and a stretched-out hand will be filled.' She nodded her large, almost square face. 'But I reckon *tha'll* have to shout mighty loud afore anybody comes running!'

Clutching the basin to her one-piece bosom, she stalked majestically to the door, her slippers making little slapping noises on the worn oilcloth.

'My mother isn't very well.' Lisa followed her, still clutching the kitchen scissors. 'She didn't mean to be rude.'

'Oh, aye?' Mrs Ellis sniffed. 'Well, *I* did.' She stood on the flags looking up and down the sloping street. 'Talking with a posh voice doesn't give folks the right to be insulting. Not in my book it doesn't.'

When Lisa went back through the front parlour into the living-room Delia was rummaging in her handbag for lipstick and mirror.

'We must keep up appearances,' she said. 'That's very important.' And holding up the mirror in the lid of a gold compact she drew a perfect cupid's bow across her thin lips, pressing them together, then fluffed up her end-frizzed hair before lighting another cigarette.

With a little cry Lisa turned and ran up the uncarpeted stairs into the bedroom at the back of the house. Throwing herself down on the bed which Jonathan had put up that morning she pulled the counterpane round her for comfort. Normally, when upset, she had retired behind her hair, drawing it over her face like a blanket, but now even that was gone. Without the long thick fall of hair she felt strangely bereft, as if, like Samson, she told herself dramatically, losing it had drained away all her strength. In spite of Patrick Grey's insistence that the house be stoved to get rid of the bugs before they moved in, a strange, sweet, sickly smell came from the walls. Outside the window were not fields and the distant view of a leafy wood, but rows of dreary terraced houses, with grey washing flapping against soot-ingrained walls.

She was a very young fifteen-year-old. She felt ugly, and she was cold. There was no food in the house, and down-stairs her mother was sitting hunched up over the fire with her thin lips painted a bright red. Back at The Laurels there were little labels stuck on Lisa's frilled dressing-table and the pink velvet chair in her bedroom. Soon dealers with catalogues would be walking round the lovely house, making bids for everything, and when the money came in it would all have to go to faceless men in loud check suits with cigars stuck into their greedy vacant faces.

Her mother was never going to accept that her life had changed for ever. Lisa knew in her heart that Delia was determined to carry on as if she were still Mrs Angus Logan of The Laurels, with a cook in the kitchen and a daily woman to do the cleaning. The way her mother had spoken to that kind little woman from next door had shown Lisa exactly how it was going to be.

There was a wild streak in Delia that positively frightened Lisa. At times it took the form of a screaming vulgarity she couldn't understand. In Lisa's opinion, for what it was worth, she told herself, there were times when her mother's

70

behaviour made nonsense of her claim to middle-class refinement.

She laid an arm across her eyes. . . . Somewhere, thousands of miles away, her father sat beneath a foreign sun by the side of a woman dripping with diamonds. With the clarity of her over-vivid imagination, Lisa could see a plump hand weighted with rings, reaching out to pat her father's knee.

I wonder if she's persuaded him into shorter shorts, she wondered, and the wondering brought scalding tears to her eyes.

Lisa was his only child – his bonny wee lass, Angus had often called her – and yet he had walked away. It was unbelievable, incredible, and yet it was so.

As her crying shuddered to soft hiccuping sobs, she sank into sleep, too weary to undress, too unhappy even to care.

'How can you stand there and tell me that you intend queueing at the Labour Exchange with a line of common people?' Delia lifted a fluted cup rimmed with gold leaf to her scarlet mouth. 'I'm sure that one of your father's so-called friends would take you as his secretary if you're really determined to give up your schooling and go out to business. You seem to have made up your mind to upset me. Isn't there some way you can claim some money from the government? Like the dole or something,' she added vaguely.

Lisa looked away from her mother's puffy early-morning face. She told herself that it was important she kept calm.

'Secretaries do shorthand and typing, Mother, and I can't do either.' She smiled, willing Delia to smile back. 'Come to think of it, there's not much I can do really. I can play the piano a little, speak a sort of schoolgirl French, ride a horse, boil an egg if I stand with a watch in my hand, and that's about it. I can't see anyone rushing to employ me, but I have to try.' She stood up and crammed a yellow beret down over the chewed and ragged hair. 'I have to *try*, Mother. We have to eat.'

Delia lit a cigarette. 'Well, I suppose if you must, then you must.' She opened her handbag and took out a ten-shilling note. 'Bring me some cigarettes on your way back, dear. And not those awful Woodbines, please! And perhaps a pot or two of those buttered shrimps from the market ladies. It *is* Wednesday, isn't it?' She put a hand to her forehead. 'It's funny, but I get the impression that every day is Monday lately, somehow. Monday, Monday, Monday. One after the other.'

'Is this all we have?' Lisa frowned at the note, her small face anxious and drawn beneath the felt beret. 'Mother. Is it?'

'Oh, my God, the fire's going out!' Delia pointed an accusing finger at the black grate. 'See to it before you go, Lisa. You're a Girl Guide. You know how to keep a fire going.'

'I *was* a Girl Guide,' Lisa corrected. 'My uniform is wrapped up in a bundle back at the house, remember? Lot 96 or something.' Kneeling down, she inserted the poker beneath the small pyramid of sticks and coal, regretting her words immediately, as Delia sprang from her chair in a fury.

'That's right! Blame me! Blame me because you can't be a bloody Girl Guide! Let us go without everything that makes life worth living; let us live in a slum, begrudge me my cigarettes, but most of all make a terrible fuss about a Guide uniform.' She hurled the china cup at the fireplace so that it fell broken into two pieces on the hearth.

Lisa closed her eyes for a moment, feeling the familiar prickle of fear run down her spine. It was all because her father was no longer here, she whispered to herself. Her mother was missing him to quarrel with, that was all. Nurtured on their shouting rows, scared witless at times, she had still known that once the storm was over the house would be full of laughter again. Delia would flutter around the room, flicking cigarette ash in the vague direction of the cut-glass ash-trays, her silken skirts billowing out as she twirled. And Angus would laugh, teasing, smiling to show all was forgotten.

Now it seemed that Lisa was to be the captive audience for her mother's petulant rages. So she must just learn how to cope. Her father had managed and now so would she.

72

'I'm going now.' Getting up from her knees, Lisa dusted her hands together. 'The fire will be OK if you put more coal on in about an hour.'

She left Delia cowering in her chair, whimpering about the unfairness of everything, weeping into a lace-edged handkerchief. The sound stayed with Lisa as she closed the front door and stepped out on to the pavement.

At the top of the street two small boys swung on a rope tied to a lamp post. In spite of the touch of frost in the air, they wore skimpy jerseys, and their faces were blue with cold. From both their noses ran green candles of slimy ropes. Lisa shuddered.

'Sken, sken, you big fat hen! We don't lay eggs for gentlemen. And if we do they're not for you, so sken, sken, you big fat hen!'

They shouted the words in unison, small faces taunting and cheeky. Lisa hurried on, hating the embarrassment of it, despising herself for caring. On the way to the town centre she passed rows of shops, and winced away from a reflection of herself with hair sticking out like chewed rope.

A coal cart clattered along the street, its driver sitting hunched up at the front, coal sacks neatly folded after the first of his morning's deliveries. Lisa walked on, past the town hall built in 1856 in the classic style, square and solid, then crossed the road before turning right down to the Labour Exchange.

She was almost past a draper's shop, its large window stuffed with draped curtain nets flanking bolts of flowered cotton prints, when she saw a notice penned in large black capitals: YOUNG LADY ASSISTANT WANTED. APPLY WITHIN.

Without stopping to think twice, Lisa opened the door, hearing the bell ping behind her as she went in.

'I've come about the vacancy,' she told a man with fair straight hair brushed back from a high forehead. She smiled a bright, trying-to-please smile. 'Are you the owner of this shop?'

Richard Carr blinked short-sighted blue eyes at the small girl across the counter smiling at him from beneath a yellow beret, with dark tufts of hair sticking out like Vikings' horns at either side. He tucked a long green Venus pencil behind an ear and riffled the pages of an order book before answering.

'I am indeed the owner, Miss.' His tight smile held a touch of patronage. 'But that notice has only just gone in the window.' He glared at her accusingly. 'You must have seen me put it in.'

Lisa's answering smile was radiant. 'There you are, then! It was meant to be. I'm a great believer in things being meant to be.' She pushed the beret back with a finger. 'Will you consider me for the position, Mr . . . ?'

'Carr. Richard Carr. But look here now. . . .' To gain the time he felt he needed, Richard Carr took the pencil from behind his ear and wrote something down on a note-pad, underlining it firmly.

Setting a great store on the way a person spoke, he told himself that this strange little girl must have talked that way since birth. In spite of the atrocious hair and the navy-blue school raincoat, he guessed she came from a class more used to giving orders than receiving them. That, he decided, was why she was speaking to him now without a trace of servility in her manner.

His face gave nothing away. 'How old are you, Miss . . . ?'

'Logan. Lisa Logan. I'm in my sixteenth year.' She glanced round the large shop, taking in quickly the large bolts of material on the shelves, the wide counter with its brass ruler incorporated along its length, the dummy by the door, draped in flowered cotton in the tucked and gathered semblance of a dress. A woman of indeterminate age appeared from a room at the back, coming forward with an ingratiating smile to serve a customer at a smaller counter set at right angles to the one across which Richard Carr surveyed Lisa, his fair head on one side.

'Experience?' He lowered his voice.

'None at all.' Lisa went on smiling through an increasing sense of desperation. 'But I pick things up quickly.'

'References?'

'Miss Adams, the headmistress of the High School. The

Mayor,' Lisa said quickly. 'He's a personal friend of my father.' Her chin lifted. 'Was,' she amended. 'My father died quite recently.'

'I'm sorry to hear that.' Richard Carr wasn't a man to be rushed into a snap decision. A businessman with a ruthless eye for a worthwhile proposition, he saw in the small girl standing there with a naked pleading in her eyes a distinct and viable asset to his business. With that voice and that accent it was just possible that young Lisa Logan could turn out to be exactly the kind of girl he'd had in mind but never hoped to find. Miss Howarth, ringing up the till for a twopenny paper of pins, knew the working of the shop like the back of her hand. She had worked for his father and could gauge the exact yardage of material by the simple expedient of holding one corner underneath her chin and extending one of her arms. But her flattened vowels betrayed her lack of education. She made no attempt, as Richard himself had done, to refine her speech. 'I think you'd best take an extra quarter of a yard,' she would say. Or, 'That's nobbut enough for a long-sleeved blouse.' And on occasions, unforgivably, 'The only way to keep your nets nice is to starch and dolly-blue 'em regular-like before they get too mucky.'

Yes, there was no doubt that what Miss Howarth lacked was finesse, whereas this peculiar small girl would add tone to the establishment. And if she was on social terms with the Mayor, it could be that his good lady the Mayoress might one-step over the threshold and lend her valuable patronage to the shop.

'You'd have to wear a black frock,' he said, his mind made up. He coughed discreetly. 'And perhaps smooth your hair down a little. We set great store on personal appearance. It's only an hour's train ride to Manchester and the big stores. The girls who work in Manchester in shops like Kendal Milne's are very ladylike. From good homes, well connected.'

'My mother's father was a Colonel in the Indian Army, and my own father was a Captain in the Scottish Highlanders. Three times mentioned in dispatches,' Lisa said quickly, adding an extra mention for effect. 'I need to go out to business only on account of him dying and leaving my mother and I temporarily short of ready money.'

In her eagerness to impress, Lisa's accent became even more swanky. Richard Carr hesitated, then, uncharacteristically for him, made an impulsive decision.

'Very well, then. I'll take you on a month's trial, starting tomorrow. Seven shillings and sixpence a week. Half day Thursday, working from eight forty-five in the morning to eight o'clock at night. Late closing at nine on Saturdays.'

Shrugging off the notion that he himself had been interviewed and not his prospective employee, Richard nodded a dismissal. His eyebrows ascended almost to his hair-line as, after thanking him breathlessly, Lisa took off like a whirlwind, out of the shop, past the window, her yellow beret bobbing furiously.

Her face shone bright pink. She was filled to bursting point with sheer joy. Nothing in her life up to now had prepared her for this soaring, blazing sense of triumph. It was as though all her future had been mapped out by a few strokes of Mr Carr's dark green Venus pencil as he'd taken down the addresses of the two people he was going to ask for references.

All her mood of previous despair was gone. She had got a job, her first, and at the very first try. She had out-smarted Mr Carr good and proper. Adrenalin pulsed through her veins as she went over the interview, word by word. She had *made* him like her; she had *willed* him to take her on.

It was of course a pity she wasn't beautiful, but personality counted for far more. Hadn't she just proved that? In spite of her awful hair, her freckles, and her shameful overlarge bust, he had accepted her. So it followed she must have something. It did, didn't it?

What she had was charm, her father's natural ability to make people like him. And although Lisa was too young to realize this fact, she accepted the attribute with gratitude.

It was a gift much tested during the long, cold winter to follow. . . .

It wasn't easy being charming to women who made her

unroll bolt after bolt of heavy velvets and velours for their inspection before deciding there was nothing they fancied after all.

Miss Howarth knew most of the difficult customers by sight, and would leave them for Lisa to deal with.

'Tell 'em to measure t'windows, then multiply by three,' she told Lisa. 'An' if they're too skinny to buy enough stuff, then let 'em find out for themselves how skimped the curtains will look when they're hung. It's their funeral, not ours.'

Lisa's feet and ankles froze into aching chilblained agony as she stood for hours in the draught from the constantly opening door. She had dyed her speech-night white frock a patchy black, and with an old black jacket of Delia's worn over the top was reasonably satisfied that she looked the part of a sales assistant.

Too depressed to argue, Delia had trimmed Lisa's hair to a club-cut neatness, and given her a stub of Tangee lipstick.

'There!' Lisa had presented herself to her mother for inspection that first day. 'Three yards of the dotted Swiss muslin? Certainly, moddom!'

But Delia had turned away, refusing to smile, pursing her lips and saying nothing.

Before Christmas The Laurels had been sold, and the asking price distributed among the growing band of creditors. When the solicitor sent his own bill, Delia had sold her engagement ring and a pair of diamond ear-rings, giving them to Lisa to take to a tiny shop where the jeweller had tut-tutted into a magnifying glass before handing over the money.

'There's still my brooches and your gold locket and chain.' Delia sat in the chair by the fire as if she was growing from it now, shrunken, defeated, deep in a lethargy that carried her, strangely uncaring, through the long winter days when Lisa was out at the shop.

'And what then?' Lisa served their evening meal, two bowls of Force followed by the inevitable bread and jam. The months of deprivation had honed her small frame down so that the flesh stretched tightly over her cheekbones,

77

throwing her huge grey-blue eyes into startling beauty. 'What then, when we've sold all the jewellery? Mr Carr is going to put my wages up to ten shillings after Christmas, but we can't live on that.' She turned to face her mother, her small face pinched with worry beneath the straight fall of dark hair. 'We haven't paid a penny in rent yet, and we wouldn't even be able to have a fire but for the coal delivered free every month. It's from Uncle Patrick. You know that, don't you? And it costs two shillings a hundredweight. Did you know *that?*'

'He'll be paid back.' Delia reached for a cigarette. 'Every penny. With interest. You always look on the black side of things, Lisa.'

The injustice of the remark made tears sting behind Lisa's eyes, but she knew better than to defend herself. Even the mildest remark was enough to send Delia into one of her tearing tempers, when a torrent of abuse poured from her thin mouth; when she would shake all over, throw whatever happened to be handy, and then collapse sobbing into her chair.

'There must be . . .' Lisa said carefully, ' . . . some way we can claim even a small allowance. Nobody is allowed to starve in this country. Are they?' She sat down at the table and picked up her spoon. 'Isn't there something called the Means Test or Parish Relief? Miss Howarth was talking about it yesterday. She says half the population of the town are on it.' She sprinkled a teaspoonful of sugar over the Force. 'It might be worth trying.'

Delia threw back her head and laughed, looking for a moment as she had looked less than a year ago when she had been full of life and vivacity. 'Oh, God, you really are naïve!' She looked down at the solid-silver spoon in her hand and pointed it at the dresser. 'Before they would give us a bean we'd have to be eating off newspapers with Wool-worth's knives and forks. Before they gave us a penny piece all our last pieces of good furniture would have to go.' Her face darkened. 'Haven't I suffered enough? Is that what you want me to be subjected to now? A pack of bullying officials coming in here and telling me what to flog before they hand out a pennyworth of charity? Is that what my parents endured years of filth and heat in India for? Is that what your father fought for in France, sleeping in trenches running with mud and rats?'

Pushing the bowl aside, she grabbed for a cigarette, lighting it with hands that shook. 'Haven't I been humiliated enough? How low do you want me to sink? Do you want me to end up like that dreadful woman next door?' Delia dragged smoke deep into her lungs. 'Do you know what she's taken to doing?'

Lisa shook her head, holding her breath, praying that if she merely nodded and agreed her mother might calm down.

'She peers in at me through the window!' Delia stabbed her glowing cigarette in the direction of the slopstone. 'I'm sitting in my chair when I hear a tapping, and when I turn round there she is, with her big fat face leering at me.'

Lisa forgot to be careful. 'Mrs Ellis? But how does she get into our yard? The outside door is always bolted. She isn't tall enough to lean over and pull it back like you say the coalman does. And anyway, if she came she would come to the front door, like she did that other time. She doesn't strike me as the sort of person who would creep about staring into other people's windows.'

Delia gave a hoarse shout of triumph. 'Well, I tell you she does! And she bangs on the wall, over and over. Some days I have to bang back just to show her.' The vixen-like face became sharp with cunning. 'I kneel on that stand-chair there and I bang like mad. With a hammer,' she added.

That night when Delia sat dozing by the fire, Lisa tiptoed through the front parlour, past the odd pieces of furniture, chairs badly arranged for the simple reason that no one ever sat in them, and the single wardrobe used for the outdoor clothes her mother never wore.

With her heart pounding against her ribs she lifted the iron knocker and let it bang against the door of Mrs Ellis's house.

It was opened almost immediately by a girl of about Lisa's own age, a brassy girl with bold eyes, and hair dried and frizzed into a curly perm. She wore a round-necked blouse of black cotton beneath a pinafore dress of green material blooming with yellow flowers. In the curly hair cotton fluff was dotted, as if someone had blown a dandelion clock over her head.

'Mam?' she called, before Lisa had uttered a word. 'It's her from next door.' She stood back, sharp eyes gleaming with curiosity. 'You'd best come in. She's through there.'

Florence Ellis was ironing at a square table set in the middle of the back room, using two irons, one heating at the fire and the other clipped into a shining slipper which glided over the starched cottons at a touch.

'You'd best sit down, luv,' she said kindly. 'You look fair beat.'

The room was so hot that Lisa closed her eyes for a moment in ecstasy. She couldn't remember being so blissfully warm. The heat came at her from the high-banked fire, and orange flames set the brasses on the stone hearth twinkling like little stars.

'I've come about my mother,' she said in a low voice.

'Oh, aye?' Mrs Ellis's broad back was noncommittal.

'I'm worried about her.' Lisa watched, sitting quietly in her chair, as the stout little woman dipped the collars and cuffs of a blouse into a basin of blued starch before pressing them through a piece of white linen. 'Do you see much of her during the day when I'm out at work?'

Mrs Ellis wiped a perspiring forehead with the back of her hand. 'Nay, luv. I never as much as set eyes on her. How can I when I'm out meself, scrubbing? I leave earlier than what you do, then when I get back at teatime it's dark. Besides, she keeps herself to herself, does your mother, as you rightly know. I'm not one for pushing me nose in where I'm not wanted. And from what I hear tell nobody else round hereabouts ever sees her neither.'

Lisa sighed. 'Then you never go into our back yard and knock on the window?'

'You what?' Mrs Ellis banged the iron down on its asbestos stand. A flush of indignation reddened the round cushions of her cheeks. Turning round, she saw the look of white despair on Lisa's face.

'It's *her* what does the knocking.'

The girl who had let Lisa in spoke from the doorway. 'I've been on short time at the mill for the past month, and the first time it happened I thought as how somebody was hanging pictures up or something, then she began the shouting.' The tightly-curled head nodded towards the dividing wall. 'It's only fair to say, Mam. It frightened the life out of me the first time I heard it, especially when I realized she's in there on her own.'

'Shouting?' Lisa tightened her hands on the wooden arms of the rocking chair. 'What kind of shouting?'

'Swear words. Filthy screaming swear words.' The bold eyes narrowed. 'I know you said not to tell, Mam, but it's terrible. An' it's not what we're used to, not down our street.'

'Joan!' Mrs Ellis sat down opposite Lisa. 'If you're going up to the top house to see Jack, then go. But mind you're back before ten.'

She leaned forward. 'Now then, luv. What's going on next door is between you and your mother, nowt to do with me. But I haven't got eyes in me head and ears stuck on the sides for nothing. An' a woman what shouts and screams herself silly when she's by herself needs seeing to. An' if you've come for advice, then that's it.'

'Seeing to, Mrs Ellis?' Lisa frowned. 'Seeing to?'

'The doctor, luv.' The big, square, ugly face softened with compassion. 'Nay, there's nowt wrong with telling the doctor what she's like. He won't pack her off to a loony-bin, not when he knows how she's had to come down in the world. It's inside your mother what's doing the screaming. I know a bit what it's like, because I was the same when my 'usband got killed on the Somme, leaving me with two kids to fetch up. I was screaming all right, but inside of me.' She thumped her chest. 'Your ma's letting hers out, that's all, an' it might not be a bad thing in the long run.'

'We can't afford to run up a doctor's bill.'

Lisa's eyes filled with shameful tears. It was the kindness, she told herself. The overpowering heat from the glowing

81

fire, and the warmth in the voice of the woman regarding her steadily through the whirlpool lenses of her spectacles.

Suddenly it all poured out. 'We were living far beyond our means, Mrs Ellis. We must have been in debt for years. Then, on the day my father's moneylenders were going to take legal action, he cracked up and walked out on us.' She lifted a tear-stained face. 'Since then the people he owed money to have never left us alone. My mother has sold everything she can to raise cash, but she won't ask for help. She's got it all twisted up in her mind that by refusing to accept even the smallest amount, she's getting her own back on my father.'

'How much do you earn, luv?'

'Seven shillings and sixpence, but after Christmas I'm being put up to ten shillings.'

'And you've nowt else coming in?'

'No.' Lisa blushed. 'A friend of . . . of my father's pays the rent and has coal delivered now and again, but you see, Mrs Ellis, my mother hasn't been used to managing. We always had maids to do the work and the shopping. She never used to bother about budgeting, she just spent and spent, and even now she still expects to be able to have her drinks and her cigarettes every day.' Lisa's head drooped. 'She's so lost and unhappy. I want to help her, but I don't know what to say. I don't know what to do.'

Leaning forward, Mrs Ellis removed the second flat iron from the fire. This wasn't the time to get on with her ironing, even though she'd be up till midnight with all the things she had to do. To tell the truth she was properly flummoxed. Her quick untutored brain was in a ferment. She could speak for the woman next door to one of her ladies, but it would never do. A posh lady like Mrs Logan would make her ladies feel embarrassed. Anyroad, she doubted if this child's mother had ever cleaned a room from top to bottom in the whole of her life.

She sighed, levering herself up out of her chair, feeling helpless and stuck for what to say. There was no solution as far as she could see, even though sympathy never came amiss whatever the circumstances.

'I know what we'll do,' she said. 'We'll have a nice cup of tea. Trouble seen through the steam of a good cuppa always seems lighter.'

Lisa was taking her first comforting sip when the knocking began on the dividing wall. It was a loud persistent hammering, almost causing her to lose her hold on the thick white cup.

'I'll come in with you, luv. Mebbe I can talk some sense into her when she won't listen to you.' The chair rocked of its own volition as Mrs Ellis jumped up quickly.

'No! Please! I'd rather you didn't.' Lisa was at the door. 'I know what to do when she's like this. I'll manage. Honestly.'

'But you're nobbut a lass.' Florence Ellis followed Lisa out into the street. Her square face was puckered with the anxiety of trying not to poke her nose in where she wasn't wanted, and yet wanting to do something to help.

'It's all right. Really!'

Lisa closed her own front door firmly, leaving the stout little woman actually wringing her hands on the pavement. She'd die if Mrs Ellis saw her mother in one of her terrible moods, she told herself dramatically. Then, squaring her shoulders, Lisa walked through the parlour into the living-room.

Delia Logan had been – not all that long ago – an attractive woman. But as she climbed down from the stand-chair drawn close to the wall, a long-handled hammer held in one hand, her face was wrenched into an evil shape, the mouth hanging open with saliva running from the corners.

'You've missed her!' she yelled. 'She's been at the bloody window again! With her curlers in and wearing that awful pinafore. She was saying how much she hated me, with her ugly fat face pressed up against the glass. Next time she does it I'll kill her! I will, you know. She's not spying on *me*, the miserable faggot!'

'It's all right now, Mother.' Gently Lisa took the hammer from Delia's hand. 'Come and sit down. See, have a cigarette. I'll light it for you.'

As Delia inhaled, Lisa closed her eyes, as if by doing so

she could shut out the sight of her mother puffing and gasping on the cigarette.

'Do you know your underskirt's showing at least two inches below your frock?' Unbelievably Delia spoke in her normal voice. 'We have to keep up our appearances, you know.'

'Oh, Mother.' Putting her arms round the thin shoulders, Lisa rocked her to and fro in an agony of pity, tempered with a fierce protective love.

Five

'A cup of Oxo's no sort of dinner for a growing girl.'

Miss Howarth bit into a beef sandwich. 'Here, have one of my butties, luv. You look to me as if you need feeding up.' She smiled, showing ivory dentures, with gums of a bright shocking pink. 'If what's in my butties has once looked over a gate, then it's all right for Daisy Howarth.' Her long face sobered. 'It's been awful these past few days listening to them telling on the wireless about the King's life drawing peacefully to its close, hasn't it? I don't reckon Edward will make much of a king. Too fond of the women for my liking. Going out dancing down in London in night-clubs, night after night. He's a loose liver, if you want my opinion.'

Her pale eyes widened in surprise as she saw the way Lisa crammed the sandwich into her mouth. 'Didn't you have no breakfast, luv? You've been looking proper peaky lately. Mr Carr noticed it. "I hope we're not overworking our Miss Logan" he said only the other day.'

Lisa forced herself to take a smaller bite. It was now the end of January, and since Christmas she had made two journeys to the second-hand jewellers at the top of King Street. Soon they would have to start selling the last pieces of silver cutlery and more transportable pieces of furniture. Food was the immediate priority. She had become used to people staring at her darned stockings and the shrunken black jacket so washed out of shape that the collar rolled over when it should have lain perfectly flat.

Constantly cold, constantly hungry, she saw her mother sink lower into depression. Delia sat crouching her days

85

away in the chair by the fire, smoking precious pennies as she lit one cigarette from another, refusing to do even the smallest task, and exploding into fury when asked.

'I'm not being nosey, luv, but you're not in any kind of trouble, are you?' Miss Howarth fiddled with her prune-coloured hair in an embarrassed way. 'I mean, a trouble shared is a trouble halved, I allus believe, and what you tell me won't go no further. May God strike me down dead if I breathe a word.'

Lisa smiled brightly, averting her eyes from the grease-proof paper bag in which a left-over sandwich lay. 'Goodness gracious, no, Miss Howarth. My mother has suffered from nervous trouble since my father . . . since he died, but when the better weather comes I'm sure she'll improve.'

'Ah, nerves.' Miss Howarth nodded with understanding. 'Give me a decent appendix or a broken leg any day. Them you can deal with. Nerves is different. Poor soul. How does it take her?'

The shop doorbell pinged, and with relief Lisa went into the shop. How could she explain to anyone that, although Delia had stopped banging on the wall, her present mood of total apathy was almost harder to bear? The worst part was that she seemed to have lost her desire to keep up appearances. Now she only washed when told to, and Lisa's fear of her ferocious rages was overridden by a much greater fear that her mother would go on sitting there, smoking herself potty.

'Three yards of white pique,' the woman across the counter said. 'It's for a dress for my daughter.' Her eyes glowed with pride. 'She's seventeen at Easter and we're taking her on a cruise. To Madeira. Like the cake, you know,' she added, adjusting the red fox pelt round her neck. 'I'm having the dress made up plain.'

Lisa stared into the glass eyes of the small pointed furry head, pitying the small creature which had once raced free through fields, its bushy tail streaming behind. She adjusted her smile. 'It would smarten the dress up if you added a woven canvas belt, something like those over there.' She pointed to a display. 'One in red, white and blue would look lovely, especially if you added a small silk scarf at the neck-line.' She reached for a box underneath the counter. 'These are the very latest. I saw Lady Astor wearing one in a copy of *The Tatler* the other week.' Draping one round her own neck she tied it in a neat knot, pulling it to one side with the same flair her mother had once shown by adding access-ories to a plain dress. 'See? Like this.'

Richard Carr's watchful eyes missed nothing. When the woman left the shop carrying a belt and scarf in addition to the dress material, he moved round to Lisa's counter.

'A very good piece of salesmanship there, Miss Logan.' He fingered his fair moustache. 'Those scarves have been sticking for a long time. Maybe we'll drape a few over the materials in the window.' His eyes twinkled. 'Did you really see a similar one on Lady Astor in *The Tatler?*'

'Either that or *Country Life.*' Lisa busied herself rolling up the bolt of white cotton pique, seeing in her mind's eye the coffee tables at The Laurels piled with glossy magazines.

She wished Mr Carr would go away, but there he stood, staring at her with his head on one side. Since coming to work at the shop she had discovered three things about Richard Carr: he was ambitious, he was a snob, but in spite of this he was basically a kind man. He was experienced in retailing, with a keen eye for what would sell. Making a go of the shop was his chief purpose in life as far as she could make out. Miss Howarth had confided that Mr Carr was a widower with a six-year-old girl, looked after by a house-keeper in a nicely set-up house out on the Chorley side of the town.

For a while now Lisa had been formulating an idea in her mind. It would mean even longer hours and harder work, but hard work could usually be translated into money, and without more money to spend on food both she and her mother would never survive. It was as simple as that.

She leaned forward, eagerness lighting up the sad contours of her pale face. 'A lot of women come into the shop to look at curtain material, then tell me how they dread having to make them up themselves.' She paused. 'They will pay a dressmaker to sew skirts, blouses and dresses, but curtains, well, they seem to begrudge paying what they call good money to a dressmaker for running up straight seams and inserting rufflette-tape.'

'And?' Richard regarded her intently. He was, in fact, more than intrigued. He never remembered coming across a girl with as much spirit and direct enthusiasm as his little Miss Logan. Employing her had been one of his better moves and, just as he had predicted, her accent and self-possession had proved a decided asset.

Lisa turned on the charm. 'I've heard there's a shop in Manchester which makes up curtains free.' She let this sink in. 'So, you see, Mr Carr, if we offered a similar service we would be bound to sell more material. So, in the long run, it would all be to our benefit. And since they finished the alterations to the Market Hall, there's a stall set up calling themselves "Lace Curtain *Specialists*". We'll have to watch them!'

Conscious that he was hesitating, half turning away, she spoke up. 'I know you're thinking that paying the wages of a machinist would kill any profit, but I would do the sewing myself. There's the machine in the back hardly ever used, and if you paid me a small commission on any orders which included making up, we'd both be more than satisfied.' Her eyes dared him to refuse. 'I *know* I'm right, Mr Carr. Within six months I expect a lot more women will buy their curtain materials from you, simply because they're getting them made up free.'

'And the tape?' Richard tapped the side of his nose. 'They'd have to pay for that.'

'Of course. They would be buying that anyway.'

'And overtime? I put you up at Christmas, you know.'

'Nothing.' Lisa spoke quickly, sensing she was winning. 'Not until it's proved to be working. Just the commission, like I said.'

Richard was stroking his moustache now with nervous strokes of a long finger. He recognized that this young girl was in a strange way his equal when it came to business acumen. He had seen her sweet-talk a hesitant customer into buying and, what was more remarkable, he had seen her change a customer's mind for her when she chose, in Lisa's opinion, a colour or type of material that would do nothing for her. And, anyway, not only was what she was suggesting a viable proposition, it could lend tone to the business. It might even double his sales of curtain material.

'So I take it you agree, Mr Carr?' As the door pinged open, Lisa's manner was brisk.

'We could give it a try.' Richard stepped back, seeing how Lisa's smile widened to welcome the potential customer.

It was a smile compounded of triumph and the thrill of achievement. Lisa knew she had won. Alone she had placed her cards on the table to see them snatched up by a man who had forgotten for a moment that she was merely a young girl turning on the charm.

Lisa Logan had pulled off her first business deal, and the sensation was one of pure joy, and a pride that lifted her way out of the over-cluttered shop into a situation where, as her imagination soared, she told herself that never again would she feel hungry, or have to storm at her mother for smoking their food money away.

'Well, yes, madam,' she told her customer. 'But I think you'll agree that this slightly more expensive velvet drapes much better? Also, the shade has that subtle difference which shows good taste. I expect your carpet is patterned? Yes? So naturally you want that to be the focal part of the room, making the curtains merely an understated influence?'

The woman gaped. How did this young girl, who looked as if she'd not long left school, know she had a patterned carpet? And what was she doing standing behind the counter of a shop talking posh like that?

'Velvet is so hard to make up, isn't it?' Lisa carefully measured the yardage against the brass rule, folded the material and took up the large shears. 'Would you like me to cut it into two lengths to make it easier?'

'Please.' The woman leaned closer. 'To tell the truth I've put off buying new curtains. My husband bought me a new Singer sewing machine last year and now he expects me to make everything with it. Curtains really get me down. And they'll have to be lined, won't they?' She pulled at the finger

89

of a leather gauntlet glove. 'Oh, dear. I'd just as soon have made do with the old ones, but we're having the decorators in and I can't for shame put the old ones back up. The linings are all shredded.'

Lisa felt as suddenly alert as if someone had prodded her hard in the small of her back. 'Oh, didn't you know, madam? Mr Carr will make the curtains up free. It's a new innovation.' She said the word in a firm, clear voice, actually tasting the feel of it on her tongue. 'If you will let us have the exact measurements of your windows we can have them ready by the weekend.'

Two round eyes narrowed into calculating slits. 'Free, did you say?'

'Excluding the tape and the cotton, of course.' Lisa smiled. 'With a 6-inch, hand-sewn hem, I'd suggest. In case of shrinkage.' She fingered the soft material. 'And, yes, you're right about having them lined. Stops them fading if the room is south-facing.'

'An' I thought there was no money about!' Miss Howarth came round to peer over Lisa's shoulder as she wrote down in a neat hand the orders for three pairs of curtains. She perched herself on the high stool, only for use when the shop was empty. 'Fancy you telling her Miss Muffet Print at sixpence a yard will make nice bedroom curtains. That's a new one on me. Miss Muffet Print's only for frocks, I would have thought.'

'Why?' Lisa licked the end of her pencil. 'If the colours are right and it's gay and colourful, what does it matter? It's for a child's bedroom, anyway, and with a pink carpet this fresh green sprigged should look lovely. See, there's a trellis of pink here and there. It should pick up the colour of the carpet beautifully.'

'Well I never!' Miss Howarth stared at Lisa in amazement. Who would have thought a slip of a girl like Lisa would know anything about soft furnishings? You could work in the trade all your life and still get no further than being able to measure a yard without having to resort to a rule.

'You've got a proper gift, luv. Did you know that?' she

asked smiling, and if there had been as much as one jealous bone in her body Daisy Howarth would have turned bright green. 'When are you going to make a start on them?'

'This afternoon,' Lisa said promptly. 'It's half-day closing. I'll ask Mr Carr for the key.' Her face lost its bright look. 'I'll have to go home to see my mother has her lunch, but I'll come straight back.'

'And see you get some dinner yourself. You look half clemmed to me.'

Lisa nodded. Because it was Thursday she had exactly six pennies in her purse. There had been a jumble sale at the Methodist Chapel the previous Saturday and Mrs Ellis had been entrusted with two whole shillings to spend on her behalf. Now Lisa was the proud possessor of a pair of black court shoes, which, lined with cardboard insoles, fitted perfectly. Into the neck of a black jumper shrunken in the wash but costing a mere twopence, Lisa had tacked one of Delia's white lace collars.

Filled with optimism, she walked into the fish-and-chip shop just round the corner from Mill Street.

Fish, of course, was out of the question. Standing in line she watched the chip-shop owner slip-slap a fillet of white fish over and across the bowl of creamy batter. 'A penny-worth of chips and two of dabs. Twice,' she said grandly, when her turn came.

'Salt and vinegar?'

Lisa nodded. 'Yes, please.'

'I'm going back,' she told Delia later, as she bit into the crunchy batter of a nicely ovalled dab, feeling the potato soft, but not too soft, underneath. 'You'll be all right, won't you, Mother?'

'I'll have to be, won't I?' Delia speared a portion of a crisp dab on her fork and looked at it without interest. 'You come and go as you like. You treat this house, if one can call it a house, like a hotel. What happens to me is none of your concern.'

Lisa went on eating. She could, she knew, have flared up and pointed out to her mother that without her meagre wages from the shop they would starve. That they were living at starvation level as it was. That if only Delia would forgo just one of her three packets of cigarettes a day they could sometimes eat potted meat, or pig's trotters from the tripe shop just round the corner from Mr Carr's. That if only her mother would do just a little work around the house instead of leaving everything for Lisa to do on Sundays, her one free day, they might perhaps, even if only marginally, survive.

'What do you do all day, Mother?' she asked quietly. 'If I bring home some marrow bones from the butcher and a pot-pourri of vegetables from the market, wouldn't you like to make some broth? Mrs Ellis told me how. It's really quite simple.'

Immediately the bright flush of anger stained Delia's thin cheeks. 'That's just what your father would like to imagine me doing, isn't it?' Pushing her plate away, she reached for a cigarette. 'I've never lived in a house without servants, and I'm not demeaning myself when I've done nothing to deserve it. Can you really see me standing at that dreadful stove stirring things round in pans?'

'Father wouldn't know.' Lisa pulled Delia's plate over. 'I'll eat this if you don't want it. I don't expect to be home much before midnight. I've three pairs of curtains to make, and it's not going to be easy. I'm not even sure I can work the flamin' sewing machine yet.' Her chin lifted. 'But I have to *try*. It's velvet, and you know how it frays.'

Delia's voice rose. 'No, I don't know! I don't know anything about curtain-making or stewing filthy bones! I don't want to know! You've developed a working-class mentality, did you know that?' The words came out jerkily between fierce puffs at the glowing cigarette. 'But *I'll* never give in. Never!'

Already Lisa, in her mind, was back at the shop, laying the material out on the worktable in the back room, slicing through it with the big scissors, studying the list of measurements, calculating, guiding the long seams beneath the foot of the hand sewing machine. Trying to apply what she had learned at school in needlework lessons to a task she might find she was unequal to.

'I'll have to go now,' she said. 'I'll put these things in the bowl for you to wash up when you feel like it.' She stood up. 'Go to bed before I come in. You look very tired, Mother.'

What she had failed to see was that Delia Logan had passed from the stage of being merely tired and depressed into the dangerous state of total uncaring apathy. Sixteen is an age when girls should be laughing with friends, going out to first dances, wearing pretty clothes. And it is also an age when, with imaginations inflamed, young girls can be single-minded in their selfishness. And what mattered to Lisa at that moment was proving to herself that she could do what she had promised herself she could do.

'I'll kill myself!' Delia's voice rose and became shrill. 'Then you'll be sorry.'

'No, you won't.' Cramming the yellow beret down on her head, Lisa started to button herself into her navy-blue school gaberdine. 'There's no need for you to do that because one day I'll be rich.' She nodded her head up and down vehemently. 'You'll see. Some day I'll have my own shop, maybe two shops or three. An' we'll buy back The Laurels, and you'll have a Mrs Parker in the kitchen, and we'll be able to thumb our noses at all the people who don't want to know us.' She touched her thumb to the end of her short nose and wiggled her fingers. 'This is only the beginning, you'll see!'

A strange and watchful expression settled on Delia's face, and suddenly Lisa turned back to put both arms round the fragile body which stiffened in her grasp. 'Just try to keep hoping, Mother. Just hope, that's all. I'm here looking after you now. I'm strong, and the best is still to be.'

Even as she spoke she acknowledged that the words had an overly dramatic ring. But she was high on a wave of euphoria, which lasted until half-past eleven that night when she folded the last of the curtains neatly, with only the hems to be hand-stitched into place. And realized she was tired halfway to death itself.

By the time the trees in the Corporation Park were skirted by daffodils, Richard Carr had taken on another assistant, a tiny girl who seemed to merge into the sewing machine in the back room, and who bent so close to the foot as she guided it through the long lengths of curtaining that Miss Howarth swore that one of these fine days she'd sew her nose into the seams.

A second machine had been bought for Lisa, a treadle model on which she did the more difficult bits, like inserting the tapes with just the right amount of frill at the top, or, more daringly, the pinch pleats she had learned to do from a book borrowed from the library. For the Town Clerk's wife she had made a bedspread to match the long chintz curtains, agonizing over the piping, but getting it right in the end.

'We're not making up bedspreads and cushions free.' Richard Carr took off his reading-glasses to polish them on a large white handkerchief, then put them back on again to examine the spread. 'Those pleats must have taken some getting even.' He flipped over a corner. 'And you've lined the middle. I must say, Lisa, you've done a good job. Anyone might be forgiven for thinking you'd served an apprenticeship in this sort of thing.'

'One can do anything,' Lisa told him loftily, 'if one makes one's mind up to it.' She frowned at a loose thread. 'You'll be paying me commission on spreads and cushions, won't you, Mr Carr? After all, I still serve in the shop and do the bulk of the sewing in my own time.' She smiled with a sudden sweetness belying her business-like approach of just a second ago. 'It snowballs, don't you see? The spread and day pillow wouldn't have been ordered without the curtains, and without the offer of making them up free we wouldn't have got the order in the first place.'

Richard hesitated, acutely aware of the fact that once again this young girl, whose pale face could lift from sadness into sparkling vivacity, was quoting her own terms, speaking to him not with grudging servility, but as if they were business partners. It was incredible, but since taking Lisa on the profits had almost doubled. Word got round, and there was nobody like a Lancashire woman for taking advantage of a bargain. And it went even deeper than that. He had seen women come into the shop merely to buy a yard and a half of 36-inch wide for a blouse, and go out with a skirt length to match, plus the pattern, plus the buttons and even a belt.

'I know you can go into the Market House and have buttons covered to match, and even a belt, but accessories make an outfit. I'm sure you know that,' Lisa would say, smiling in a conspiratorial way. 'There was an article in *Vogue* only last month showing a model wearing a simple cotton dress with a crocodile-skin belt and a silk neck-tie. It looked a million dollars.'

'Nay, love, I can't afford no crocodile nor no pure silk.' The customer had laughed out loud.

'Well, of course not. Who can?' Lisa had laughed with her. 'But there are imitations which look just as good.' With a flip of her wrist she had unhooked a rayon scarf from a stand and twisted it round her own neck. 'See? Especially with the bow tied like this.'

And to Richard's amusement and admiration, yet another of the scarves he had given up all hope of selling had gone into the neatly wrapped parcel of material.

Lisa had mastered the technique of selling almost overnight. He was more than impressed by her enormous capacity for sheer hard work. Superior intelligence shone from those great eyes. Were they grey or blue? She was no more than a child, and yet she faced him now with the maturity of a woman twice her age, with a confidence that left him speechless.

'We'll work out suitable terms,' he said at last. 'I'm not a mean man.'

'And I don't want you to get too big for your boots and leave,' he told himself as he moved away, his expression bleak as he envisaged the shop without Lisa's bright presence.

'Tha's got our Mr Carr on one leg.' Daisy Howarth twinkled at Lisa over the mid-morning cup of tea. 'But don't go underestimating him. He's a hard nut like his father were afore him. Wouldn't give his best friend the skin off his rice puddin', the old man wouldn't.'

At three o'clock that afternoon the telephone rang, and as Richard was out of the shop Lisa answered it.

'This is Mrs Patrick Grey,' a sweet voice said, giving her address. 'I need two sets of curtains for my sitting-room, but I'm not able to come down into town to choose the material. I wonder if Mr Carr would come round? He came once before and brought some samples of material with him. Do you think that would be possible?'

Lisa stood with the telephone receiver pressed close to her ear. The shock of hearing Patrick Grey's wife speaking widened her eyes and jerked her chin up. When she found her voice it was even and business-like, but her pulse had quickened so that a bright flush stained her cheeks.

'Of course we can help, Mrs Grey,' she said clearly. 'Mr Carr is out of the shop at the moment, but when he comes back I'll give him your message. Will you be there if he rings later this afternoon? I'm sure he'll come to see you.'

'I'm always here, my dear.' Lying back on her cushions, Alice Grey's delicately arched eyebrows were raised as she replaced the receiver. Mr Carr must have taken on another assistant, because that had certainly not been Miss Howarth answering the telephone. When she had phoned the last time Miss Howarth had said, 'Hang about a bit, luv, whilst I find a pencil. I'd lose me head if it weren't fastened down to me neck!'

'She's a nice woman, Mrs Grey is.' Miss Howarth came over to peer at the message written down in Lisa's neat schoolgirl hand. 'It's Grey the builders. Grey and Son Limited, General Building Contractors. I know them. Out on the Hoghton side. She's a semi-invalid, but he's a right mess.' A finger was tapped against Miss Howarth's beaky nose. 'One for the women, he is, from what I've heard tell. Still, what a man can't get at home he's bound to . . . .'

'Miss Howarth!' Richard had come into the shop unnoticed. Over by the door two potential customers hovered, one of them already wearing an expression which said that she for one wasn't going to wait to be served by an assistant who would obviously prefer to talk to her friend. 'If you have time . . . .'

The quick temper so assiduously kept in check flared his nostrils and sparked anger from the light blue eyes. The first customer waited meekly for Miss Howarth to spread a length of dotted net across the counter, but the second escaped, letting the door bang to behind her to show exactly how she felt.

Lisa followed her employer into the back room. Miss Howarth had said that Mr Carr was a bully when roused, but this was the first time his anger had been directed at her.

'I'm sorry. We didn't see. . . .' She looked up into Richard's tight face. 'I was explaining to Miss Howarth about this order.' Holding out the piece of paper with Alice Grey's address on it, she smiled. The smile failed to work.

Richard Carr believed that his private life was best kept completely separate from his working existence. He felt it was entirely his own business that at lunchtime he had driven home to be told by his housekeeper that the temperature his little daughter had been running for two days still showed no sign of coming down. The six-year-old Irene lay in her bed with parched lips and flushed cheeks, talking rubbish. Rambling. Tossing and turning and saying her head hurt. Richard tried to focus his attention on his assistant standing before him, her eyes pleading in the white oval of her face.

Was this the girl who at times had him tied in knots with the cool logic of her thinking? Making him feel as if her intelligence was superior to his own? Showing him by a glance, a word, that she understood the mechanics of retail selling as well if not better than he did himself? Just look at her in that washed-out cardigan and the black skirt bagged out of shape at the back. How, in the name of heaven, had she ever managed to get the better of him? Why, he could sack her on the spot and have the choice of at least a hundred applicants for her job.

'Mrs Grey wants you to go to her house with some samples. I said as it was half-day closing tomorrow you would go then. Probably,' Lisa added, realizing her mistake too late.

If the doctor hadn't called by the time he got back, Richard would personally grip him by the throat and drag him to Irene's bedside. What was the good of being told to wait to see if measles spots came out when it could be meningitis or worse? Richard turned a cold and baleful glance on Lisa.

'You will go yourself, Lisa. I will give you the bus fare there and back, and you will never again promise a customer that I will do *anything*!' Anxiety made his voice harsh. 'You understand?'

'But I can't go, Mr Carr. Not to the Greys' house.' The words sputtered from Lisa's mouth like boiling water from an overfilled kettle. 'I can't, because – because I have that order to finish for the orphanage.'

'Hah!' Richard slapped his hand down so sharply on the long worktable that a box of pins scattered to the floor. 'We must be mad making up twenty-four sets of curtains free. You never thought your idea could backfire like that, did you?'

'But we got the order!' Lisa flashed back, forgetting her place. 'And they're simple to do. No linings or anything and no patterns to match. May has already done half the side seams. And it's a colour that wasn't moving. . . .' She turned away. 'Anyway, I can't go to Mrs Grey's house. For personal reasons, that's why.'

Just for the space of a brief moment Richard forgot the tearing anxiety inside him. In that moment he no longer felt like an employer being cheeked by a young employee. This girl, this thin waif of a nobody who had come in from the street and demanded a job, yes, let him face the truth, *demanded* to be taken on, was besting him once more. She was actually turning her back on him and walking away.

The anger inside him caught in his throat. His hand shot out to grip Lisa by the arm, whirling her round to face him.

'You either go to the Greys' house tomorrow afternoon, or you take your cards and walk out of my shop right now.' The wrist round which his fingers tightened shocked him by its fragility, but he would put this small girl in her place if it were the last thing he did. 'Which shall it be?'

'I'll go to the Greys' house tomorrow,' Lisa said at once, rubbing at her wrist and walking with quiet dignity back into the shop.

As she left, Richard stared after her, bewildered and baffled, uncertain for once in his life, and his confidence seeped out of him like the air from a pricked balloon.

Lisa caught a red Ribble bus out of the town and, climbing the stairs, had the top deck all to herself. She was wearing a pale grey flannel suit that had once belonged to her mother, with the collar of a white blouse pulled out, and her dark hair had been brushed until the auburn lights gleamed. She knew she looked older than her sixteen years, and the thought gave her comfort.

There was a gnawing hunger in her stomach, but it was a familiar sensation. As pay day was tomorrow and Delia still had two packets of cigarettes in hand, Lisa was satisfied that the week's budgeting hadn't gone too awry.

Smoking away food money was terrible, but dealing with a mother to whom cigarettes were as milk to a baby was even more terrible. She had tried to take them off her once, but Delia's hysterical wailing, and the pleading in her hooded eyes had been too much to bear. Lisa squeezed her eyes tight shut and offered up a fervent prayer.

'Please, God, don't let her go back to the way she was before, shouting and screaming. Keep her quiet, because we're managing. Things won't always be as bad as this, and as long as I keep on the right side of Mr Carr, he won't give me the sack. I've got to make myself so valuable to him, he won't dare to get rid of me.'

When she walked up the long drive to the Greys' house, she sighed with relief at the sight of the garage, its doors fastened back showing that neither Jonathan's car nor his father's was inside. If she was lucky she would be able to do what she had to do then go away without either of them being the wiser.

Shivering with apprehension, she pressed the bell set high in the big front door, then followed a maid in a white apron down the hall.

'The girl from the curtain shop, Mrs Grey.' Lisa moved forward into the high-ceilinged sitting-room, automatically switching on the professional smile she kept for customers.

'Mr Carr couldn't come, madam. I hope you don't mind me coming instead.' She hoped the dismay didn't show on her face as she saw the woman lying on the wide chesterfield with a rug thrown over her legs, her face a pale mask against the faded chintz cushions.

Alice Grey had once been a beautiful woman, and even years of pain and suffering had not completely obliterated the sweetness in her expression. Hers wasn't a sickness of deprivation or poverty, but the gradual erosion caused by a virulent illness. The wasting disease that over the years had been held in check by treatment and drugs was obviously in its terminal stages, leaving Alice Grey a tortured wraith of a woman with blue eyes that burned feverishly and hands that plucked nervously at the mohair rug.

The room had a Regency décor with none of the ugly angular appearance of what Delia had loved to call the 'structural look'. On a mahogany desk sat a Victorian inkstand in the shape of a flower surrounded by tiny leaves. It was an overly embellished object which Delia would have scorned to own, and yet to Lisa it epitomized the softly gracious beauty of the whole room. There was, she noticed in one swift glance, not a single hard line to break the gentle contours of furniture polished to a mirror shine, or to clash with the serenity of the hanging drapes.

'They don't look too bad, do they?' Alice intercepted Lisa's glance. 'Drawn back they would last a little longer, I suppose, but pulled across they're threadbare in places, and the next time they're cleaned they're going to drop to bits.'

She began to cough, not violently, but enough to warrant a pressing of her thin hands over her chest as if to contain the spasm. 'It's the talking,' she explained. 'My husband tells me I talk too much, and my son says he'll stick my mouth up with plaster one of these days.' She held out her hand. 'They cosset me too much, the pair of them. Said I shouldn't be bothered with new curtains; but I don't always do as I'm told. Now then, my dear.' She nodded towards a small bucket chair. 'Draw that up and we'll look at these samples. I've an idea of what I want . . . at least I thought I had.' She lifted a hand to a forehead beading with sweat. 'Perhaps you could . . . .'

When Alice began to cough again Lisa leaned forward and firmly took the pattern book from her. She realized now that she had come prepared to hate Alice Grey for being such a fool. For not finding out about her husband and Delia. For allowing her husband so much freedom. But now she saw that here was a woman so sick that if her husband had kept three mistresses she would have been none the wiser.

'If this were my room,' Lisa said softly, 'I would have curtains in a silk the colour of rain clouds, not thunder clouds, more a soft pearl. Not in a stiff material, but soft, very full, maybe four times the width of the windows. Light and elegant, with curved pelmets covered in the same silk, and hanging down to the floor, not touching the window sills like these.' Her eyes glowed. 'And if money were no object I'd have this suite re-covered in Regency stripes, dark mulberry and off-white. This pastel chintz is pretty, but it gives too much of a cottagey effect to a room that cries out for long, smooth lines and understated elegance.'

'Well I never!' Alice spoke quickly without coughing. 'Fancy you having ideas like that!' She smiled. 'You know, I reckon Mr Carr's a lucky man having you as his adviser. Did you learn all that at one of those art colleges? You don't look old enough to have been to college though. Did that just pop out of your head?'

'Out of my head.' Lisa wrinkled her nose at the thought of what Mr Carr would have said if he'd heard her referred to as his adviser. 'Do you like the sound of it, then, Mrs Grey?'

Alice nodded, putting a finger to her pale lips in a conspiratorial way. 'We'll have the curtains just the way you said, *and* we'll have the suite done up. And I won't tell my husband how much it's going to cost till it's all done.' Her cheeks flushed with sudden colour. 'He's so good to me, my dear. He'd give me the moon if it would get me better. They don't grow them like my Patrick very often these days.'

Lisa swallowed the lump in her throat. In different circumstances she could have liked this gentle kindly woman so much, even loved her. There was a childish warmth about Patrick Grey's wife that made you want to put your arms round her and will her to get better.

The very air of the gracious room was like a blessing, and Jonathan's mother was like an angel with her fair hair a faded nimbus round her thin face. But she was already tiring. The effort of talking was proving too much for her. Lisa stood up abruptly.

'If you don't mind, Mrs Grey, I'll get on with measuring the windows.' Her trained eyes did a swift assessment. 'Both windows are exactly the same size, so it won't take long. If I lay this newspaper on this chair I can reach by standing on it. Then, if you agree to leave everything with me, I'll be getting back.'

'Yes.' The whisper from the sofa was as soft as a sigh.

'That's my son coming back from the yard,' she said after a while, as Lisa climbed down from the chair. 'I can always tell the sound of his car.' The thin lips curved upwards in a proud smile. 'He drives it as if he were on the last lap of the Monte Carlo Rally. He often comes home early to make sure I'm all right.'

Lisa spoke quickly, feeling her mouth tremble. 'I have to go, Mrs Grey. Now. This minute.' She was fighting the urge to rush from the room. 'Goodbye, Mrs Grey. Forgive me, but I have to get back.'

'Of course, dear.' There was a slightly baffled expression in Alice's blue eyes, but an innate politeness, born of kindness, made her stretch out a hand. 'I've enjoyed talking to you so much. You'll come again, I hope?' She sighed. 'You remind me of someone, but I can't think who. Please come again, my dear.'

Lisa hesitated by the door, clasping and unclasping her hands round the large envelope of patterns in a frenzy of agitation. If she could only get out of the house before Jonathan came in from the garage – escape down the path and out into the tree-lined road. If she could get away without him seeing her. . . .

As she stepped outside, shutting the big front door behind her, she came face to face with Jonathan walking towards her with his long, loping stride, his face completely abstract. He stared at her like a man in deep and sudden shock.

'Lisa Logan! What the hell?' His eyes were almost black, like hard stones, in his grim furious face. 'How *dare* you come here?' Giving her no chance to explain, he gripped Lisa's arm, marching her quickly down the path, out of the wide gates and along the pavement, only stopping when they were well away from the house.

'What have you been saying to her?' A lock of black hair fell over his forehead as he jerked his chin back in the direction of the house. 'If you've upset her; if you've said one single word about your blasted mother. . . .' Heedless of the curious glances of a passer-by walking her dog, he dug his fingers into Lisa's shoulders, forcing her back against a privet hedge. 'God, you *wouldn't?* Nobody could be that cruel!'

Lisa stared into the blazing eyes, blinking at the violence she saw mirrored there, opened her mouth to protest, then heard him say, 'What do you want from my father? Blood? Now you've seen for yourself the way she is, do you blame him for wanting to keep what went on between him and your mother a secret? She worships him, and he worships her. Yes, he does, and always has. Have you seen him lately, or did you prefer to come begging for more at the house rather than at his office?' As he pushed Lisa even further back, she felt the prickle of the hedge against her back. 'He's a broken man, Lisa Logan. Like your own father, he's come to the end of the road, but my father's not quitting. By God, no! He'll look after my mother and cherish her right to the end, and do you want to know why? Because she's no slut like yours. My mother is pure gold, and she's dying.' His contemptuous gaze raked Lisa up and down, taking in the smart costume and the pristine whiteness of the collar with its scalloped edging. 'You're doing OK, that's obvious, but then your sort always do. Leeches, that's what you Logans are. Greedy and grasping for more, even from a woman living on borrowed time. I always thought you were an insufferable little prig, and now I know for sure. Oh, God, but you make me sick!'

The injustice of it all finally lifted Lisa out of her abject misery and fear. In spite of her numbness, her quick brain was working like a ferment. Let Jonathan Grey find out for himself how wrong he'd been, how quick to judge and condemn – but she'd be damned if she'd explain.

Out of the corner of her eye she saw a red bus trundling to a stop not ten yards away. Breaking free from his grasp, she ran to hurl herself on to the boarding platform. Then, as if expecting Jonathan to follow her, she clattered up the steps to the upper deck, causing the conductor to whistle after her in surprise.

It wasn't until she had handed over her twopenny fare that the trembling began.

She thought of her mother, crouching over the inevitable fire, smoking, always smoking, lighting one cigarette from another. Refusing to go out, sinking deeper into the well of bitterness, her ribs showing when she undressed and her stomach sticking out where once it had been taut and flat. She thought about her own bedroom in the cold damp house in Mill Street, with its view of the sloping back yard and the grey houses facing across the cobbled back. She reminded herself that only by the grace of Jonathan Grey's father were they able to live there at all and, swallowing her pride, she acknowledged that if Patrick withdrew his patronage they would be out on the street.

The only solution was work and more work, cutting down on her sleep, forcing herself to eat even less, making herself so indispensable to Mr Carr that never again would he threaten her with the sack. And some day, some far-off glorious day, they would pay Patrick Grey and his son back, every single penny, and with interest, she added, bitterly.

With her father's theatrical flair for seeing every crisis in terms of high drama, Lisa imagined herself facing Patrick Grey, throwing the money down at his feet. Jonathan would be there, standing in the background, his dark head bowed as he realized how badly he'd misjudged her, pleading with her to forgive him with a suspicion of tears in his eyes.

Give me two more years, she prayed. Then she would be eighteen and have saved up enough money maybe to start up on her own. She could turn the little front room into a workroom with a trestle table and a machine beneath the window. She would have made a name for herself by then, and if Mr Carr didn't like to see his customers going to her, then he could . . . he could jump off the end of Blackpool pier!

She would be rich and she would be famous, and knowing what men were like she would best them at their own game. Every man jack of them, she added for good measure, her own eyes sparkling with angry tears.

When the bus turned into the Boulevard she got off, muttering to herself that she would finish the curtains for the orphanage that same day or die in the attempt. She would then make a start on the silk curtains for Alice Grey. Lisa's eyes lifted to the spring-lit sky as, imagining the feel of the soft material beneath her fingers, she was comforted and held strangely at peace.

PART TWO

PART TWO

Six

'There's going to be a war,' Richard Carr said. 'That Hitler's not going to keep his promise, no matter what old Chamberlain says. Starting up on your own at a time like this would be more than foolish, it would be proper daft.'

He stared at the eighteen-year-old Lisa, trying to remember how she had looked when he had taken her on as a shop assistant two years ago. Then, she had looked like a skinned rabbit, all eyes, with tufts of badly cut hair sticking out from beneath an atrocious yellow beret. Now her hair swung shining clean, club cut almost to her shoulders, black in some lights and auburn in others. Gone was the washed-out cardigan and the seated skirt, and in their place she wore a plain black dress, darted at the bust to fit what he always thought of as her Edwardian figure, pinched in at the waist, and swirling in cross-cut panels round her shapely legs.

Four times he had raised her wages, so that – including the commission she earned – she sometimes took home as much as two pounds. That was more than a lot of men in the town were earning, if indeed they were lucky enough to be in full-time work.

Now Lisa left most of the sewing to the two machinists in the back room, concentrating on advising customers as to colour, the balance between patterned and plain, plus the contrast of texture. She trotted out such terms with confidence, as if she enjoyed the feel of the words on her tongue. Let a customer tell her exactly how much she could afford to spend and Lisa would set to work with merely a sketch of a room, using pattern to improve its proportions, concentrating mainly on neutral colours, with green or turquoise for a sophisticated effect, peach or coral if a warmer look was desired.

'The last thing folks will be doing if war comes is doing up their houses.' Richard heard the desperation creep into his voice. 'But there'll always be a need for curtains, and your job here with the shop is secure. Safe.' He swallowed hard. 'Look. I'll give you another five shillings to stop on. What do you say?'

With a total feeling of detachment Lisa watched a deep flush spread slowly over the smooth skin of her employer's face. With a bit more colour in his face Mr Carr was more than passably good-looking, she told herself. Kind, too, when he let himself be, but aggressively masculine in spite of his daily preoccupation with spotted muslins and bolts of locally woven cotton.

'I'm sorry, Mr Carr,' she said, 'but an extra five shillings a week isn't what I had in mind. I want to be my own boss, make my own mistakes, and hopefully reap the benefit when I've learned from them.'

'And take custom away from me.'

Lisa's laugh rang out, setting her eyes dancing and sparkling with amusement. 'Now tha's talking,' she said, in such an exact mimicry of Miss Howarth's flat vowel sounds that Richard's own eyes twinkled.

'Miss Logan, Lisa. Will you at least think it over?' All at once he dropped his hectoring tone. 'Will you come to my house, say on Sunday, for tea?' He put up a hand as if to stop a stream of traffic. 'That way we can talk things over without fear of interruption.' He jerked his head towards the back of the shop where the whir of the sewing machines had suddenly stopped. 'Maybe we can work out a different arrangement. If you're still determined to strike out on your own at least I might be able to let you have materials at cost. I still know a thing or two about pricing, don't forget. In most cases I buy straight from the mills like my father did in the old days. The world outside can be a very frightening place, you know.'

'I've gathered that, Mr Carr.' Lisa's voice was very low, but just when Richard thought she was going to open up and tell him something about her fiercely guarded private life, she turned on him her strange sweet smile. 'Thank you, Mr Carr. I *will* come to tea on Sunday. But I won't change my mind,' she added, moving away as a customer came into the shop. 'It's made up.'

'Look, Mother, I won't be away for more than three hours at the most.' Lisa tried, not very successfully, to hide a sigh of exasperation. 'If I stayed in I would be working on this new set of designs. One of the Entwistle girls is getting married, and her father is giving them a house up by the park for a wedding present, so they can afford to have new everything. Curtains, spreads, lampshades. They even want me to choose the colour scheme for the bathroom, right down to the towels and face flannels. I'll be up till midnight working anyway.'

Delia's dark eyes were sly. 'One of these days when you come back I won't be here. Then you'll be sorry.'

'Where will you be, Mother?' Lisa studied her reflection in the round mirror over the sink. 'You know what the doctor said. It's all in your mind, this aversion to leaving the house. Only you can overcome it.' She turned round. 'Mother! You're not even listening to me. You remember what he said? Surely?'

Wearily Delia passed a hand over her brow. 'It's these headaches making me a bit forgetful at times. They're like a red-hot needle stabbing into the side of my head. I've got one now.' Her eyes lost their brief lucidity and glazed over. 'I remember a lot of things I don't tell you.' A small expression of triumph slid over her face. 'Like when Patrick Grey's son Jonathan came that day.' She stared into the fire as if in a trance. 'I remember that well, but I wasn't going to tell you that, was I?'

'Jonathan? Jonathan Grey came *here*? When? When exactly?' Lisa felt a shock so acute it actually tingled in her armpits. How could her mother forget something like that so easily and readily? And deliberately? Horrified, she went

111

to kneel down on the rug, trying to force the woman staring so abstractedly into the fire to meet her eyes.

Delia smiled a deliquescent smile. 'I shouted through the letter-box telling him to go away and never come near us again.' She blinked. 'Anyway, it was only a message from his mother, and I know all about her, don't I? Playing the invalid to get her husband back. And she's won, hasn't she? Look at her, living in the lap of luxury, while I . . . oh, my God, I know her sort. If she saw how I'm living now she'd be laughing. A woman like her would think I'd got my just desserts. The mealy-mouthed faggot.'

'Mother!' Lisa's voice was high with disbelief. 'Mrs Grey is dead! She died at Christmas. Not last Christmas but the one before!' She took hold of Delia's wrist. 'I wrote to . . . to Uncle Patrick to say how sorry I was. You remember that? You have to remember because you said I must be mad.'

'And now you think it's me who's mad.' Delia's expression was complacent. 'But he's still paying the rent, isn't he? And having the coal delivered.' Her eyes filled with tears. 'Did you say Alice Grey was dead, Lisa? Dead for a long time?' She began to wail, rocking herself backwards and forwards. 'If your father knew how badly Patrick Grey had let me down, even though he's free to marry me, he'd come back. He only went away because of Patrick, because he couldn't share me with another man.' With the tears sliding down her cheeks she smiled suddenly, like a child forgetting a grazed knee at the offer of a sweet. 'You must write to your father, Lisa. You must write a letter pretending I don't know anything about it. Not pleading. Just putting him in the picture.' Delia turned back to her perusal of the leaping flames. 'He wasn't all bad, your father. Weak at times, but not all bad.'

She was quiet for a moment, then in a conversational tone, she said, 'Isn't it time you were going, dear? It's a long time since you went out to tea. You must tell me all about it when you get back.'

The change in Delia was so swift and incredible that Lisa could only sit back on her heels, astonished. 'Yes, I'll tell you all about it, Mother.' She got up and reached for the jacket of the same grey suit she had worn the last time she saw Jonathan Grey. Was her mother really losing her mind, and if so, how could she behave so rationally in between her bouts of forgetfulness? She hovered uncertainly by the door. 'Mother? I must go now. This meeting at Mr Carr's house could be a most important step up for us. If he makes it well worth my while then I may stay on at the shop, but he doesn't know that.' She gave a tweak to the Peter Pan collar of her silk blouse. 'If I can work more or less freelance, but with him paying the overheads, I might get a bit put by before I branch out alone.' She hesitated. 'You'll be all right, won't you?'

To her horror, Delia gave a shrill trill of a laugh. 'Just like your father. Always off to clinch some business deal.' Her face sobered. 'But none of his deals ever came off. They were out to get him, you see, just as they'll get you. The name of Logan is a dirty word in this town.'

So much in a ferment was Lisa's mind that the journey by bus out to Mr Carr's house on the outskirts of the town wasn't half long enough for her to get herself rightly sorted out, as Miss Howarth would undoubtedly have said.

Her mother's behaviour baffled and worried Lisa, but then Delia had always behaved unpredictably: up in the clouds, or sunk deep into the depths of depression, and some of the time putting it on.

'You're a two-headed woman!' Angus used to shout. 'I never know which hat you're wearing, and neither of them suits you, if the truth be known.'

Resolutely Lisa put aside all thoughts of her father, blanking her mind into stony indifference. Sometimes she marvelled at the fact that his blood even ran in her veins. He had fathered her, that was all. She stared through the window at the quiet Sunday afternoon streets, seeing nothing.

But Jonathan had called to apologize, she was sure of that. He had gone away appalled at Delia's behaviour, and soon after his own mother had died. The silk curtains, made with such care and delivered by Mr Carr, would be hanging at the tall windows, but Alice Grey would never have the pleasure of drawing them to shut out the dark evenings, never admire the way their pleats fell in a muted extension of the pale washed walls. And yet the rent continued to be paid. Lisa pressed her lips close together. Now that it could no longer be construed as a kind of blackmail to keep the truth from Patrick's wife, why hadn't it been stopped? Jonathan had something to do with it. Instinctively she knew that.

But even as Lisa asked herself the question, the answer was plain. She could guess at the things Delia would have shouted through the letter-box, and now more than ever the Greys, father and son, would be determined to play down Delia's existence in the only way they and their kind knew. By the silent power of money. With money anything was possible. Without it a person was helpless, as helpless as a reed broken by the wind.

When Lisa walked into Richard Carr's sitting-room at the back of the large, red-bricked, semi-detached house her determination to best him was apparent to him at once in the tilt of her head and the light of battle in her wide grey-blue eyes.

'This is Irene.' With obvious pride, Richard drew a chubby, golden-haired little girl into the circle of his arm. 'Say hello to Miss Logan – to Lisa.'

A pair of cornflower-blue eyes stared up at Lisa without expression, and a rosebud mouth set into an obstinate line.

For a minute Lisa was puzzled. The round face topped with a mop of yellow curls seemed strangely familiar. Then she remembered. Once, a long time ago, her father had given Lisa a doll with a face just like the expressionless one gazing up at her. The doll's eyes were supposed to have closed when it was laid back, but something had gone wrong with the mechanism so that the vivid blue eyes had stared endlessly at nothing, infuriating her with their pot-hard indifference.

'Hello, Irene,' Lisa said, then smiled to show it didn't matter when the child ducked her head and ran from the room.

'That's right, love. Go and tell Millie we're ready for tea.'

Richard motioned Lisa to a chair, holding out his hand for her jacket. 'Sorry about that. I'm afraid she's very spoilt. She chatters away nineteen to the dozen with my house-keeper, but with strangers she clams up. You'll be lucky if you get a word out of her all afternoon.'

He stood awkwardly, holding the jacket, with its designer label, in his hands. It was the first time he had seen Lisa in anything but the obligatory shop-black, and the sight of her in the silk blouse with her full breasts clearly outlined and straining against the pearl-button fastening made him avert his face, then as suddenly turn to stare at her again. She was so incredibly lovely. There was something very vulner-able about her, in spite of the familiar challenge in those sea-grey eyes. A fervent longing swept through him. He wanted to pull her to her feet and hold her close against him, telling her that if she insisted on leaving nothing would matter to him any more. Not the shop, not his carefully hoarded profits, not the ominous rumble of war clouds on the horizon, nothing at all if she went away, if he did not see her every day. Physical desire, held in careful check since his wife died, rushed the blood to his face.

Now he knew why he had broken his strict rule of never mixing business with pleasure. Of never meeting his assis-tants out of working hours. Quickly he turned and carried the jacket into the wide hall, curbing a desire to press its satin lining against his face before he hung it on the hallstand. When he went back he avoided Lisa's eyes, in case his own betrayed his agitation.

As he stood by the fireplace, gripping the edge of the mantelshelf, he was saved by the rattle of teacups as Millie Schofield wheeled the trolley into the room.

Nodding briefly to Lisa, she spoke directly to Richard: 'I'm sorry, Mr Carr, but there's no doing anything with her.' She set a silver teapot down on the tiled hearth and capped it with a quilted cosy. 'She's skulking out there and won't come in. Even her favourite strawberry jam won't 'tice her out of the kitchen.'

Lisa studied Millie Schofield with interest. She reminded her of Norma Shearer in a film she had seen called *The*

Barretts of Wimpole Street, all oval, unthinking face and eyes not quite true. When she straightened up from the hearth, Lisa saw that she was almost as tall as her employer, or could it have been because of the queenly way she held herself with her brown hair piled up on top of her head, secured at the back by a tortoiseshell comb? Lisa, used to seeing Richard treated with deference and even servility, found herself immensely intrigued by the woman with a Christian name which in no way fitted her face. She surfaced from her assessment in time to hear Richard making the necessary introductions.

And that in itself was strange. Brought up with servants, Lisa tried to imagine her mother introducing one of her small staff to a guest, and failed. Delia had always treated her maids with proper disdain.

'If you don't mind, Mr Carr,' Millie was saying, 'I'll take Irene out for a walk. I know you said you have work to get getting on with, so she'll be better out of your way.'

She doesn't like me, Lisa told herself. I've done nothing but sit here smiling politely, but I've made an enemy. Then, as Richard passed her a cup of tea with a hand that trembled imperceptibly, her eyebrows drew together in a frown. What was going on in this strange household where a child was allowed to dictate her own pattern of behaviour? Where a woman who was merely the housekeeper spoke to her employer with such familiarity, and where the master of the house appeared to be on the verge of losing his temper?

Richard ran an impatient hand through his thick hair. 'When we've finished eating we'll get down to business.' He passed a plate of thinly cut salmon sandwiches, then sat down opposite her. 'Before you leave here I want your promise that you'll stay on at the shop.' He was staring at her mouth in a way that made Lisa feel a crumb must be lodging indelicately on her chin. Raising a small, embroidered napkin she dabbed at her lips.

'You don't understand,' she said quietly. 'I have to make – it is essential that I make far more money than I can ever earn working for you, Mr Carr.'

'Richard,' he said in a strangulated voice.

'Richard.' Lisa said his name without a trace of self-consciousness. The atmosphere of the overheated house was getting underneath her skin. The front door had banged behind Miss Schofield and the child, but their presence was still there, hanging in the air like a disapproving cloud.

When they had finished the meal Richard wheeled the trolley back into the kitchen, refusing Lisa's offer of help with the washing up.

'Millie will do it.' He rolled back the top of a bureau and took out a bulging file. He came and sat down beside her, spreading it wide on his knees. 'These are the figures for the past year.' He riffled through the papers. 'You don't need me to tell you that since you began the scheme of making up curtains free, and since you started making something of a name for yourself as an interior designer . . .' he said the last two words with an air of masculine patronage that irritated Lisa, ' . . . the profits have almost doubled.' He nodded and she saw with surprise that his face wore an odd expression, almost of despair. 'I admit I haven't been altogether fair to you. Oh, I put your wages up from time to time, but I refused to recognize your true potential. Now I do.'

'Since I said I'd like to leave and set up on my own.' Lisa gave a little laugh, holding out her hand for the topmost sheet of figures. 'That's understandable. You're a man, Richard, so you find it hard to accept that a girl could just walk in and put her finger on the obvious remedy for increasing your revenue.' She was beginning to enjoy herself, now that she could see she held the winning cards. 'You resent the fact that you weren't the one to see what could be done, and now you want to cut me in.' She touched his wrist lightly with her forefinger. 'I'm right, aren't I?'

He flinched at her touch, his fresh complexion flushing to an angry red. 'You're always right, damn you, Lisa Logan. I've seen you nearly every day for the past two years. I've watched you work and I've seen the way you can wheedle blood from a stone. I don't know where you get it from, but it's there, inherent in you. You look like something off a bloody chocolate box, and yet you'd best a Rothschild in a business deal.' He ran a hand through his hair, beside himself with tearing emotion. 'You'd pinch the pennies from a dead man's eyes if you could add them to your wage packet without anyone seeing!'

She made a sound compounded of hurt and a flaring anger at the injustice of what he was saying. This wasn't how she had planned it at all. She had come, she realized now, prepared to listen, OK, maybe out of a certain curiosity, to hear a plan she would have the pleasure of turning down. And now the score was all wrong. This man she had thought to be as unemotional as a flat stone was seething with an uncharacteristic emotion in what should have been a meeting controlled by her, motivated as she was by her desire to see him crawl as he finally came to understand that not even he could stand in the way of her ambition.

'Have you ever been hungry?' Her voice was deathly quiet. 'I don't mean hungry for the next meal, but hungry when there isn't going to *be* a next meal?' She glanced round the over-furnished room. 'Have you ever seen everything you owned taken from you to pay debts incurred by someone who used money like it grew on trees? Have you ever had to hang your clothes round a fading fire to dry, praying that they wouldn't be too damp to wear the next day? Have you ever had to exist on seven shillings and sixpence a week, and be grateful every single day that a man you loathed was paying the rent as well as having just enough coal delivered to stop you freezing to death? Oh, yes, Richard, you're right! I *would* have snatched the pennies from dead men's eyes, and spent them too, because twopence would buy a cabbage I could have made into soup.' She felt her face flame so hotly that her eyes watered. 'And if I don't get my mother out of the house we're forced to live in she's going to go mad. Insane. So now you see why money is my God! Because without it, as far as I can see, there is no God! He doesn't live down our street because it's hard to pray on an empty belly. That's why!'

As his arms came round her she tried to move away, but he held her fast. Held against his chest she heard his voice, low, roughened with compassion. 'Lisa. Lisa, oh, my little love. You should have said. You should have told me. I'm not a hard man.' He raised his head. 'I must have been blind. I try not to involve myself.'

'With your workforce?' she sobbed against his chest, and felt him nod.

'My father always instilled in me that the dividing line between caring and involvement must never be crossed. And I've tried to follow his example, Lisa, though it wasn't easy taking on the running of the shop at twenty-eight, with a new wife and a baby to keep happy.'

His arms tightened round her, and she made no move to draw away. Her father used to hold her like this when she was troubled, as though his strength was the only thing keeping her from disintegrating. Richard smelled like her father too, a mixture of tobacco and Coal Tar soap, a reassuring scent keeping her safe.

At first his kiss was no more than a brushing of his lips against her skin. A tickling of the fair moustache on her closed eyelids, her nose, her chin. It seemed as if he would never kiss her mouth, but when he did, holding her face still between his hands, the searching movements caught her emotions, blotting out the world outside, soothing and possessing, so that in a strange paradoxical way she became a child again.

He ran her home, insisted on doing so. He had asked her to marry him and she had refused, but he wouldn't, he said, take no for an answer, and in the meantime he would pay her three pounds a week, a sum that made her gasp.

In the first flush of his declaration of love he had become her master, not in the obvious way of employer and employee, but with a glorying masculine pride of possession, swearing that with him around nothing would ever hurt or worry her again.

And for the time being, because her whole being craved for even a temporary contentment, she relinquished her fighting spirit and was as docile and feminine as this strong man, almost old enough to be her father, obviously wanted her to be.

'Is this it?' Richard tried to look noncommittal as he stopped the car outside the little terraced house in Mill Street. Two whey-faced children abandoned their game of hop-scotch chalked out on the flags and came to stare with open curiosity at the black saloon car.

'Yes, the one with the mucky step.' Lisa spoke flippantly, hiding what she refused to admit could be shame. She had seen the women in the street down on their hands and knees, mopping not only the step but a semi-circle of flags outside their front doors, and told herself that never, never would she lower herself both physically and mentally to do the same. 'Thank you for the tea,' she said, suddenly overcome with shyness. 'I'll be thinking over what you said.' She walked quickly round the car, only to find Richard standing on the pavement beside her.

'I'll come in and meet your mother. It might as well be now as later,' he added, ignoring the way her eyes widened with dismay. 'There's no need to look like that, love. From now on your worries are mine. Right?'

The little house was wrapped in silence as they made their way through the front parlour, past the unpolished furniture set out as if it was waiting to be collected by the owner of a saleroom.

'Mother? I'm back. I've brought . . . .' Lisa's voice tailed away as she walked into the back living-room, expecting to see Delia crouched in her chair by the fire, huddled into a shapeless cardigan, a cigarette dangling between her lips. Then, as she saw what lay huddled on the floor, her throat thickened so much that she could hardly speak.

Delia was lying on the floor with the rug rucked up underneath her twisted legs. She was partly beneath the table, and when they pulled her out and Lisa lifted her head gently she saw with a sudden stab of horror that her mother's mouth was twisted to one side with saliva running from it.

Delia was conscious, but when she tried to speak the words came out like mirror writing, jumbled back to front, slurring, indecipherable words, stopping short of the end syllables.

'She's had a stroke.' Richard pulled a cushion from a

120

chair and laid the jibbering head on it. 'Where's the nearest phone?'

Lisa took her mother's left hand, shuddering at the leaden weight of it. 'Oh, God, I don't know.' She found she was shivering uncontrollably. 'The man in the top house on this side will let you use his phone. He's a secretary of a union, and if he's out I think there's a kiosk about three streets on along the main road.'

When Richard had gone she took off her costume jacket and laid it across Delia's chest, tucking it in round the thin shoulders. As she did so the grotesque lopsided mouth wobbled. 'An? Ang . . . ?'

Lisa closed her eyes in disbelief. It was her father's name Delia was trying to say. After all this time, in spite of everything, his was the name she called in that strange guttural moan of a voice.

'He's not here just now, Mother.' Holding her tears tight inside her, Lisa smoothed the hair back from Delia's furrowed forehead. 'Just lie still. The doctor will be here soon. He'll know what to do.'

There was a half-smoked cigarette lying on the oilcloth surround. The ash had burned itself out, but a cylindrical-shaped burn mark showed plain round the edges. Lisa shuddered. If the cigarette had fallen on the rug, her mother could have been . . . the whole house could have gone up in flames. While she was eating scones spread with strawberry jam and being kissed by Richard Carr, her poor pathetic little mother could have been burned to death.

The face she turned to Richard as he came through the door was a mask of pain.

'The ambulance is on its way.' He came and knelt down beside her. 'It's what the doctor would have done anyway. This way is quicker.'

'She's so cold,' Lisa whispered. 'The fire must have gone out long ago. How long do you think she's been lying here?'

'Not long, love.' Richard kissed her face. 'I'll go upstairs and fetch a blanket. I can't see them getting here for at least ten minutes.'

Lisa heard his feet pounding on the uncarpeted stairs.

When he came back they wrapped the blanket round the still figure with the unequal staring eyes. She leaned against him, drawing solace from his nearness, so grateful for his presence that their future relationship was cemented in that moment.

Outside the small sash window over the slopstone the sky had darkened. The room was full of shifting shadows, and Richard endeavoured to conceal his horror at the smell of poverty emanating from the huddled heap of skin and bones beneath the blanket. Never in a million years could he have imagined that things were as bad as this. This woman, this grey-faced woman who was Lisa's mother, had no more flesh on her than a starling fallen from a nest. Never a sensitive man and totally lacking the imagination to identify completely with others, what would normally have been compassion turned in Richard's case to a searing anger.

How had they . . . ? In his silent fury 'they' could have been anyone – the local authorities, the ministry, the medical profession, even the government down in London. How could bureaucracy let this be? Richard's deep-rooted sense of integrity showed itself in the jutting of his jaw, the flushing of his sensitive fair skin. This woman's husband deserved a flogging, a whipping with a cat o' nine tails till his back hung in strips like a peeled cane.

Even as he cursed a man he had never known, Delia's face changed to a ghastly putty colour. With one side of her face rigid and unmoving, the other side twitched and contorted itself into a tortuous expression. Underneath the blanket one knee raised convulsively. Then was still.

'Now you just have to stop it,' Richard was to say over and over again in the weeks that followed the quiet funeral and Delia's burial in a corner of a bleak and windy cemetery. 'Feeling remorse is natural when someone close to us dies. We blame ourselves for not being more considerate, more loving, especially when death comes suddenly.' He was very sure of his facts. 'Your mother, from what you tell me, had stopped wanting to live a long time ago.'

'Ever since my father went away.' Lisa had sobbed out

the truth on Richard's shoulder, sensing without seeing the tightening of his jaw and the repugnance in his eyes. 'Or since her lover deserted her.'

Once again she was seeing events as if they were played out on a cinema screen, her mother as the deserted wife with Patrick Grey in the role of villain. 'You can't imagine what she was like years ago. My mother was so joyous, so gay, so dressed just right. Her appearance was as important to her as food and drink. More important.' She began to cry again. 'My father used to say she didn't eat enough to keep a bird alive, so when she wouldn't eat the meals I made her it was harder for me to realize . . . oh, Richard, the doctor who signed the death certificate said she was suffering from malnutrition. Can't you see that was – *has* to be my fault?'

'Stop it,' Richard said again. 'You'll have to stop blaming yourself, Lisa. The doctor wasn't being critical, he was merely stating a fact.' Shaking her, he held Lisa away from him. 'Some people are born to be survivors, some are not. But you are,' he said more gently. 'You never stopped work even though I told you people would understand and wait a while for their orders. I don't know how you did it, if you want the truth. Oh, yes, the good Lord definitely made you a survivor when He doled out attributes.' His kiss was firm on her trembling lips. 'And when we're married you'll never need to worry again. You're never going to feel so alone again, darling. Not with me around.'

He was so practical, so much in control, that Lisa could only marvel at his solid unflappability. Of course, he had never known her mother, she reminded herself, and it was possible that coping with funeral arrangements and the awful trappings of death brought out the organizing ability of a man like Richard.

He had arranged immediately for her to stay with Miss Howarth, refusing to condone the idea of Lisa living alone even temporarily in the house in Mill Street. Her grief came in recurrent waves, almost paralysing her with its intensity, and it was at moments like this that the ignoble thought crept into her subconscious: had Delia's death rid Richard of the burden of a future mother-in-law who would have

123

done him less than credit? What people thought mattered to Richard. He wasn't a cruel man, but Delia's shuffling, chain-smoking presence in his house would have been an affront to the respectability he cherished so much.

Lisa was alone in the little house in Mill Street one Sunday morning, sorting out her personal belongings, emptying drawers so that the saleroom men could come and take away the furniture, when a knock came at the door.

'Hello there, Lisa Logan!'

Jonathan Grey stood there, tall and slightly rakish-looking in a long, belted raincoat with the collar turned up against the rain, and a dark brown trilby with a wide brim dipping over one eye.

'Jonathan!' Lisa was so surprised, so filled with an emotion she couldn't define, that she could only gape at him, foolishly regretting her old skirt and the blue turban covering her hair.

'We got your letter about your mother and about the house.' He was very formal, very solicitous. 'May I come in?'

In the back living-room he shook the rain from his trilby into the slopstone, then laid the hat down on the bare table. His silly little sideburns had gone, she noticed, along with the neat moustache. She was suddenly lost for words, so aware of him that she began to tremble.

'Thank you for the letter about my mother,' he said. He stared straight at her with a whimsical expression. 'My father didn't feel . . . didn't feel he could reply.'

'Of course not.' Lisa flushed. 'A letter might have given my mother ideas.'

He was standing too close to her. She saw the flash of irritation in his eyes. 'It was over long ago, and you know it.'

Against her will Lisa felt her mouth curl upwards into a smirk. 'I will soon be able,' she said clearly, 'to repay the considerable debt I owe your father for the two years' rent and the monthly delivery of coal. It's all written down. I've kept a record of every penny. So will you tell him, please?'

Making her jump, Jonathan banged the flat of his hand

down hard on the table. 'God, but you never let up, do you? You're still that same impossible kid I shoved under a wave in the sea in Brittany!' A Machiavellian twinkle came into his eyes. 'You look about as fetching in that bloody turban as you looked in that terrible rubber bathing cap you wore. Remember when I kissed you at the dark of the moon?'

'No!' Her denial was swift and absolute. 'I do not remember.' She turned her hot face away from his penetrating gaze. 'What happened to your moustache? Did your fiancée make you shave it off? I remember her at school, you know. A big girl with mousey hair.'

'Average height with auburn hair.' Jonathan grinned. 'So you know Amy, do you? I suppose you saw the engagement in the paper? Her parents put it in.' He hesitated momentarily. 'And you're to be Mrs Richard Carr? Thick-set, middle-aged bloke with a ginger tash.'

'Not forty yet, broad-shouldered and fair,' Lisa flashed back. 'How did you know?'

'I have my spies.' He picked up the trilby and pinched the brim into an even wavier shape. 'Look. I have the car outside. Leave all this.' He nodded at the half-packed carton on the beef-tea-coloured oilcloth. 'It's stopped raining. Come out for a spin. You're as pale as a vanilla blancmange. And take that bloody scarf off your head. I'm not taking you in a pub looking like that.'

'Why *should* I come for a drink with you?' Lisa realized she was beginning to feel light-headed. Sorting her mother's few belongings into two piles, one to throw out and the other to keep for what she supposed could be called sentimental reasons, seemed to have drained her strength. She had started a period that morning and the familiar cramp spasmed inside her with a dull aching grind. 'You do nothing but insult me.'

Flourishing the brown trilby as if it were a courtier's hat plumed with feathers, Jonathan held it over his stomach and bowed low. 'See that patch of blue sky out there? Over those mucky chimney pots? The sun is coming out, Lisa Logan, and I know a place where we can sit and watch it sparkling on the River Ribble. I will expunge my boorish behaviour by paying you lavish compliments.' His eyes twinkled. 'That is, if you will remove that thing from your head and wash your face. I will not flirt with a dirty face. What man could?'

For a crazy moment their eyes held. 'You shouldn't say things like that,' she told him, flustered, turning away. But even as she spoke she was untying the knot on top of her head, shaking her hair loose and dabbing at her cheeks with her handkerchief. 'What if we're seen?'

'By your fiancé?'

'Or yours.'

'You're not serious?'

Lisa considered. 'No, I'm not. Today I don't give a damn.'

'That's what misery does.' He flicked the rim of the cardboard carton with his finger. 'You can grieve for so long, then wham! You have to take off and to hell with it all. For a little while. Ready?'

'Ready,' she said, and when he helped her on with her coat and she felt his fingers lightly press her neck, she wanted to turn round and cry against his chest. But, holding herself stiffly, she walked before him to the front door, seeing Mrs Ellis's net curtains twitch as she climbed, showing too much leg, into the passenger seat of the low car which crouched at the kerb like a shiny green beetle.

'I came round,' Richard grumbled. 'I suddenly couldn't bear to think of your packing things away in that room.' He pushed his thick straight hair back from his forehead, a gesture she was to become familiar with whenever he was holding his irritation in check. 'The woman next door came out and told me you'd gone off with a man in a green sports car.'

'Jonathan Grey,' she told him. 'His father is the one who let my mother and me live rent-free for all that time. We had things to discuss.'

'Such as?'

'Such as the money I intend to pay his father back. When I've saved it,' Lisa said.

They were in the back room of the shop, quiet for the moment with Miss Howarth and May gone for a meat-pie

126

and a cup of tea in Tippings café in the Market House. Lisa was finishing off and neatening a zip along the side of a day pillow which matched the folded curtains of marigold-splashed cretonne on the worktable.

'I will give you the money.' Richard turned back a corner of a curtain, examining the finish in an absent-minded way. 'You don't need to wait till we're married, I'll give it to you now. The sooner you put all that business with the Grey family behind you the better.'

'No!' Lisa threw the cushion down in disgust. She had never liked the large flowery pattern anyway, but there were times when a customer's wishes had to be adhered to whatever her own reservations. 'Don't you see? For my mother's sake that debt has to be paid, and by *me!*' Her eyes seemed unfocused in their fierce resolution. 'When my career really takes off – and it is going to, Richard – I am never going to owe any man a penny. My mother used to say I was like my father, and in some ways I suppose I am, but not in that way. Never, never will I see my debts piling up, bills shoved in drawers, letters unopened. It can happen so easily, Richard, but it's not going to happen to me!'

'But we're going to be married!' He was honestly bewildered, and as usual it showed in the flushing of his sensitive skin. 'I will be your husband, responsible for your debts.' He tried a smile. 'I've told you, Lisa. When you marry me there won't be the need for you to work. We've discussed it over and over.' A patronizing chuckle crept into his voice. 'You can keep up with your designing if you want to – I agree it would be a shame to drop that when it's going so well.' He spread both hands wide. 'It's a wife I want, and a mother for Irene, not a career-mad woman dashing off here, there and everywhere with a portfolio of patterns underneath her arm.'

Lisa stared at him in disbelief. 'Then I won't marry you,' she said coldly.

In a second, disregarding the fact that Miss Howarth and May could have walked in by the back door, she was in his arms. And his arms were strength, reassurance, an Angus-smoothing of her hair, a driving away of the past two years.

127

When he kissed her she felt that source of strength seep into her body, as she knew that with this man the memory of her mother's haggard twisted face might fade from her memory.

'Are you sure I will be able to make you happy?'

As he held her away from him, Richard's face was a study. 'But just being with you is happiness. Or, to put it another way, if you left me my life would have no meaning.'

'Oh, Richard. . . .'

His confidence restored by Lisa's response to his kiss, Richard touched the tip of her nose lightly with his forefinger. 'You'll be surprised how poetical I can be when I get carried away.' All at once his face sobered. 'I just want to take care of you, absolve you from all anxiety, *cherish* you. Does that make me into some kind of monster?'

'I'll never be your shadow, Richard. I warn you. There's a part of me that will always want to stand on its own two feet.'

A glimmer of determination flickered for a second in the light-blue eyes. 'I'll stand back from you,' he promised. 'If that's what you want.'

'It's what I *need*,' she said simply.

'Then so be it,' he said, his eyes and face alight with love.

PART THREE

Seven

One early summer evening in 1941 Lisa Carr tucked her baby son into his cot, looked in on her husband who was deep in a sweat-drenched sleep following a severe dose of flu, then went downstairs.

'Your turn now, Irene.' Lisa heard the jollying tone in her voice, despising herself for it. Her stepdaughter, a matronly, overweight eleven-year-old, raised blue eyes ceilingwards, then went on reading the book on her lap.

Lisa dabbed at the wet patch on the front of her skirt. Why had no one ever told her that boy babies peed upwards? Only by turning her head sharply sideways had she missed getting it full in her face. For a moment she considered recounting the incident to the stolid child on the sofa, then knew it would have been a waste of time. Irene Carr had an invisible sign on her forehead which read: 'Don't make jokes to me, because I won't laugh, so there!'

'Time for bed.' Lisa felt exasperation thick in her throat as Irene turned a page with a languid hand. She fought to control her annoyance. The day had called for every ounce of her slipping control. Millie Schofield's face had set into its tragedy queen's mask when Lisa had asked her to stay on after her finishing time of six o'clock.

'I do have a life of my own,' her expression said, but Lisa had ignored her. The only way to tolerate the housekeeper's presence was to ignore her. Quietly, to herself, Lisa had rationalized the position. Without Millie's brooding presence she would find herself tied to the house at twenty-one, a slave to her husband, her baby, and a stepdaughter who hated her with a concentrated venom. Just for a moment Lisa allowed herself the indulgence of a healthy surge of pure hatred against the strange woman who, without being a relative, was an integral part of the household. There was something about Millie's long-suffering face that made Lisa more determined than ever to insist on following her burgeoning career. The shop had been inundated with orders for black-out curtains, which Lisa's ingenuity had fashioned into unobtrusive necessities as she lined velvets and brocades with the shiny black cotton, positioning the ugly material on the outside.

Irene turned another page, sighing as if willing Lisa to move away.

'Will you please put that book down?' Lisa spoke slowly, forcing a calmness she was far from feeling. 'Go upstairs and run your bath. I'll be up in ten minutes to see you into bed.'

'I'm hungry.' Irene widened round blue eyes. 'It's ages since I had my tea.'

Picking up a fluffy rabbit from the floor, Lisa held it against her face in a small unconscious gesture of comfort. 'You've had three biscuits since then.' She tried to instil a teasing note in her voice. 'Look at your tummy. It's like a little football.'

'It's not as fat as yours was before Peter came out.' The round eyes narrowed. 'Millie said you must be having twins.'

Lisa coloured to the roots of her hair. There was something very wrong in the way this child discussed her with Millie. Irene nodded her curly head up and down twice.

'Millie says she's sorry for Peter.'

'She's what?'

'Sorry. Because you give him milk from a bottle instead of from you-know-where.'

'Oh, my God!'

Irene's face set in a satisfied smugness. 'It's wicked to use God as a swear word. It's worse than saying damn.'

Lisa closed her eyes to shut out the sight of the round fat face. Her fingers itched to slap the hamster cheeks until they flamed an even brighter crimson. Then, as Irene trotted slap-footed en route for the kitchen and the biscuit tin, the

132

urge to smack her disappeared, to be replaced by a desire to take the matronly figure into her arms, whispering words of affection, a pleading to be accepted.

Sighing, she picked up the open book from the sofa and pushed it out of sight on the shelf underneath the coffee table. The answer, she knew, was to insist to Richard that Millie went. But that would mean staying at home all day, presumably turning her back on her pattern books, her sketch pad, her increasing clientele who asked her advice on anything from the colour of their bathroom curtains to the bridesmaids' dresses at their daughters' weddings. Three outside workers now made up clothes from Lisa's own designs, plain and expensive, each one adapted to the buyer's figure, disguising her faults, emphasizing her better points. Her creations were unique, and soon she would have labels made to sew into them. Her own trademark – LISA LOGAN, she had decided, the alliteration giving greater impact than Lisa Carr. She winced as she heard the clang of the biscuit tin. Lisa Logan dresses, evening gowns, hostess frocks, housecoats, curtains, spreads, cushion covers – all with her imprint. And someday, who knew? Fabrics woven to her own design at one of the town's cotton mills? Shops in other towns?

Slowly she walked through into the kitchen to the sight of Irene cramming a whole shortbread biscuit into her mouth. The bulging cheeks and the slyness in the flicking glance from round blue eyes snapped the last vestige of Lisa's control.

Snapping the lid back on to the biscuit tin, she whirled round in time to see Irene pushing a second, or was it a third, biscuit into her mouth. There were crumbs down the front of the child's dress, her eyes watered with the effort of swallowing without chewing, and suddenly Lisa did what she'd been longing to do for a long, long time.

Almost without volition her hand came out to slap one bulging cheek, and as Irene's lips parted in a wide gasp of surprise a shower of crumbs spluttered out to dribble down her chin.

'I told you you'd had enough to eat!' Now that she had

133

done the unforgivable, Lisa's anger was immediately spent. Irene Carr wasn't a child. Lisa doubted if she had ever been a child. They had heard only the week before that Irene had won a scholarship to Lisa's old school, and come September she would be setting off each day wearing the familiar uniform of navy-blue and sky-blue, squashing the cap down over her white-gold curls, the box pleats of her gym slip pulled out of line by her already sprouting chest. With her gift of mimicry Lisa had impersonated some of the mistresses, walking like one, talking like another, only to be met by Irene's blank, indifferent stare.

'I shouldn't have done that. I'm sorry.' Lisa was almost weeping as she tried to pull the stiff, resisting girl into her arms. 'Look. I know I have an awful temper.' She spoke quickly, trying to take advantage of Irene's stunned reaction to the hard slap. 'It's upsetting your father seeing us always at loggerheads with each other. He thought we would be friends.' She dropped her arms to her sides. 'I'm not trying to be your mother, love. I'm not trying to take anyone's place. But you're stuck with me.' Lisa smiled ruefully. 'And I'm stuck with you, so can't we make the best of it? Please?'

Already the marks of her fingers were beginning to show red on Irene's left cheek. If Irene had burst into tears, even tears of rage, Lisa felt she could have coped. But the round china-blue eyes were as hard as flint, dry and cold with a hatred that was almost tangible.

'Your father stole money from his friends.' Irene backed away, spitting out each word. 'He should have gone to prison. Millie told me. But he went to Australia so the police couldn't find him. And you lived in Mill Street.' She took another backward step. 'You made my father feel sorry for you, Millie said, and that's why he married you. An' I'm going to tell him now what you've done. An' if you follow me, then I'll push you downstairs.' She pointed a finger. 'If you touch me I'll scream!'

Utterly defeated, Lisa let her go. She walked over to the sink and ran cold water into a glass. There was a pain just below her ribs as if she had been punched violently by a balled-up fist. She accepted in that moment that Millie

134

Schofield would have to go. Veiled animosity was one thing; putting Irene against her by telling the child half-truths was another. Richard was right. Her place was here in this house, being a full-time mother to Peter and a full-time something or other to his daughter. Lisa took the glass over to the table and sat down.

She could not imagine a life dedicated to domesticity. She would still make time to work on her sketches, talk to clients on the telephone, live vicariously through Richard's anecdotes about the shop. Be the kind of wife he had always wanted her to be. Lisa sipped the water slowly, putting off the moment when she must go upstairs.

She loved her husband. And oh, dear God, how he loved her! Behind the horn-rimmed spectacles he had taken to wearing full-time, his eyes would glow with pride as he looked at her. Their love-making was as soothing and satisfactory as if it were a blessing.

Even the war seemed to be happening to other people, in some far-away place, only the shortages and the news bulletins intruding into their new-found dream of contentment. When she'd tell Richard of her decision to stay at home and conform to his blueprint of how a wife should behave, Lisa could clearly anticipate the relief and joy on his face.

Like her father before her, Lisa's impulses and decisions were never half-toned. Her day would come, she told herself, when Peter was at school, the war was over and Irene was married.

Muttering to herself, Lisa rinsed out the glass and upended it on the draining board. Immediately she was all contrition. She would make herself love Irene, even if it killed her, and she would force the strange child to love her back. She could make anyone like her; hadn't she proved it over and over again? It was a gift that her father had possessed in abundance.

Just for a moment Lisa imagined her father, laughing in the garden at The Laurels on a sunlit day, with his red-gold hair and vivid blue eyes, a circle of friends hanging on his every word. She heard the soft Scottish burr in his deep voice, remembered the twinkle in his eyes as he winked at her. He would have made what he would have called 'mincemeat' of Millie Schofield, sent her packing, then exerted all his charm on Irene so that she too drowned in his charm.

Once again the bleak feeling of rejection stilled her into sadness, leaving her feeling lost and lonely. Walking quickly into the wide hall she ran lightly upstairs.

Richard, pale now that the fever had subsided, sat up in bed, his head lolling uncomfortably against the mahogany bed-end. He looked as neat and tidy in his striped pyjamas as in the dark suits he wore at the shop, with a white handkerchief, ironed by Millie, pushed into the top pocket. Without the horn-rimmed spectacles his eyes looked young and defenceless, and the sight of him made Lisa feel better and strengthened her resolution.

'Feeling better?' She took a pillow from the foot of the bed and put it behind his head. 'I suppose Irene told you I smacked her?'

He nodded. 'I told her she must have asked for it.' He frowned. 'Do you think it was wise, though? She's gone off to bed in one of her sulks.' He stretched out a hand for a glass of cloudy barley water and took a sip, wrinkling his nose. 'I wish Millie would put lemon in this. It tastes disgusting.'

'There's a war on, love.' Lisa sat down on the bed, smiling at him. 'I wouldn't queue for half an hour in the hope of a lemon. Would you?'

He couldn't understand her calmness, Lisa knew that. Without the sparkling lenses of his spectacles to hide behind, his stare was wary. He had expected her to storm upstairs in the wake of his difficult daughter, tearful maybe, justifying the slap, and instead here she was, talking about lemons, the shortage of, apparently unperturbed.

'I've decided to stop working full-time,' she said straight out. 'The shop will carry on without me, and now that clothes rationing is almost on us women will be using their coupons for more important things than dresses.' She met his astonished gaze. 'Besides, now we've finished more or less with orders for black-out curtains, people will be making do for the duration. May's gone to make uniforms anyway, and where would you get girls to do the sewing even if there was anything to sew? It's into the Forces, or munitions, or the Land Army. Our kind of work doesn't fall into the reserved-occupation scheme exactly, does it?'

Richard blinked. The arguments about his wife's insistence on working had been long and fierce. He had tried reason, bullying, even bribery, and nothing had worked. Now here she was, looking as if butter wouldn't melt in her mouth, dark hair swinging forward on to her cheeks as she leaned forward, her expression as bland as one of Millie's creamy rice puddings.

'It'll never do,' he said biliously, 'you and Millie in the house all day. That's what you always said. Isn't it?'

'I did, and it won't. So she'll have to go.'

'Millie go? Where?'

'I don't know. Anywhere!'

'But she's always been here.' Richard looked embarrassed. 'Since before my . . . since before Irene's mother died.' He reddened slightly. 'You won't be happy being at home all day washing socks and scrubbing out.'

In his obvious dismay he used the northern phrase without thinking, then winced as Lisa laughed.

'Scrubbing out? Not much chance with wall-to-wall carpets all over the house.' She took his hand in her own. 'Come on, Richard. Don't tell me you've been pleading with me to settle down like a good wife and mother all this time just for the sake of saying it?' She juggled the hand up and down. 'It's Millie, isn't it? You don't like the thought of me working, but you like even less the idea of her leaving your employ.' Lisa raised dark eyebrows. 'Because that's what she is, Richard, in your *employ*.'

'In other words, a servant?'

'Yes, if you want to be difficult.'

'And you were used to giving servants the sack?'

'My mother was. If they deserved it.'

'And Millie does?'

'Yes, if you must know. Yes!'

A painful silence settled between them. Lisa saw that he

was disturbed and angry. She turned her head away from him. All right then – she would be angry, too. For heaven's sake, she was the one who was making the sacrifice, giving up something she held dear. As usual when disturbed, her thoughts came out in her head in clichés. Richard wasn't playing this scene at all the way she had expected him to. Instead of being totally overwhelmed by her offer, all he could think about was his housekeeper!

'She's been discussing me again with Irene. Telling lies about my father. Setting her against me. I tell you honestly, with Millie here there's not the slightest chance of Irene and me being friends. If you won't tell her to leave, then I will.'

'You won't, you know.'

When Lisa turned round she saw with surprise that two spots of hectic colour burned high on Richard's cheeks. His voice was low but it had the ring of authority. He was, as Miss Howarth would undoubtedly have said, in one of his moods. On his high horse, impervious to reason.

'Anyone would think Millie has some sort of hold over you,' she said slowly.

'Nonsense!' Lisa's eyes widened as she watched with fascination the tide of colour flood his fair skin. Richard was blushing like a young girl, caught in the grip of an emotion without the power to control it. She looked at him with growing disbelief.

'You've slept with her, haven't you?' The words said themselves, even before she grasped their implication. 'You have, haven't you?'

Instead of replying, Richard suddenly swung his legs over the side of the bed, pushing back the blankets, but when he tried to stand up his knees buckled beneath him and he fell back, his eyes closed.

'It was a long time ago. Long before you.'

Lisa felt as if she'd been winded. It wasn't as if she was a prig or a prude; it was just that the thought of the tall, horse-faced Millie, with her high-piled hair and her sliding eyes, slipping between the sheets for a night of passion, couldn't be grasped. Millie Schofield was a spinster, natural-born. The idea of her small, buttoned-up mouth opening to a man's kiss was obscene. Good Lord, there was more warmth in a Wall's ice-cream than in the whole of that elongated torso.

'It was just after my wife died.' Richard kept his eyes tightly closed as he made his confession. 'She – Millie – had been a tower of strength.'

Blackpool Tower, Lisa thought hysterically.

'She came to my room one night after Irene had been playing up, to tell me she'd got her to sleep at last.' He laid a hand over his closed eyes. 'Anyway, it just happened.'

Lisa found her voice. 'But she's older than you!'

'Five years, that's all.' Richard spoke with a breezy insensitivity. 'It was just the once because the next morning I told her it had been a mistake.'

'A *mistake*?'

'Yes. And she understood and agreed, what's more. It wouldn't have done, not with her living in as she was then.' Richard removed his hand from his face and opened his eyes. 'That was when I got her the room over the shop down in the village. She's all alone in the world, you know. I upped her wages so she could afford the rent.'

'Paid her off?'

He winced at her crudity. 'I wouldn't put it like that.'

'Well, I would.' Lisa got up from the bed and walked over to the window, lifting the net curtain and staring down into the deserted avenue.

'I told you. It was a mistake.' Richard gave a deep sigh. 'I suppose you find it all hard to credit?'

Lisa answered in a muffled voice. 'I find it almost impossible to believe.' She turned round. 'And I suppose you've convinced yourself it didn't matter? I suppose she was a virgin? A near-middle-aged virgin who could take it all in her stride, then dismiss it as just one of those things?'

'Don't use that word. I don't like it.'

'What word? Virgin?'

'It's not ladylike.'

'And what you did – no, what you *didn't* do afterwards was the behaviour of a gentleman? My God, Richard. I'm not a man-hater, but the more I learn about them the more

I think I should be. It's a man's world, isn't it? First my father, then Patrick Grey, taking what they need at the time they need it, and to hell with the women who are daft enough to comply.' She shook her head from side to side. 'Poor Millie. No wonder she can hardly bear to look at me. You must have known she couldn't shrug a thing like that aside. Because of what you did she's been in love with you all these years, living on hope that one day you'd turn to her again. Have you really been kidding yourself that she'd forgotten?'

'I thought you disliked her?'

'I did. I still do. But as far as this goes we're sisters under the skin, Richard. In this case I'm with her against you. Can't you see?'

'You're not suggesting I should have *married* her?'

When Lisa went to bed at midnight Richard was snoring through an aspirin-induced sleep. He had insisted that she slept in the spare room until he was better, and for an hour or more Lisa tossed and turned in the narrow bed, going over and over their unsatisfactory confrontation.

Poor, poor Millie, with her dour manner and grim face, eating her heart out for a man who had once made love to her. By mistake! And poor Richard, too insensitive to realize that a woman like Millie, by sleeping with him, would consider herself committed to him for ever. Lisa turned her pillow over, seeking a cooler place. Now, more than ever, it was essential that the housekeeper left. They would have to see that she didn't suffer financially, though at her age it wouldn't be easy for her to find another situation.

When the sirens went Lisa sat up in bed, staring wide-eyed into the darkness. She wasn't afraid. The town was well away from the heavy bombing concentrated mainly on Liverpool and Manchester. There was an Anderson shelter at the bottom of the back garden, but they had never used it, as up to now the only casualty had been a cow in a field over on the other side of the town. But even as the wailing sound fell away, she heard the plane, a heavy, trundling beat in the sky, a rhythmic pounding filling her ears and striking dread into her heart.

She was half out of bed when the bomb fell. It came first as a whistling swish, then as a crunch, rattling the windows, and as if in protest the baby began to cry in a loud piercing howl.

Out on the wide landing Lisa bumped into Richard, shivering in his pyjamas, clutching the cord of the striped trousers round his middle.

'It's all right,' he said. 'For my guess, it's just a lone bomber dropping its load on the way back. You see to the baby and I'll go in to Irene.'

Unbelievably, Irene had slept through the noise. When Richard came into the nursery where Lisa stood, wondering what to do next with the crying baby held against her shoulder, the All Clear went. In the dim light from the shaded lamp they stared at each other, embarrassed by their momentary panic.

'Go back to bed.' Lisa patted her baby son's back. 'He's going off already. It was just the unexpected noise. Go back to bed before you catch more cold. I'll go down and make a cup of tea. We'll know where it landed in the morning.'

'Come into my bed,' Richard said, when she carried the steaming mugs of tea into the big front bedroom. 'I'm not sneezing now. I can't get warm without you.'

He was just like a child, Lisa thought, as they settled into their familiar position of spoons in a box. He thinks he's so strong, so much a man of his own destiny, but really he needs me just as much as the baby does. Tenderly she pulled up the blankets and tucked them round his neck. Soon she herself drifted into sleep, aware that in some subtle way their relationship had changed irrevocably.

No longer would she look upon her husband as a substitute for the father who had rejected her. From now on, even at twenty-one, she was the wiser, the more mature. This man, who had once been her boss and now was her husband, would no longer have the power to make her feel subservient, even as she fought to be independent. She had his measure, as Miss Howarth would undoubtedly have said.

She awoke long before the first streak of dawn lightened the blacked-out window, her thoughts crystal clear.

Because of Richard's insistence that everything be shared equally between them, all profits from the shop and from her own earnings going into a joint bank account, she had no money she could call her own, despite the fact that she had desperately tried to hold back a bit in order to repay Patrick Grey. She had thought she needed protection. Losing first her father then her mother had made her vulnerable. Marrying Richard had subjugated for a while her desperate need for total independence. Now, although she was too tired to formulate a reason, she accepted that she was free.

The ringing of the telephone down in the hall propelled Lisa out of bed with the force of a stone hurled from a catapult.

'Is that Mrs Carr?' said the voice on the telephone. 'I don't want to alarm you, but the bomb in the night fell on the shops across the market square. Yours wasn't damaged too badly, but the front windows have gone. I think it might be as well if your husband gets down there. This is Sergeant Wilkes,' he added, 'speaking from the police station.'

'Thank you.' Lisa replaced the receiver, then ran upstairs to dress. She heard Millie letting herself in at the back door and, closing the bedroom door on a still-sleeping Richard, she tiptoed along the wide landing.

Millie was wearing her morning face, grimly set into the habitual lines of suffering. Lisa found it impossible to meet the untrue eyes. Quickly she explained where she was going.

'I'm going now without telling Mr Carr what's happened. If he hears he'll insist on coming down. Tell him I didn't want to wake him.' She turned at the door. 'The baby should sleep on. He had an extra bottle in the night.'

Millie's silence meant she had heard. As Lisa left the house Millie was already setting the table for Irene's breakfast, taking the cream off the milk for the huge bowl of cornflakes, cutting the bread into 'soldiers' for the boiled egg she had saved from her own ration. Now with that silly young girl out of the way she could slip into the fantasy which sustained her day by day. This was her house, that was her husband asleep in bed upstairs, and soon her precious little girl would come down and eat up all her breakfast. The baby . . . well, Millie hadn't quite placed him yet. He was just a little animal to be fed and winded. A pity he wasn't fair like his father. Millie frowned. From where had he got that bright red hair and those pale blue eyes? Like a blazing beacon his hair, glinting in the sunshine when she put him out in his pram. Maybe the colour would fade as he grew. At least he wasn't dark. Like her . . . like his so-called mother.

The damage wasn't as bad as Lisa had expected. By some strange quirk only one of the plate-glass windows had shattered. She was sweeping up the glass, picking up the bigger pieces with her fingers, when she looked up and saw Jonathan Grey watching her.

He wore his army captain's uniform with a debonair style, the neb of the cap pushed rakishly to one side, and his greatcoat more Russian in length than British. He stepped in through the broken window to stand beside her, looking down at her with a remembered air of whimsicality.

'You've cut your finger,' he said.

Lisa flushed bright red. 'You made me jump appearing suddenly like that.' She nodded towards his suitcase. 'Are you coming or going?'

'Going.' Jonathan took her finger, held it for a moment, then, putting it in his mouth, began to suck the blood away.

The totally unexpected, intimate gesture shook Lisa to the depths of her being. The long, almost sleepless night had left her worried and anxious. What to do about Millie? The matter of how she was going to live up to her impulsive intention of staying at home with the house and the children posed questions she was too tired to answer. Now, as Jonathan sucked seriously at her finger, she was aware of his dark, uptilted eyes regarding her with amusement, the clear brownness of his skin. She was twenty-one, that was all; this man knew her and why she was as she was. He was young, incredibly good-looking in his captain's uniform, and there was at that moment a crazy excitement in being close to him.

'Now we must wrap it up.' Jonathan examined the finger

critically. 'Isn't this where you lift your skirt and rip a piece from your petticoat?'

'There's a First Aid box through in the back.' Lisa led the way, asking herself why she was trembling. It was the association he had with her past, she told herself, as Jonathan wound a narrow bandage round her finger. It was him appearing suddenly like that, and any minute he would say something insulting the way he always had, and they would be back on familiar ground.

'How is your wife?' she asked as lightly as she could. 'I saw the picture of your wedding in the paper.'

Jonathan smiled down at her. She had forgotten how tall he was, but maybe that was because Richard was of only average height.

'She's OK. It's my old man who's the problem. We live with him, you know.'

'In the same house?'

Jonathan nodded. 'He drinks,' he told her baldly. 'He's got to the stage now where he's seldom sober, but he still goes down to the yard and fuddles his way through the days.'

'That must be hard on your wife.'

'She says it's her duty. Everyone has a cross to bear and my old man is hers. Apparently,' Jonathan added, smiling at Lisa with his mobile mouth.

All at once Lisa knew the smile was for smiling's sake. She changed the subject quickly. 'Richard's in bed. With flu. Otherwise he would have been down here.'

'Then you wouldn't have cut your finger.'

'No.' Lisa stared at the bandage tied with a comical bow like rabbit's ears on the top of her finger. But if she had, Richard would never have sucked the blood away. The very idea would have nauseated him. Richard had a hygienic temperament, she suddenly saw.

'I never would have thought it,' Jonathan was saying, his head on one side and the wicked glint back in his eyes.

'Thought what?'

'That such an ugly duckling could turn into such a beautiful swan. Motherhood suits you.'

'How did you know?'

'Amy told me. Read it in the paper. "A son for Lisa and Richard Carr. A brother for Irene." Irene?'

'My stepdaughter.' Lisa wrinkled her nose. 'Richard put that in thinking it would please her.'

'And it didn't?'

'She hates the baby. I caught her pinching his cheek the day I brought him home. She hates me, too.'

'*Your* cross?'

Lisa nodded. She found she was holding her breath as Jonathan glanced at his watch and gave a low whistle.

'I must run.'

She followed him back through the shop and out on to the pavement. 'I suppose I can't ask where you're going?'

The Jonathan smile was back again. 'Well, I might be going where I'll get sand in me butties. OK?'

People were beginning to hurry past on their way to work, stopping to stare at the broken windows. Suddenly Lisa wanted to snatch up her jacket from where she had thrown it over the counter, take his arm, and go with him to the station. Wait until the train drew away, savouring the last glimpse of the dark head, sending her prayers with him for his safe return.

She laid a hand on his khaki sleeve. 'Don't come to any harm, Jonathan,' she whispered foolishly. 'Come back safely.'

'Lisa?' His eyes were questioning. When his lips touched hers, soft and fleeting, she had an urge to wind her arms round his neck. Then he was gone, striding away from her with his loping walk, turning the corner, leaving her standing there, bewildered by the emotion flooding her body.

She turned back into the shop, and when Miss Howarth came in Lisa was staring in disbelief at a bolt of cloth with a hole going all the way through it.

'Shrapnel,' Miss Howarth said at once. 'That Hitler's got something to answer for. Fifty yards of best brocade ruined. The mean-minded faggot.' Her arms came round Lisa, holding her close against a flat sloping bosom. 'Nay, don't take on so, love. It's nobbut a bit of stuff. Better through that than through thee or me.'

'Oh, Miss Howarth,' Lisa sobbed. 'Isn't the war awful? It's come home to me this morning just how awful it is.'

That night Lisa told Richard that of course Millie must stay; that with the onset of clothes rationing she realized that her dreams of expanding her own side of the business must wait until the war was over; that she would work from the shop.

'Part-time would be best,' Richard said. 'You could work in the mornings, then take the baby out in the afternoons. To the park, or the clinic,' he added vaguely. 'You'd meet other mothers that way. Company your own age. Compare weights and things. Stop all this worriting about a so-called career. That way you'll have the best of both worlds.'

Lisa looked hard at her husband, seeing the concern in his face, pale from the aftermath of his illness. He was *old*, she thought suddenly – exactly twice her own age.

'Oh, Richard,' she sighed, as his arms came round her, holding her close.

Eight

Four years after the ending of the war Richard Carr had his fiftieth birthday, and it was at about this time that Lisa accepted a truth she had been unwilling to face.

In spite of her growing success she was a very lonely woman.

With the end of clothes rationing her career had expanded in every fresh line she took up, in spite of the post-war depression. The simple patterns and designs, so much the Lisa Logan hallmark, appealed to women starved of colour and imaginative lines. She used mainly her favourite Monet colours of lilac and soft pinks, giving her work an easily recognizable stamp of individuality.

Millie Schofield came in daily, even at weekends, giving Richard what Lisa supposed most men secretly wanted: two women catering for his every whim. It was, Lisa supposed, a ménage à trois, in the non-sexual sense, a situation she was forced to tolerate if she wanted to make money and yet more money. So the three of them lived in an uneasy truce.

Irene had been accepted at a Teachers' Training College in Yorkshire, and her earnestness moved Lisa almost to tears. She was still plump, but her golden hair and milkmaid complexion gave her, Lisa knew, a ripe attraction appealing to older men, especially those who still hankered after their mothers.

Peter, at eight, grew daily more like his grandfather, Angus Logan. Tall, thin, with hair as bright as a copper warming pan, he gave no trouble, either to his parents or to his teachers at the local school. Millie could stuff him with food to her heart's content without adding to his lean frame.

'That lad's got hollow legs,' Richard said one evening, puffing contentedly at his pipe. He smiled at Lisa as she sat on the floor beside his chair surrounded by drawings, sheets of figures and samples of materials.

'It's time we opened another shop.' Tucking a strand of hair behind an ear Lisa looked straight at him. 'Now that we sell as much dress material as curtain yardage, we're very short of space.' She sat back on her heels. 'Richard, I've seen an empty shop in Nelson Street, and just round the corner on some waste land there's a small warehouse. That's empty too.'

Before he could speak she held up a finger. 'No, don't say anything. Hear me out first. I've been doing a lot of thinking, and that little warehouse wouldn't take much converting to a factory. I'd start with, say, a dozen sewing machines and two lay-out tables, and there's room at one end for a partitioned-off office for the administrative side.'

The expression on Richard's face brought a note of pleading into her voice. 'Richard! Listen! Please! The overheads would be negligible. Now the war is over hem-lines are coming down, skirts getting fuller. Women are going crazy for the New Look. They're longing to spend money on clothes after years of austerity and square shoulders.' She held out a sketch. 'See! That's the way they want to look. Nipped-in waists and the feel of material floating round their legs. *Our* material, yards and yards of it. The days have gone when three yards of 36-inch made a dress, and a pair of cami-knickers had to be got from a single yard.'

Richard had lost the thread of what she was saying. How lovely she was, even lovelier at twenty-nine than as a young girl. No longer hankering after a sun-kissed complexion, Lisa now accentuated the magnolia creaminess of her skin by drawing attention to her large grey-blue eyes with smudged grey eye pencil, and mascara brushed on her long eyelashes. The little job he allowed her to do kept her happy, and he had to admit she had a rare and unique talent for design. He even thought he understood the reason for her

148

wanting to branch out into what he liked to think of as a man's world of business.

After what Lisa's father had done, getting himself hopelessly into debt, it followed that his daughter needed to prove she could succeed, just to show she was Angus Logan's daughter in name only. Richard sucked at his pipe, smiling on her with tolerance, rather proud of the way he'd worked that little problem out for himself.

'So, in view of what I intend to do,' Lisa was saying now, 'I'd like to be entirely responsible for this new venture.' Her voice came out just a fraction too loud. 'Richard, I'd like my own bank account, and my own cheque book.' She went on firmly: 'I'll need a loan to get started, but I know you'll help me there. Our credit is high at the bank.' Rummaging in a folder, she held out a sheet of figures. 'Look. I've worked it all out in rough. It's scary at first glance, but I know my timing's right, and the customers are already there. They know me and ask for me. I'm having to *reject* orders, Richard. I've got a long waiting list, so it would be criminal not to expand!' Her eyes were suddenly wary. 'And I want to do this on my own. It's my idea and I want to feel free to do it my way. Can you see that?'

For a moment Richard said nothing, then he knocked out his pipe with such fury that Lisa looked up from her folder, startled.

'Good God, what kind of talk is all that? We're married, for heaven's sake! You're not some silly single career woman who thinks she can succeed on her own. You're my wife and we *share*. And sharing means having a joint bank account for a start off! I'm the one responsible for you and your debts, and I always will be.'

'My debts?' Lisa spluttered into an angry torrent of words. 'My debts? Oh, come now, Richard. I've more than doubled the takings. I've worked hard and every single penny I've earned has gone into the business. What bloody debts of mine have you ever had to pay?'

'If you're going to swear. . . .'

'You *make* me swear. You try to pretend that what I'm doing is merely a nice little sideline, a hobby to keep me

149

happy. And as long as my earnings are mingled with the business you can go on pretending. You won't let me *be*, Richard. You have to stand back this time and let me be. Can't you see?'

'Your earnings?' Richard snorted. 'I thought we were the same firm. In every way. I haven't objected to you working, have I? If I hadn't been willing to keep Millie on you'd have been forced to stay at home doing the housework like any normal wife. Millie's been doing your job for years.'

'You hypocrite!'

'Keep your voice down. She hasn't gone yet.'

'Call her in, then! She'll side with you, that's for sure.' Lisa took a deep breath, almost sick with disgust. 'You *insisted* that Millie stayed on. You like it this way. . . .' She gestured at the drawings littering the carpet. 'All right, then. I'll go to the bank myself, using your credibility to get a loan. If we're in the same firm that shouldn't be too difficult.'

A flush of anger heightened the colour in Richard's cheeks. 'And you say you love me?'

Lisa sighed. 'I love you. There's a part of me that even enjoys your supportiveness. It's very important for a wife to feel she's being taken care of.' She gathered the sketches together. 'But loving you doesn't turn me into your shadow.' Her mouth quirked upwards. 'Come on, now, love. You'd soon lose your respect for me if I wanted to live my life vicariously through you and Irene and Peter, wouldn't you? You'd hate there to be no more to me than that.'

That night Richard made love to her, and when it was over went immediately to sleep.

Lisa stared wide-eyed into the darkness.

She was a lucky woman, she told herself. She, who once had nothing, had a home, a husband who loved her, and a job she enjoyed. She would *make* him go with her to see the empty shop and the warehouse, make him agree to her plans. She could make anyone do anything if she tried hard enough.

All at once the loneliness swamped her again, leaving her bereft and as lost as a tiny child whose hand has slipped from a parent's grasp.

When Richard saw the shop he agreed it could be a viable proposition and, shaming her by his generous capitulation, set the wheels in motion for the purchase. The warehouse, however, posed a stumbling block neither of them could have anticipated.

'It was bought for redevelopment before the war,' the solicitor told them. 'Since then nothing has been done. I've made inquiries, but as far as I can see the owner has shown no further interest in the property.'

He coughed politely behind a blue-veined hand. 'My client is not a man easy to approach. Something of an odd-bod, I would say.' The second cough was even more discreet than the first. 'My advice would be to contact him directly. He seems to view the legal profession with suspicion. Put the telephone down on me, to be frank.'

'And his name?' Richard asked before Lisa could speak, wanting to give the impression, she knew, that all this business was his own idea – that he had brought his wife along merely to humour her. 'It might be worth having a word with him, as you say,' he conceded.

The solicitor consulted a slip of paper in a dark green folder. 'Patrick Grey, the builder and property developer. The firm of Patrick Grey and Son, General Building Contractors. The office and main yard are in Reading Street, but if you would like his private address . . . ? I would have to ask his permission, of course.'

'That won't be necessary.' Lisa refused to look at Richard. Oh, dear God – the Greys. Patrick and his son Jonathan. Was she never to be rid of them? Since that last disturbing meeting with Jonathan during the war, when he had kissed her, leaving her struggling with feelings she could not define, she had seen him twice. Once from her seat on the top of a bus, as he was striding along the pavement, hatless, the collar of his raincoat turned up against a biting wind. And once as a head in a crowd round the war memorial in the park on Armistice Day. Both times he had been alone, and both times she had wanted to go after him and tell him of her thankfulness that he had come back safely from the war.

He was a part of her life, probably the only person who

knew her from the old days when she had been young Lisa Logan, ashamed of her sprouting chest and her freckles. He was, she supposed, a friend who would always be her friend, in spite of the intervening years when he had most likely forgotten her existence.

With an effort she brought her concentration back to the business in hand.

Twenty minutes later she faced her husband on the wide pavement outside the solicitor's office. 'I'm going to see Patrick Grey now. It's got to be done straight away.'

'Then I'm coming with you.' Richard's face was set in determined lines.

'No!' Lisa almost stamped her foot. 'I have to do this my way. Back there . . .' she jerked her head, ' . . . you took over from me, Richard. You talked to that man as if I didn't exist. You still can't accept that I'm capable of seeing all this through on my own, can you?' She put a hand on his arm, only to have it shrugged away as the tell-tale flush of anger again reddened his fair skin.

'But first I'm going to the bank.' She nodded twice. 'To spoil the look of my new bank balance.' Her mouth twitched. 'Don't look like that, Richard. It's a debt of honour, that's all, and if I didn't feel it was money I've earned myself these past years I would wait. This is something I've wanted to do for a long time.'

'And I don't come into it?'

'Not into this. No, Richard.'

When he turned to walk back to the shop, a stocky, bewildered man with his pork-pie trilby pulled low over his forehead, Lisa watched him for a moment before going in the opposite direction to the bank on the corner.

When she came out she quickened her steps, almost running along the pavement. She was glad she was wearing her new cherry-red suit with the fluted peplum to the jacket and the long, full skirt. When a man leaned out of the driver's cab of a passing lorry to whistle at her she smiled at him, enjoying the feel of the skirt round her legs and the bounce of her hair on her shoulders.

It was all beginning to happen, just as she had dreamed

it would. Soon she would be part, in her own right, of the exciting business world, free to expand her ideas, on her way to wiping out for ever the legacy of defeat left by her parents. She would never be another Angus, nor yet another Delia, running from defeat, or wallowing in it. Never. Never. Never!

The builder's yard, behind a high brick wall, led to the office, a one-storey building with two modern picture windows. Lisa's heart beat faster as she walked through the outer office, past a girl typing with two fingers at a huge machine.

'Mr Grey? Mr Patrick Grey?' At the sound of Lisa's voice, the girl sighed deeply, picked up an eraser and rubbed at the sheet of figures.

'Through there.' She nodded at a door. 'Just knock and go in. Blast! I'll have to start again.'

Leaving her tearing the paper out of the machine, Lisa walked to the door and opened it.

Her first sight of Patrick Grey jolted Lisa into an immediate reaction of acute dismay. Surely this grizzled man with the puffy face and eyes sunk deep into cushions of mottled flesh couldn't be the Uncle Patrick she remembered from years ago? The man she remembered had been as handsome, in a rather more fleshy way, as Clark Gable in *Gone With the Wind*, brown-skinned, with black wavy hair springing back from a high forehead, and a strong tanned neck rising from an open shirt.

She moved forward, hoping the shock wasn't reflected in her expression. His neck hung in loose folds over his collar; the long sideburns had gone; and his big face was as red and mottled as a slice of polony, his nose bulbous and lumpy, his eyes glazed like a fish on a slab in the fish market.

'Mr Grey?' She had come prepared to speak with authority, but heard her voice come out in a strangulated whisper.

Patrick Grey had been for years an alcoholic. Never quite sober, he spent his days craving the next drink which soothed for the moment, then left him trembling in anticipation of another. One part of his fuddled brain told him that the business had been run for the past few years by his son, but the other half still insisted that he came daily into his office, going through the motions, impervious to the sly glances of his workmen, and willing the hours away until he could weave his unsteady way into the nearest bar.

'Yes? What is it, lass?'

It was obvious he had no idea who she was. Lisa swallowed hard. 'It's Lisa. Lisa Logan when you saw me last.' She hesitated. 'You knew my parents. My mother, Delia. I'm her daughter. Don't you *remember?*'

For a moment Patrick stared at her with watery, blood-shot eyes, then the big face seemed to crumple. 'Lisa. Little Lisa. Nay, but tha's grown into a bonny lass. Nay, when I saw you last you were no bigger than two pennorth of copper. An' just look at you now! Well, who would've thought it?'

The protruding eyes grew moist. Lisa made a conscious effort to subdue the sympathy flooding her heart.

'I've come about the empty warehouse off Nelson Street. I'd like to make you an offer for it,' she said clearly.

'What warehouse?' Patrick waved a hand at a stand-chair. 'Sit down, lass. Warehouse? Nay, you'd best ask my son about that. He's the one throwing good money after bad, buying bloody ruins.' A hand crept down to a drawer on the left of the desk then, trembling, came to rest on the wide pink blotter. 'Nay, I remember you when you was as skinny as a whippet. Now look at you!' He glanced at his hand as if its trembling astonished him. 'I was heart sorry to hear about your mother, aye, heart sorry.'

To Lisa's horror she saw a tear slide down his cheek. 'She was a fine woman. A pity she got the wrong end of the stick. Took things too seriously your mother did.' Lifting his head he stared into Lisa's shocked face. 'But I did what I could for her, and no man can do more than that.'

When Lisa opened her handbag and pushed an envelope across the desk at him, Patrick picked it up and turned it over.

'What's this, lass?'

Lisa bit hard at her bottom lip. The scene wasn't being

154

played at all in the way she had imagined it would be, but she wasn't going to spare him. He didn't deserve to be spared. Just for a moment she heard her mother pleading with him on the telephone: 'Please, Patrick? Please . . . ?'

'It's the money I owe you. For the rent on the house in Mill Street, and for the coal you had delivered every month. My mother swore she would pay you back one day, so in her name . . . here it is.'

'Aw, lass. Aw, lass.' Patrick raised a ravaged face. 'I don't want this.' He was obviously struggling to bring some sort of coherence into his speech. 'You think I did what I did through guilt. You do, don't you?'

'Yes.'

'Well, it wasn't guilt, oh, no. There wasn't no onus on me to do a thing. I'd been trying to tell your mother for a long time that what had been between us was finished.' He bowed his face into his hands. 'But she wouldn't take no.'

Lisa sat quite still. He was right. Even in his fuddled thinking this man was right. Delia had never been one to take no. Rejection of any kind had always thrown her into a frenzy.

'I'd still rather you took it,' Lisa mumbled, hating herself for doing so. 'My mother would have wished it. For her sake you must take it.'

'Aw, God!'

As the raucous sound broke from Patrick's throat Lisa stood up, pushing the chair back so that it almost toppled over. Tears were sprouting from the big man's eyes, were running down his mottled cheeks, and he was making no move to wipe them away.

'Alice,' he sobbed. 'Oh, Alice. Come back to me, Alice. . . .'

For all her deliberately acquired poise, Lisa felt her insides dissolve with pity. This man was sick, so sick that in spite of the voice of reason telling her he was as sodden with drink as a piece of blotting paper left to soak in water, her inborn kindness took over. Moving quickly round the desk, she laid an arm over the heaving shoulders.

'Uncle Patrick.' With no feeling of revulsion she began to

stroke the thick grey hair. 'I'm sorry.' She picked up the envelope. 'Forget it. I'm going now. Try not to be so . . . so upset.'

In the outer office the girl was still typing with two fingers, her small face a mask of agonized concentration. Hesitating for a moment, Lisa noticed a chocolate box at the corner of the desk. In strong black capitals someone had printed SWEAR BOX, and when Lisa picked it up it gave a slight rattle.

'Yours?'

The girl sighed. 'Yes. Mr Jonathan had the idea it might help.' Her hand reached out for the eraser. 'I've only been here for three weeks, but I'm getting the hang of it. I am really. It's just that when I make a mistake I let fly. I'm good at everything but typing, and when I swear I put a penny in the box.' Her sudden grin lifted her small face into surprising beauty. 'And I always seem to be cussing when Mr Jonathan's in.' She nodded towards a leather-topped desk by the far window. 'He says I know more swear words than he heard in the war. Better ones,' she added, not without pride.

'And when the box is full?' Lisa rattled it again.

'We're going to buy cream cakes. All round.' The eraser was applied vigorously to the letter rolled into the typewriter. 'Bloody hell! I've forgotten to protect the carbon again. Now there'll be a bloody great smudge.'

Without stopping to think, Lisa took the folded notes from the envelope and pushed them through the slit in the top of the box. 'Have those and the next year's swearing on me,' she said. 'And persevere with the typing. It'll come in time.' Her face was all at once calm again. 'A long time ago I taught myself how to use a sewing machine, so I know how you feel.'

Before the girl could close her mouth or even begin to speak, Lisa walked quickly out of the office into the yard, past a lorry loaded with bricks, through the door set into the wall and out into the street again.

When she heard the voice calling her name she was so engrossed in her thoughts that for a moment she kept on walking, her high heels making a tapping sound on the pavement.

'Lisa!'

She turned her head to see Jonathan Grey standing there, staring at her soberly, an expression of disbelief on his face.

'I thought I was imagining things when I saw you in the yard just now.' He touched her arm. 'I had to come after you to make sure.'

His eyes were darker than she remembered, but they still had that glint of mockery in their depths, one eyebrow raised as he stared at her with obvious pleasure. 'Is it too much to hope that you'd come to see me?'

There was a special look in his eyes, and to her dismay Lisa felt a warm tide of colour flood her face. He was only teasing. Jonathan had always teased, but her legs had turned to water, and her heart was pounding in her breast. With an effort she forced herself to speak calmly.

'I came to see your father about the warehouse in Nelson Street.' Her chin lifted as she fought to control the totally unexpected tide of emotion. 'I want to buy it.' Before he could dare to laugh, she told him of her concern for his father. 'He's in such a state. I've never seen a man in such a state before. I think you should go to him, Jonathan.'

'My father is always in a state. Whisky-induced.'

'Please, Jonathan.'

'OK, OK. But you mustn't run away.' He touched the tip of her nose lightly. 'I'll only be a minute and when I come back you have to be here. You can't walk back into my life like this, then disappear. It wouldn't be right.'

What sort of talk was that? Walk back into his life? Lisa stood self-consciously on the corner of the short street, the full, fluted skirt of her cherry-coloured suit billowing up in a wind that seemed to have sprung up from nowhere.

Had they ever had a normal conversation? Ever once? She thought not. Teasing, fighting, every single meeting somehow charged with some sort of drama. It came to her as she waited that at every single watershed in her life Jonathan had been there. She tucked a strand of hair behind an ear, her expression one of deep concentration. Or was it that his presence *provided* the excitement and the drama?

'I've rung for a taxi. Sylvia will see him into it. He's OK.'

'Sylvia? The typist?'

Jonathan laughed. 'Face of an angel and language of an Irish navvy. Once she gets the hang of our ancient typewriter she'll be invaluable. The last girl never made a mistake, but she left because of the old man's goings-on. Sylvia, now, she just gets on with what has to be done. Says she never remembers seeing her father sober, so she knows what to do.' He took her arm. 'Now we're going to see the warehouse in Nelson Street, and on the way there you can tell me why on earth your husband wants to buy it. I wouldn't have thought it was in a posh enough district to tempt.'

'*I* want to buy it, not Richard.' Lisa's voice was crisp. 'Along with the empty shop on the corner. I'm going into business on my own account. Lisa Logan fabrics, dresses, soft furnishings. I want the warehouse for a small factory, and the shop as a centre for distribution and retail trade. Mail order,' she went on. 'I've applied for the trademark, but in the meantime, working as I am now, there are enough orders to keep at least five machinists busy. I know what I'm doing, and with hard work I'm going to succeed. I *am*, Jonathan.'

'Well, of course you are,' he said, without breaking his stride. 'Why the defensive air? Your father was one of the most brilliant businessmen I ever knew. He had flair; if he'd stuck to his stocks and shares instead of trying to pit that brain of his against the bookies, he'd have touched the stars. Of course you're going to succeed.'

Lisa turned to stare at him in amazement. 'Did you really feel that about my father? I got the impression you despised him.'

'Because of what he did? Oh, he'd gone too far down the road to ruin when that happened, but I realized his potential. Surely most folks did?'

Lisa looked quickly at the dark face, serious for once, and felt tears prick behind her eyes. 'Do you know, you are the first person to say anything good about my father.' Her voice was barely audible. 'Thank you. And thank you for believing I can achieve what I intend to achieve. It matters. It really matters, Jonathan.'

His hold on her arm tightened, and they walked along in silence. Anyone seeing them would have thought they were husband and wife, or lovers content in their quietness, stopping now and then to smile at each other, their steps matching, a beautiful woman out walking with a tall, more-than-presentable man. Made for each other, the more sentimental watcher might have said.

When Jonathan unlocked the door of the warehouse the smell of neglect and dampness wrapped round them like a shroud. The windows were thick with the grime of years, and the floorboards were rotted in places, encrusted with dirt.

'Not much of a place.' Jonathan stretched out a finger and touched a wall. 'But structurally sound.' He smiled at Lisa as she walked the length of the building, opening a door, coming back to gaze up at the high ceiling with the single light fitting, cobweb-trimmed. This was not the Lisa he remembered, unsure of herself, flaring into instant retaliation, covering her insecurity by rudeness. This beautiful girl had grown somehow into an awareness of her own potential. Her confidence had a touching quality about it, as if it had been painfully acquired over the years. When she spoke at last her voice seemed to bounce back at him from the bare walls.

'Subject to the surveyor's report being OK, will you sell, Jonathan?'

'Subject to the surveyor's report, I may consider it.'

'And if your father says no?'

'My father is incapable of saying either yes or no. The business passed into my hands a long time ago.'

'I upset him, Jonathan.'

'By reminding him of his inglorious past?'

'By giving him the money my mother owed him for the rent and coal in Mill Street.'

'That was cruel, Lisa.'

'I know. *Now* I know.'

Jonathan was walking towards her. It was the natural thing to do with the length of the big room separating them. And suddenly her whole instinct was to back away, to put as much distance between them as possible. She closed her eyes for a second and when she opened them he was standing close to her. Her eyes were exactly on a level with his mouth.

'Don't you think it's time we buried the past, Lisa?' He spoke hesitantly, his mouth slowly forming the words. 'What happened gave us no chance to be friends. You with your loyalty to your mother, and me with my loyalty to my father. I came to see you once, to ask you to forgive me, but your mother . . . she shouted me away.'

'She killed herself, Jonathan, waiting for your father.'

'That's not true!' He gripped both her hands. 'You're making another drama out of it. I thought you'd changed, but in that respect you're just the same. My father never intended to marry her. He was married already. He's still *married* to my mother even though she's dead.' He looked down at their joined hands. 'Face it, Lisa! Stop play-acting and face the truth!'

Before she could answer Jonathan bent his head. Her great grey-blue eyes sparkled with anger. To stop her contradicting him he touched her lips lightly with his own. Her mouth was moist, sweet-tasting, and he could not move away. Gently he kissed her closed eyelids, the soft contours of her cheeks, lingering at the corner of her mouth before he pulled her up against him. And this time the kiss was a burning heat flooding his body. Strands of her dark hair were entwined in his fingers, and he could feel the softness of her full breasts against him.

'Lisa,' he groaned. 'Oh, Lisa. This is how it was always meant to be. . . .'

Once, long ago, on a darkened beach in Brittany, she had pushed him away when he kissed her, sending him sprawling on the sand. Then, she had been a child, but now she was a woman who accepted that their desire was mutual. Her limbs felt heavy with a deep languor, and yet she was shaking. There was no strength left in her. At that moment she wanted him so much she would have lain down with

160

him on the dirty floor, and the knowledge saddened and appalled her at one and the same time.

'Jonathan,' she whispered, when the kiss ended. 'That shouldn't have happened. I am married and so are you. I can't hurt Richard, and you mustn't hurt your wife.' Her voice was laboured, as if every word was spoken with difficulty. 'I want you – oh, please don't be shocked – I want you, and I know you want me. But we can't hurt people. There's been too much hurting between our two families.'

As her mouth moved against his cheek she felt the slight stubble rough and exciting. 'There must be a reason why we . . . why we feel like this, but let's not talk about it, please. It's all happened before, can't you see? We can't take over where your father and my mother left off. It's . . . oh, God, it would be obscene!'

There was no anger in his face when she pulled away from him, just a sad perplexity. 'I am not my father, and you are not your mother.' His eyes were almost black with the intensity of his longing. 'I have a *need* of you, Lisa, and you have a need of me.'

'Wasn't that what *they* had?'

For a long moment they clung together, as cobwebs danced in a sudden shaft of sunshine through the dirty window. Their faces were dazed, and when they walked together towards the door into the street they stumbled as if they were sleep-walking.

They parted on the windy corner, nothing resolved, nothing arranged.

'I'll be in touch directly,' he told her, his expression stiff. Then, without further words, he walked away from her with his long, loping stride, his head bent.

Back at the shop Lisa walked straight through into the workroom at the back, grateful for the dinner hour which meant that May and Miss Howarth were walking round the Market House with its fawn-coloured paving and stalls bordered with fancy green terrazzo patterns.

Richard was serving. She could see him standing at the

161

counter, a pencil behind a neat ear, his head inclined towards his customer with his usual deference.

There was a length of sprigged cotton material spilling over a worktable, and Lisa picked up a fold, running it through her fingers.

Low down in her stomach she could feel a dragging physical pain of longing. Love wasn't like that, she told herself fiercely. Love didn't happen suddenly like that. Love was tender, soft and quiet, not a grinding ache of the guts. Deliberately she tried to disgust herself.

Her mother had been like that. Like a bitch on heat, she told herself, lusting after her lover. Jonathan Grey's father. And she, Lisa, would have none of it. She wasn't like that.

Richard came into the room and at once she turned her head away.

'How did it go? The warehouse,' he added, seeing the blankness in his wife's face as she turned to face him.

'Fine,' she said. 'If the price is right it's all settled.' Then, surprising him, she came and laid her head on his shoulder. 'Oh, Richard,' she whispered. 'You are so good to me. So good.'

Nine

'I would have preferred,' Lisa said, 'to have talked about this to your father.'

She was sitting opposite Jonathan in Patrick Grey's office, the width of the masive desk between them. Something had gone wrong with the oil stove and he was wearing what she took to be a golfing sweater underneath a tweed jacket. Sylvia, showing her in, had advised Lisa to keep her coat on.

'It's cold enough to freeze your bloody cockles,' she'd said, then clapped a hand over her mouth. 'Whoops! I'll never learn.' She had grinned widely. 'Anyroad, thanks to you, Mrs Carr, I've plenty of swear words to go at yet before I need to put me hand in me pocket.'

'Where *is* your father?' Lisa took a firm grip on herself, determined not to betray her agitation by as much as a flicker of an eyelid. She would not meet Jonathan's eyes. She *dare* not meet his eyes. She was there, she reminded herself, to talk business. She was the wife of a man who had done nothing to deserve a truant wife. She didn't want to know anything personal about Jonathan Grey. She refused to look at his ardent mouth, and she had in the past week decided to shut him out of her heart because, dramatic as it sounded even to herself, that was the only way she could go on living.

Jonathan couldn't take his eyes off her. She was wearing a winter coat in a dark shade of violet, and with the collar pulled up round her lively, expressive face her eyes took on the same shade. Unlike her, he had made no promises to himself, and desire rose in him like a lick of flame. He stared down at his hands, clasped before him on the blotting pad, imagining what they could do to her. With a great effort of will he forced himself to speak calmly.

'My father has gone into hospital. Voluntarily. What they are doing to him is terrible.' He didn't spare her. 'They are forcing him to drink whisky, then giving him something to make him sick. Violently sick. When he turns his head away from the next drink they force it down him, and so it goes on. Before they've finished with him he'll throw up at the sight of a bottle. So my father's got his come-uppance, wouldn't you say?'

Her great eyes were liquid with compassion. Jonathan clenched his hands together to prevent himself from reaching out to her.

'I'm sorry I told you. The last thing I want to do is hurt you,' he said in a low voice. 'Oh, Lisa . . . oh, God . . . what are we going to do?'

Now she was looking straight at him; their eyes were holding hard. Neither of them could look away.

'Jonathan.' It was merely a saying of his name, and in another moment he would have moved round the desk, taken her into his arms, covered her mouth with his own, tasted the sweetness of her, lost himself in the softness and beauty of her. . . .

'Shall I bring the tea in now, Mr Jonathan?'

The two faces that turned towards Sylvia as she came through the door were dazed and expressionless. But without a perceptive bone in her squat little body, the typist noticed nothing.

'If you don't mind, Sylvia.'

Jonathan sighed. And the moment was gone, the danger past.

'The surveyor must have worked overtime on the report.' Lisa took a folder from a slim briefcase. 'My solicitor has it in hand. I'm using the same one your father always dealt with. I can't see any complications. Apart from the price.' She tucked a strand of heavy hair back behind an ear. 'He tells me it is well below the current market value. I don't want charity, Jonathan.'

164

He shook his head, smiling, the ache for her suddenly replaced by a sensation of such tenderness that he felt he could die of it. This was the Lisa he remembered. Fierce, determined, standing up to him, playing the part, he suspected, of a hard-bitten career woman. He stroked his chin thoughtfully. And yet, *was* she playing? The old dramatic Lisa he had once known had somehow been replaced by this cool and beautiful woman, talking figures to him now, pointing at the columns with pearl-tipped fingernails, sure of her facts, estimating positively, with an optimism tempered with a realistic grasp of the situation.

'D'you know, Lisa Logan, I think you're going to make a go of this!' His tone was so suggestive of masculine bewilderment that she laughed out loud.

'Now you're talking like Richard,' she said without thinking, then before he could comment she looked up and thanked Sylvia for the cup of tea with a biscuit in the saucer, placed before her on the wide desk.

'I've just thought who that girl reminds me of.' Lisa smiled as the door closed behind the wide bottom encased in a flurry of tartan pleats. 'Or what she reminds me of. A pantomime babe.' She put the biscuit to one side and took a sip of the hot tea. 'One in a row of girls all pretending to be thirteen when they're past twenty. With young-old faces and turned up noses, and too many teeth.'

'She's pure gold.' Jonathan raised an eyebrow. 'Pure *bloody* gold.'

Laughing with him, Lisa was taken off guard. She hadn't known that laughter between two people could suddenly fade, leaving an intimacy more powerful than before. Jonathan had always laughed like that, tilting his dark head back, showing his strong brown throat – but had the irises of his eyes always been so dark? Almost black, merging with the pupils. Such lazy, beautiful, dreamy eyes, the kindest eyes she ever remembered seeing in a man.

'Have you any children, Jonathan?'

The question surprised her. She hadn't been conscious of formulating it, even in her mind. Business was what she had come to talk about. The warehouse, the shop, settling on a fair asking price, perhaps even going on to a proposed estimate for the building work necessary to make the place decent enough to pass the Factory Buildings Inspector. She frowned and bit her lip. 'Forget that. I don't know why I asked.'

Jonathan looked down at the folder on his desk and she saw a shadow flit across his face. 'No children,' he said quietly. 'Amy can't have babies.' He raised his head and smiled at her. 'Your son? He'll be a big boy now?'

'Almost nine.' In spite of her immediate realization of Jonathan's obvious sadness about his own childless state, Lisa could not keep the pride from her voice. 'Peter is at the local school. Doing well. He's so much like my father it's laughable. Tall, red hair. But he has my husband's prosaic approach to life. He's not brilliant, but he gets there by hard slog.' She smiled. 'I suppose I am a bit obsessive about him, but he really is a grand lad. You'd like him, Jonathan.'

Because she regretted her lack of sensitivity in talking about her son to this man who had just told her he would never have a son of his own, Lisa tried to make amends by telling him about Irene.

'She resented me from the beginning, and now she's away at college I feel a sense of such relief I can't explain it.' She frowned. 'It isn't a cut-and-dried case of the girl clinging to the memory of her own mother. From what I gather, Irene wasn't even close to *her*.'

She stopped, closing her eyes in an effort to stem the overwhelming urge to confide, to blurt out her despair about a situation growing daily more intolerable.

'Tell me, love.' Jonathan's deep voice steadied her, even as the shameful tears pricked behind her eyes.

'I've never talked about it before.'

'Then it's time you did. I'm here, love. Listening.'

'We have a housekeeper.' Lisa felt for a handkerchief in the pocket of her coat and began to twist it round her fingers. 'She was there when I married Richard.'

For a moment Millie's long-suffering face materialized before her, the uneven eyes watching slyly. Lisa shivered.

166

'Richard isn't a weak man, far from it, but she, this
keeper, has him under some sort of spell. His loyalty
runs ... least on the surface, but I sense he looks to her
her. She made The lace edging on the handkerchief tore
to do, which wasn't ... sent her away long ago. I almost did
rice puddings. So I suppose I've go ... clouded at the memory. 'But I
if you look at it like that.' ... ned foolish. And anyway she
... ly I could never replace
... the thing I wanted
... aking creamy
... uppance

'And Richard insists she stays?'

The softly spoken question was so intuitive that Lisa had
to look away. 'It's got beyond that,' she whispered, biting
her lips as Sylvia came into the room again with a query
about a pile of invoices.

'Let's get out of here.' Jonathan stood up as soon as the
door had closed behind the typist. 'I want to have another
look at the warehouse before I give you a written estimate.
OK?'

She ought to have let him go alone. Lisa knew that, but
already their meeting had progressed far beyond that of
builder and client. She felt drained of emotion now, so
achingly vulnerable that at that moment she felt had he
stretched out a hand she would have let him take her
anywhere. When he took her arm outside in the street and
pressed her close to his side, her legs felt weak and her heart
thudded so loudly she felt he must surely hear it.

He took her in his arms as soon as the door of the empty
warehouse swung to behind them.

'Oh, Lisa. My darling. My own unhappy Lisa. I love
you,' he whispered. 'I think I have always loved you. What
a mess we seem to have made of our lives.' His lips moved
slowly over her face, kissing her closed eyelids, lingering at
the corners of her mouth. 'Tell me you feel the same. Admit
you feel the same.'

Her response to his kiss gave him her answer. After what
seemed an eternity, when time ceased to be, Lisa pushed

him away, forcing her trembling legs to ... ... my
blindly taking her out of his reach. ... ... telephone
'We must stop it!' Her voice w... ... our father, willing
'We must never ever be alone ... ...
the tears streaming down h... own poor mother, doesn't
mother, creeping out to ...
to ring; and you, Jon...
to deceive your w... ... of his voice startled her. 'Are you
deserve it.' ...ess

'Amy? ...pare my wife with my mother?' He moved
trying to take her in his arms again. 'Oh, God! How wrong
you are!'

Holding herself stiff in his arms, Lisa looked up into his
ravaged face. 'I don't want to know, Jonathan! Whatever is
wrong between you and Amy, I don't want to know!' She
shuddered. 'I said too much, and I'm sorry. Can't you see,
we're spoiling it already. And I'm not unhappy.' She
avoided his kiss. 'I'm not *happy*, but then who is? But I'm
not unhappy.' She looked round the bare building. 'I'm too
busy to dwell on what I am. I'm going to make a go of this,
and you must get on with your life and forget me. As I will
forget you.'

Jerking away, she faced him as, long ago, she had faced
him on a darkened beach in Brittany, eyes blazing, hands
balled into fists as though squaring up for a fight.

They were no more than two paces apart. To the casual
observer coming across them suddenly they were merely two
people talking – intimately perhaps – but as Richard opened
the warehouse door and stepped inside his nostrils flared as
if he were an animal scenting danger.

He nodded at Lisa. 'The girl at the office back in Reading
Street told me you'd be here.' He walked towards Jonathan,
holding out his hand. 'Mr Grey? We've never met, but I've
heard a lot about you. The name's Carr. Richard Carr.
Lisa's husband,' he added unnecessarily.

They were getting ready for bed before Lisa had an opportu-
nity to speak to Richard about his rudeness to Jonathan

Grey. Dazed and bewildered by the strength of her own
...tion, she had listened, unbelieving, as her husband, red
...the tweed trilby which always seemed too small for
tousled, face ...ered at any suggestion Jonathan had
him to do the alterations... said. 'A wide boy. Like his
town. It's hardly the time to rake up ... his shirt, thick hair
just starting in business on your own. Folks ... been mad setting
memories. It won't be long before they begin to put two and
two together. The Logans and the Greys? Weren't they the
two families where one bloke hopped it to Australia because
his wife was having a bit of that there with his friend?'

The round blue eyes were shiny with barely controlled
anger. When he buttoned his pyjama jacket Lisa saw his
fingers shake. There was no point in arguing with Richard
when he was in this truculent mood – she had decided that
a long time ago; but it wasn't like him to be crude. She
turned her back as she unfastened her bra, before slipping
a lace-trimmed nightdress over her head.

'It's late,' she said. 'I have to catch the eight o'clock train
in the morning to Manchester to see about the shop fittings.
I could have ordered them from samples, but the firm I've
chosen has complete mock-up shops set out in the factory.
So I feel it will be worth the visit even though I can't really
spare the time.'

'Leave that off.' Richard's voice was low, thick in his
throat, so low that Lisa thought she had got away with
pretending she hadn't heard. Ignoring him, she adjusted the
ribbon straps of the nightdress over her bare shoulders
before slipping off her stockings, suspender belt and panties
beneath the long satin folds, as if she were undressing on a
beach.

'Goodnight, Richard.' Getting into bed, Lisa presented a
cheek for what she hoped against hope would be no more
than a husbandly peck. When he fastened his lips over hers,

forcing her teeth apart, she beat at him with ...

that he drew away, staring down with asto....en a bit

set face.

'Do you know how long it is sinc... ..my looking after

he forced a bony knee betwe...

embrace. 'All right, all was happening. In all the years

abrupt with your buil... ...ad never seen him like this. 'Richard!

your interests.' ...oice shook. 'Please! I'm tired. I don't feel

She couldn'...

of their l...

Pleas...

li'...

'But you'd let *him*, wouldn't you?'

Lisa struggled to move away, but he held her fast, his face above hers, eyes blazing.

'I saw you together.' He gripped her wrist, holding her arm high above her head. 'I'm no fool. I saw the way you were looking at him. And as long as you're my wife you don't look at any other man like that!'

With an almighty effort she tried to get out of bed, but he pinned her beneath him. She could actually feel the heat from his face, and when he took her roughly she lay still, twisting her head away from him on the pillow, knowing instinctively that to fight back would only inflame him further.

It was soon over. He rolled away from her, and quickly she slid from the bed.

In the bathroom she locked the door, tore off her night-dress, dropped it into the linen basket, and ran the taps into the bath. Somehow she had to get clean, to wash away his touch, to lie back in the warm water and let it soothe and restore her to herself.

The door handle moved, rattled, and she heard his voice from the other side. When she gave no answer he began to pound on the door, softly at first, then with increasing anger.

Peter would hear. In her imagination Lisa saw him coming on to the landing, his small face puffed with sleep beneath the thatch of red-gold hair, clutching his pyjama trousers round his middle. Quickly she stood up, stepped over the side of the bath and draped herself in a large white towel.

'I'm going downstairs.' Through the crack in the door Richard faced her, a belligerent expression on his red face, his eyes Irene's eyes, shiny and blue. 'I want to talk to you.'

He was sitting at the small table in the kitchen when she joined him. There was no shame on his face for what he had done. He was wearing his brown woollen dressing-gown and had found time, Lisa noticed, to lay the collar of his pyjama jacket neatly over the dressing-gown collar. The fair hairs on his chest were almost white now. Lisa found she had to turn her head away.

'There doesn't seem to be a lot left for us to talk about, does there, Richard?' She sat down, facing him across the table. 'In my book, what you did to me was rape. Or is that too strong a word for you to stomach?'

'A man can't rape his own wife.' Richard's high colour deepened only slightly. 'Stop being dramatic. You've been married too long to play the prude.'

A sharp pain stabbed at her temples, and she pressed it away with a finger. She felt sore where he had forced her to unwilling surrender, and his total lack of sensitivity filled her with a creeping disgust.

'I love you,' he said, 'but I won't stand being made a fool of. Especially with that dago from the builder's yard.' The blue eyes turned sly. 'Anyway, he's got his own problems from what I've heard.'

'What have you heard?' Lisa forced her voice to steadiness.

'Millie tells me his wife caught the drinking habit from her father-in-law. Looks like a slut with mucky clothes, shouting in shops and showing herself up in the market.No wonder your friend makes a grab at other women. Millie tells me no decent man would touch her with a barge-pole.'

'*Millie* tells you?' Lisa wasn't ready to absorb the meaning of his words, not yet. All she could do was sit quite still and stare at the nauseous matt of white hair on her husband's chest. Beneath it his skin looked red and damp. Lisa shuddered. She didn't like his skin, she thought wearily. For a long time she hadn't liked the touch of her husband's skin. '*Millie* told you?' she said again.

He was blustering now. 'Well, she does overhear things when she's out at the shops. She's not like you, always running around doing a man's job. Women gossip,' he added, 'and sometimes they bring the gossip home.'

'Home?' Lisa shook her head from side to side, feeling the damp strands on her neck. It was strange how the part of her which should have been fighting mad was subdued deep inside her with a sadness she could barely tolerate. Of course this was virtually Millie's home; it had been her home for longer than it had been Lisa's. Millie Schofield loved this bullying, bewildered man with a steadfastness his own wife could not compete with. Nor did she want to. All she wanted to do at the moment was to creep upstairs into the spare room and curl up on her side in the bed kept ready for guests who never came. And think. . . .

Think about Jonathan with a wife who drank, the Amy she vaguely remembered from her schooldays, a girl with a mane of auburn hair who had looked after Jonathan's father, saying he was her cross. From a long time ago she heard Jonathan's voice saying that.

'Would you care very much if I . . . if we parted?' Lisa's mouth seemed to be having difficulty stretching round the words. 'I've failed you, Richard. In so many ways I have failed you. Wouldn't it be better if we went our separate ways?'

'No!' The shouted word brought her sharply out of her dream-like trance. 'Don't say that!' The face across the little table was wrenched out of shape by a blinding, tearing anger. 'That's what you'd like, isn't it? To run away as your father ran away.' Richard shot out a hand and gripped her wrist, taking her by surprise. 'You'll never go, because if you did I'd see to it that you never saw Peter again. He's *my* son, and if you go then you'll have no claim to him.' The clinging fingers dug deep into her soft flesh. 'Besides, I couldn't live without you. You're mine and I'll never let you go. Lisa! Look at me!'

Wearily she looked at him, at the naked fear in the hard

172

blue eyes, at this man who could change in a second from being a shouting bully to a whining coward. And in that moment the remnants of Lisa's love for him died, to be replaced by a pity so overwhelming that the enormity of it made her feel physically sick. When he came round the table, kneeling down on the bright-coloured oilcloth covering the kitchen floor and laid his head in her lap, she stared down at the incipient bald patch on the top of his head.

All at once she was a fifteen-year-old girl again, standing behind her father's chair on the evening of the Conservative Ball. She was stroking his neck and comforting him in the only way she knew. She had tried to replace that beloved father with this man. And she had made a terrible, terrible mistake.

'I want to sleep alone, Richard,' she whispered. 'We've both said too much, and it's very late.' Fleetingly her hand touched his hair. 'Nothing will seem as bad in the morning.'

'It *is* the morning.' Pulling himself up by a corner of the table, Richard nodded towards the clock on the wall. 'But yes, you're right. After a good sleep you'll feel different. You'll see.'

It wasn't too difficult to avoid being alone with Jonathan. The building permit came through more quickly than anyone could have believed it would, and now the warehouse and the little corner shop reverberated to the sound of hammers and saws, with men in overalls carrying planks, climbing ladders, installing work benches, restoring the neglected building.

Lisa worked long hours. Already she had absorbed the techniques of buying, so that she could cost every single dress down to the last stitch, the price of a zip, every inch of trim, leaving a fair margin for profit.

She interviewed a dozen machinists, choosing them carefully, making sure that, if they were married, arrangements were properly made for their children to be cared for, knowing that on a budget so tight that its implications kept her awake at night, there would be no concession to absenteeism. She accepted without conceit that she had been born with natural good taste. She knew instinctively that accessories made or marred an outfit, and through working in Richard's shop she knew which designs would appeal to the fashion-starved, more affluent women of the town and its surrounding countryside.

She knew she was not designing for ultra-rich clients who spent their lives at charity balls or travelling down to London to visit the top couturiers. Her clients would be women who saw themselves as the ultra-thin models in the glossy fashion magazines, while still accepting that their clothes were not too outrageously different. A Northerner herself, Lisa knew that value for money was still their first consideration and that a ceiling price of twenty pounds a dress was inevitable.

Just as it was also inevitable that, in spite of her resolution, she would one day find herself alone with Jonathan Grey.

She was waiting on the station platform for a train to take her to Manchester on one of her twice-weekly visits to the war-scarred city, when she saw him making his way towards her. The train was drawing in with a rush of sound. Lisa felt herself urged forward by the touch of Jonathan's hand on her arm.

'I'm not travelling First,' she said weakly, as he opened the door of an empty compartment.

'Today you are,' he said grimly, pulling the door to with its leather strap, sitting down opposite her on the shabbily upholstered seat with its little squares of linen for headrests.

By the look on his face she knew that if anyone had tried to get in he would have quelled them with such a glance that they would have felt obliged to move further down the platform, but the train began to move and he leaned forward and took her hands in his own.

'I followed you,' he said. 'Now then, Lisa. What are we going to do?'

She could only stare at him wordlessly. He looked pale and ill, as if he hadn't been sleeping. There was a bruised look round his dark eyes and a small pulse throbbed in his jaw-line.

'There is nothing we can do.' She looked out at the grey

174

morning slipping by the dirty window. 'I am married and so are you.' She swallowed the lump in her throat. 'I won't let history repeat itself.'

'I am dying for you, Lisa,' he said softly. 'You must know that. It's taken a long time for us to find each other, but now we have there's nothing we can do about it.' He began to stroke the pulse at her wrist. 'We should have waited, but we both married the wrong people, and now we have a second chance. If we don't take it we are craven cowards. Don't you see?'

'No, I don't see.' She spoke so low that the clattering of the train wheels almost drowned the sound of her voice. 'You have seen Richard. You know I have a son. What are you suggesting? That I leave them and go away with you?' Her voice rose a little. 'That you leave your wife who has cared for your father all these years? And what about him? One family was destroyed. Do you want to destroy two more?' She stared straight into his dark eyes. 'Oh, Jonathan, we are neither of us the kind who can walk away. I could never emulate my father in doing that. I could never, never do to my child what he did to me.'

He came to sit beside her. 'Stop being so . . . so sensible, love. The past is the past, just that. You can't torture yourself with it for ever.'

'My past is me.'

'That's ridiculous.'

'No, Jonathan.'

He saw then what he had never seen before – the almost spiritual beauty of her lovely face, and the sight saddened him. He saw in that moment that the years spent with her mother in the little house in Mill Street had made her into a woman of great compassion, and the loving of her brought unmanly tears to his dark eyes.

'Richard will never let me go,' she was saying. 'He would keep Peter from me.' She sighed deeply. 'My husband has a ruthless streak in him. Peter is such a joyous little boy, Jonathan.' Her chin lifted. 'Thank God I have my work. Without that . . . .' She bent her head in a gesture of such melancholy that he felt his heart would break.

The train clattered on. When it reached Darwen a businessman got on, sitting opposite them, opening his briefcase and taking out a sheaf of papers which he studied with an abstract attention. Jonathan stared at him, hating his very guts.

He thought of his wife, of the way she was, the way circumstances had made her, of her slipshod ways, her bitterness at the way life had deprived her of the child she wanted, giving her instead an old man to cherish. He thought about her bouts of drinking when she turned on him, damning his father to hell, and the way she rallied to take up what she called her 'cross' again, sinking into a martyrdom which was almost harder to bear.

He glanced sideways at Lisa, at the rise and fall of her full breasts beneath the lilac woollen dress, revealed by her unbuttoning of the fur-trimmed coat in a darker shade. And it seemed the clitter-clatter of the train wheels echoed his frantic questioning. There had to be a way . . . there had to be a way . . . a way . . . a way.

Regardless of the milling crowds, he took her in his arms on the wide platform of Exchange Station at Manchester. For a moment he tasted the sweetness of her lips.

'You're crazy,' Lisa whispered as she pushed him away. 'You might not care who sees us, but I do!'

Two women, wearing identical camel-hair coats, turned to stare at them strangely, but blind to reason Jonathan gripped Lisa's arms.

'You go away from home.' His eyes were wild in their pleading. 'You travel. As I do. You don't have to account for your every moment.'

'And?' She glared at him, but he would not meet her eyes.

'We could be together.' He shook her none too gently. 'Lisa. We're two grown-up people, not children. You're so locked in the past. You're casting me in the role of my father, and you're seeing yourself as your mother. But that's gone! You're being as pig-headed as you were when you were a kid with freckles and your hair in plaits. OK, OK, so you can't leave Peter, and OK, so I can't leave my wife with my father, but hell's bells, there's a way we can take

176

what there is. I'm in love with you, and you're in love with me. Listen to me! We can both do what's right and still take time off for loving.'

'There's a word for what you mean.' She was trembling now. 'Why don't you say it?' She jerked away from his grasp. 'Is that what you want? Furtive phone calls? Clandestine meetings? Lying to your wife? Then tiring of all the messy secretive business and wondering how to end it? Making love to me, then going home and making love to your wife? I suppose you still make love to your wife?'

As he stared at her with despair and disbelief, she saw that her assumption had hit hard. And in that moment her weakening resolve strengthened.

'Please go,' she whispered. 'We're making a spectacle of ourselves. Besides, I'm going to cry, and I haven't to cry.'

As angry as he was, as baffled and infuriated, he saw that she could take no more. So he let her go, watching as she walked away, the full skirt of her coat swaying, the heels of her black court shoes making little clicking noises on the platform.

And because she was crying Lisa failed to see the two women in identical camel-hair coats trying to hail a taxi outside the station. Hurrying across the busy street, she saw nothing of the way they nudged each other and narrowed their eyes into suspicious slits.

'You were holding hands! You were *seen*, Jonathan! I even know who she was!' Amy Grey's face was wrenched out of shape by the force of her emotion. 'You've been seeing her for a long time, that Lisa Logan.' She faced him with hands clenched over the front of a none-too-clean apron.

'She's a married woman, but she calls herself by her maiden name. That shows the sort she is!' She began to cry. 'A walking clothes-horse, that's all she is, and you haven't the sense to see it. What have you told her? That you have a wife tied to the house, cleaning up after your father when he's too drunk to know what he's doing?' She caught her breath on a sob. 'Do you know what he did this afternoon? He opened a drawer and peed on his shirts. Too drunk to

177

realize he wasn't in the bathroom. And all the time you've been seeing *her*. Oh, God, you should have married *her*, then you'd realize what it's like. She wouldn't do what I've had to do. Not her, not fancy-pants Logan.'

Amy Grey had once been a big, beautiful girl with a laugh that could be as hearty and infectious as a child's. Now her auburn hair, streaked with grey, was pulled back from her shiny face, held in the nape of her neck by a rubber band. A long way from being an alcoholic, she still drank too much and the resultant puffiness of her face blurred her features into plainness. At first her caring for her father-in-law had sprung from genuine kindness; now some days she matched him drink for drink, letting the housework go, slopping around in bedroom slippers, swinging from resigned martyrdom to burning resentment.

Jonathan stretched out a hand to her, trying not to see the way she flinched away. 'You're wrong, quite wrong,' he told her. 'I haven't been seeing Lisa.' His voice deepened into sadness. 'True, I did see her the other day, but I've known her a long time, Amy, longer than I've known you. She's a part of my childhood, but I won't be seeing her again. So you see . . . .'

'You promise?' Amy came closer, so close he could smell the whisky on her breath. 'I'd die if you left me, Jonathan. You're all I have.' She gazed up at him piteously. 'Perhaps if I see another doctor and maybe have that operation, I'll be able to have a baby.' She laid her head on his shoulder, then lifted his arms round her waist. 'They are bitches, my so-called friends, both of them, trying to make trouble.' She sighed and snuggled closer. 'I believe you. It's just that . . . just that . . . .'

'I know.' Jonathan stared over her head round the gracious room with the curtains Lisa had made so long ago still hanging at the tall windows. 'I know, Amy.'

His dark eyes closed, so that the anguish in them was hidden.

There were times during the next few years when Jonathan would stop for a moment, look at the man he had become,

178

and be filled with such doubt and self-loathing that he would actually bury his face in his hands and groan aloud.

He would examine his frenetic life-style, his fourteen-hour day at the yard, his sporadic conquests of women who were no more to him than a temporary satisfaction of the flesh, and cringe away from his own weakness.

Inherited from his father? He didn't know, but with the old man dead and gone, and his wife refusing to sleep with him now that all hope of having a child was abandoned, he felt at times as if he dwelled at the bottom of a well in a sludge of sorrow.

He saw Lisa's name everywhere. The weekly newspaper ran a regular advertisement of her latest ranges. Lisa Logan dresses. Lisa Logan sheets, pillowcases and bedspreads, all patterned with the dainty designs she had made her trademark.

Once, in a fit of unbearable loneliness, he went into the small shop on the corner of Nelson Street hoping to see her, asking for her by name, only to be told that Mrs Carr was down in London and would be there for another two weeks.

'If you'd like to leave your name, sir?' The girl behind the counter had stared at him with open curiosity. 'I'll see Mrs Carr gets any message.'

He knew then that he must forget her. He told himself he was lucky to have a business so thriving that work could and must be his salvation. Contracts were flooding in as rows of terraced houses, built over a hundred years ago at the time when the cotton mills were flourishing, were being knocked down. They were being replaced by uniform blocks of flats, destroying the intimacy and close-knit communities of the little streets. And in many cases destroying also the lives of the people who lived in them.

Not that any of that was the concern of this new Jonathan Grey, a man who was making money so fast that he had to employ a full-time accountant if he wasn't going to hand most of it back to the government in taxes.

And as the years passed, his memories of Lisa faded, as memories do. Just now and again he would stop what he was doing and see, in his imagination, her swaying walk as she left him on the dingy platform, and his heart would contract with longing.

So he signed yet another contract, knocked down another row of houses, built another block of concrete monstrosities, worked at his desk until the print blurred before his eyes. Then he went home to a loveless marriage and a wife who now spent money as if it had indeed grown on trees.

'Get on with your life,' he would tell himself. 'What else is there to do?'

PART FOUR

Ten

In 1958, when Irene Carr was twenty-eight, she came home one day from the junior school where she taught the mixed infants and, marching into the large front room of the red-bricked house, held out her left hand.

'I'm engaged,' she announced baldly.

Lisa, working that day from home on a set of sketches for her first mannequin parade, turned from her drawing-board.

'To Edwin Bates? Oh, love, I *am* pleased. I never imagined you were as serious with him as all that.'

For a moment the puny, tweed-clad man, a fellow teacher at Irene's school, appeared in Lisa's mind's eye like a puff of ectoplasm by her stepdaughter's side. Hardly reaching Irene's chin, an ineffectual little man in his middle forties with a moustache too big for his face, Lisa had never dreamed he could be a possible suitor. A born bachelor, she would have sworn, but now Irene was showing off his ring, an opal set in a raised claw setting. Her birth stone, Lisa remembered.

'I'm really glad,' she said again. 'Edwin strikes me as being such a kind man. I always have thought that men who teach very young children must be special. Patience,' she went on, ignoring Irene's stony expression, 'that's the quality they have. Infinite patience and gentleness. I'm so happy for you.'

'Well, you would be.' Sitting down on the sofa, Irene spread the full skirt of her shirtwaister dress. 'It means I'll be leaving home, and that's what you've always wanted, isn't it?'

'That's not true,' Lisa said insincerely. She had stopped

183

trying to love this strangely embittered young woman a long time ago, and their relationship had developed into a resigned acceptance of each other's presence. There were no rows, no more fierce confrontations. A wry smile lifted the corners of Lisa's wide mouth. 'Well, maybe you're right. It *is* time you had a place of your own.' She pushed the drawing-board aside. 'You must let me make your wedding dress.'

With an expert professional eye she assessed the waistless, lumpy figure, the round face seemingly devoid of cheekbones and topped by a short floss of spun-gold hair. 'I've got it! The new sack line skimming your waist will be perfect.' Her eyes narrowed as she concentrated. 'We mustn't cover your hair with too much veil. Maybe a tiny coronet with a circular veil fastened with a spray of orange blossom.' Her voice came alight with enthusiasm. 'Oh, yes. It will be such a joy to me to make you a lovely dress. See . . . I'll make a rough sketch. You have such beautiful skin, so I'll cut the neck-line fairly low. . . .'

'No!' Irene cried out in immediate anger. 'You're not turning me out like a dog's dinner. I refuse to let you! What do you want? To use me as a walking advertisement for your everlasting fashions? "The bride wore a Lisa Logan dress." Is that what you'd like to see in the paper? You've always sneered at the way I dress. Yes, you have. Even when I was a child you'd have starved me to make me as thin as one of your flamin' mannequins if you'd got the chance. You patronize me. And I won't be patronized!'

'I've never sneered at you.' Lisa twisted the pencil round and round in her fingers. 'I would have been proud of you, if you'd let me be. I know you're a marvellous teacher, and I hope you and Edwin have lots of children of your own. You need someone of your very own, Irene, and Edwin will make a wonderful father.'

'Better than yours did!' A blush like a scald rose slowly from Irene's thick neck, suffusing her face with colour. 'And at least when I do have a baby I won't neglect it. When my baby comes I'll stop work to look after it. At least I have *my* priorities straight.'

'Irene.' Lisa spoke softly, determined not to lose her temper. 'Do you *really* believe that I neglected Peter? Has he grown up the way he has, winning a scholarship to Oxford, turning out into the well-adjusted independent young man he is, because of lack of care? Be honest now. Have you ever known a happier being than Peter? Hasn't it been better for his development that he had a mother vitally interested in a challenging career rather than one who stayed at home feeling frustrated?' She sighed. 'Can't you understand that there's something inherent in me forcing me to succeed?' The grey-blue eyes were pleading. 'Just for once, Irene, talk to me, not as if you were a child and I was your wicked stepmother. You're only ten years younger than me. Do you honestly believe I neglected *you*?'

'Millie brought me up.' Irene's tone was flat, the dolly-blue eyes as hard as glass marbles. 'If my father hadn't met you and become infatuated . . .' she corrected herself, ' . . . obsessed, he would have married Millie.' She glanced over her shoulder at the closed door. 'Oh, I know you think of her as a servant, but she was *living* with my father till you came on the scene.' The creamy neck deepened again to crimson. 'You told him a hard-luck story, and he stopped Millie staying overnight. He put her in her place good and proper, but being the way she is she still couldn't bear not to see him every day. So she stopped on as housekeeper, coming in every day. That's what *real* love means. She demeaned herself, just to be near him, doing the work you should have done if you hadn't been determined to go out to work making money we don't need. *You* just want to be famous. Millie only wanted to be his loving slave.' Tears sparkled and were quickly blinked away. 'Millie says my father is going to be ill if he doesn't stop working so hard, influenced by you, but I don't expect you've even noticed. If you want the truth, I think of Millie as my mother! I always have, and I always will!'

When she jumped up and left the room in a graceless, plodding run, Lisa sat quite still, gripping the pencil hard between her fingers. Like a hollow, sad echo, Irene's words lingered: 'Millie was living with my father till you came on the scene.'

Lisa stared unseeing out of the bay window at the small front garden with its high privet hedge fronting the lawn. Richard had said . . . he had admitted that his relationship with Millie had been more than that of housekeeper and employer, but it had been only once, he had sworn. One of those things, he'd inferred. And all the time the dour woman with the untrue eyes had been his mistress. The old-fashioned word slipped naturally into Lisa's fevered thinking. She shivered as if a damp chill had suddenly seeped from the cream-washed walls.

But Irene had been a mere child. Eight years old. How much could a child of that age have known about what went on behind a closed bedroom door?

And Millie? Millie with the smooth face, the tall, willowy figure, the devious slipping eyes? Oh, yes, she would have waited. Bided her time, grown older along with Richard, knowing that in the fullness of time he would have capitulated and married her.

As usual when distressed, Lisa's thoughts came out in articulate platitudes. She sighed heavily. What chance had she ever had in this house with all that brooding devotion emanating from the kitchen?

It was a long time now since Richard had stopped wanting to make love to her. She was fully aware that the physical side of their marriage had held it together. She also accepted that nothing had been left between them to compensate. He would never understand the strong emotional urge to make and keep money that inspired her material ambition. And now it was too late.

Or was it? Lisa began to tremble. At thirty-eight she was still a youngish woman. She could start afresh on her own now that Peter was grown-up. She could . . . oh, yes, she could.

And starting right now she would go and talk to Millie.

But in spite of her resolution her heart was beating with dull, heavy thuds as she walked through the hall into the breakfast-room and on into the scullery beyond.

Millie was ironing. She was ironing the jacket of Richard's striped pyjamas, paying it as much attention as if it were one of his white go-to-business shirts. Lisa felt pity well up inside her as she looked at the still slim woman, past her sixtieth birthday, but with scarcely a thread of grey in her high-piled hair.

'Millie?' Lisa's voice sounded alien, even to her own ears.

'Yes, Mrs Carr?' The iron slid silently round the collar. The untrue eyes lifted for a second. 'We're eating cold tonight. I hope you don't mind.'

There was a tap dripping in the stone sink and it gave Lisa an excuse to turn away.

'Millie . . .' she said again, as the door bell rang, a harsh electric jarring, as if someone had kept a finger there, cutting off for ever what Lisa had been going to say.

The policeman standing there played his distasteful role according to the rule book.

'Mrs Carr?'

Lisa nodded.

'Are you alone?'

'No. Why?'

But even as she asked, Lisa knew what he had come to say. And when he told her, an immediate numbness settled on her, blanking her mind to the meaning of his words.

'It was in the street,' the policeman said. 'Quick and sudden.' He coughed apologetically. 'Witnesses said your husband just fell down as though he'd been pole-axed.' He jerked his chin towards the police car standing at the kerb. 'If you'd like to come with me, I'll take you to the hospital. To where he's lying temporarily.' His glance went over Lisa's shoulder. 'Your mother? Perhaps she'll come with you? It might be better. . . .'

Millie's scream rent the air like the vicious tearing of a sheet of emery paper. 'He's dead! Oh, God! Go away! It's not true! Go away and stop your lying! It isn't true! I won't believe it. Oh, God, help me! Someone help me. Please!'

Irene got to her before Lisa could bring her leaden limbs to move. Standing there as still as if she'd been carved from stone she watched them sway together, clinging, crying, till

187

Millie's screams died to low moans, mingling with Irene's desperate sobbing.

The young policeman's mouth dropped open as Millie pointed a finger at Lisa.

'She doesn't care! She's never cared! Look at her, the cold devil! All she's ever cared about is herself! Oh, Richard . . . Richard!'

Sinking to her knees, Millie tore at her hair, the immaculate high-piled hair. Lisa watched in detached horror as it came loose to fall round her face and down to her shoulders.

'Unfasten her dress.' The policeman stepped inside the dark panelled hall. 'A glass of water, love. Where's the kitchen? Through there?'

Irene spoke to him, ignoring Lisa. 'I'll see to her.' Gently she raised the hysterical woman. 'Come with me, Millie. Upstairs. Come and lie down. I'm here. Come on. Come with me.'

'I'll get my coat.' Lisa's voice was dull and expressionless. 'Just give me a minute.'

There were no tears. The pain inside her set her features into stony indifference. As the police car drew away from the kerb a damp fog hung over the rooftops of the neatly spaced houses set behind high privet hedges. She didn't speak a word.

The tears came on the day she picked Peter up from the station on the morning of the funeral.

'I'm sorry,' she whispered. 'It's seeing you, love. I'll be all right in a minute.'

Peter put his arms round his mother. His own tears had been shed in the privacy of his room at the college. He was wearing a black tie. Lisa could see it at the open neck of his duffle-coat, and somehow the sight of it had opened the flood-gates of her grief. Much to Richard's disgust, Peter had never been a tie man. His hair, his vivid red-gold Logan hair, straggled long over his collar, and that too had driven his father to distraction.

'For Christ's sake!' Richard had once shouted. 'What do you think you look like?'

'As a matter of fact, Christ wore his hair quite long, Father,' Peter had retorted.

'You know, Mother,' he was saying quietly now, 'I never really knew him.' His rather prominent Adam's apple moved up and down in his thin neck. 'Oh, I loved him, because he was my father, but I never got close, not really close.'

Lisa moved away and mopped her eyes with a handkerchief. Sitting side by side, they stared through the windscreen at the grey winter's day, then, as Lisa stretched out a hand to switch on the ignition, Peter said unexpectedly, 'Why did you marry him, Mother? You had so little in common. I've often wondered.' He smiled at her shocked face. 'Oh, I know what you're thinking. You're thinking that's a terrible thing to say on the day of his funeral; but Father dying hasn't turned him into a plaster saint. He was always trying to *diminish* you, to make light of what you've achieved. He'd put you down in company, make you look foolish, and that you're certainly not. You stayed with him because of me, didn't you?'

A boy like this, to have known so much, to have known and said nothing. . . . Lisa held her breath, wondering what was coming next.

'He was a good father. A better one than most. But what I could never understand was the way he sided with Millie and Irene against you. Oh, not openly, but in little subtle ways. I'd have tackled him about it before I went away if I hadn't known it would've been a waste of time. I wasn't exactly afraid of him, but I was sometimes afraid of incurring his displeasure. He was a gentle bully, if there's such a thing.'

'Well . . . well. . . .' Lisa turned to look at the gangling boy, huddled deep into the duffle-coat, the scars of a youthful bout of acne showing faintly on his smooth cheeks. 'Why have you waited until now to say all that?'

'Because I could see you had worked out your own salvation, and because that is what life's all about, isn't it? A person working out their own salvation, making a marriage work or letting it go. But I ached for you, Mother. There were times when I really ached for you. There wasn't much in it for you but your career, was there?'

The kindness in his gruff voice, the understanding, the perceptiveness, caught Lisa unawares, so that the tears filled her eyes again. 'Thank God I've got you,' she wanted to say, but swallowed even the thought. If there was one thing she had to do right, that thing was to send him back the next day free, unburdened by a widowed mother who relied on him for emotional comfort.

'I wasn't going to tell you until after the funeral,' she said, 'but I've made up my mind to go away.'

Now it was Peter's turn to look surprised. 'Where to, Mother?'

Lisa fiddled with the button at the neck of her plain black coat. 'First I'm going to settle the house and the shop – your father's shop – on Irene. When she marries she will have a home, and Millie . . .' she tightened her lips, ' . . . Millie will stay on, I'm sure. Irene will want that.' Her voice was high and brittle. 'They're very close, you know. Your father would have approved, I'm sure.'

Peter's expression was noncommittal, but she went on quickly, daring him to pass comment. Some things were sacred surely; most things she would discuss with this too-wise son of hers, but not that, not Millie's relationship with his father.

'Gordon Conway, the man I've taken on as my assistant, is perfectly capable of running the other shop and the warehouse, without me to oversee.' She gripped the tortoiseshell handle of the bag on her knee until her knuckles turned white. 'I thought about Manchester, but it's a place I can't identify with somehow.' For a moment she closed her eyes and saw Jonathan's ravaged face as he stood with her on the station platform. 'No, not Manchester. London's where I've set my sights. I've repaid the mortgage on the shop and the warehouse, so I'm free to start afresh. With real quality merchandise this time. I'll have a different clientele down there, not a minority of women who appreciate high fashion. The bank will help out, I know, especially if I pledge a new

190

shop as collateral. I'll redeem any promissory note in no time, you'll see.'

Peter whistled between his teeth. 'All I wanted was a cuddly mummy,' he grinned, 'and what do I get? A tycoon wearing a hat with a spotted veil!'

As the car drew away from the kerb one part of Lisa's mind concentrated on her driving; the other part dwelled on the note received that morning which was tucked into the zipped compartment of her leather handbag: 'If you want me, ring this number. I *implore* you to ring this number . . . . Jonathan.'

She had opened the short letter, running her fingers round and round the figures. 2956. The telephone number of Grey's the builders. Jonathan's office number. Well, of course, his office number. How could it be otherwise? For a brief moment she had seen in her imagination her mother dialling that very same number, eyes dark and wide in the pale oval of her face, pleading with Jonathan's father to see her, just once more. 'We must talk,' Delia had said. 'I have to see you!'

And when Irene had come downstairs into the hall she had pushed the letter into her bag, feeling her face flame.

'Are you all right, Mother?' Peter asked.

His voice, gruff with concern, relaxed her hands on the wheel.

'Perfectly all right, love,' she said, then drove on, chin held high, dark wings of hair swinging forward on to her cheeks beneath the small, black velvet pill-box hat. Oh, yes, she was all right. She was a survivor. Now who had once said that of her? She was Lisa Logan, businesswoman in her own right, a Lancashire woman, and women from Lancashire did not live their lives pining for the unobtainable. No, by gum, Lancashire women co-operated with the inevitable.

And who had said that? Lisa had no idea, but it fitted.

'You'll see a great change in Millie,' she said, as the car swung into the drive of the house with its curtains drawn against the cold winter morning.

Eleven

Gordon Conway lingered outside the smart boutique tucked away in a side street off London's Upper Regent Street. He had made the train journey from the north many times in the five years since his employer had moved away, but he always lingered before stepping inside the shop, his trained eye taking in the simplicity of the window dressing. He never failed to look up at the letters engraved above the glass door: LISA LOGAN.

He was always impressed. A go-ahead man himself, he still considered Lisa's achievement awesome; there was no other word for it. Here, in the very centre of what he liked to think of as swinging sixties London, she had given full rein to her individuality, selling the modish styles which might have been frowned upon by the affluent matrons in the big country houses surrounding the mill town he had left behind that morning.

At thirty-nine Gordon Conway was an impressively handsome man. There was an animal virility in his big frame, and more than a hint of sensuality about his firm mouth. In spite of his workaday life among sprigged cottons and shiny brocades, there was no lack of masculinity in his appearance.

When Lisa had taken him on years before, he had been in the throes of a nasty divorce, shaken by the sordidness of the publicity, but now the 'other woman' was a distant memory to him, and much to his own surprise he had been celibate for longer than he would have admitted.

For a while he wandered round the lower floor of the elegant shop, feeling the deep pile of the beige carpet beneath his feet, watching the women ruffling through the carousels of crochet dresses, hipsters, trouser suits and kaftans. Only for the very young, he decided, the new breed of youngsters swarming into London with money to spend on clothes they would wear today and discard tomorrow. The real heart of the Lisa Logan empire, he knew, beat upstairs, where valued clients were able to choose at leisure, be fitted or measured, eventually going away starry-eyed, clutching the distinctive violet bag, feeling that the dress inside it compared favourably with an Yves Saint-Laurent design.

'Miss Logan always knows what suits me,' they would tell their friends. 'Isn't she marvellous? So beautiful. I wonder just how old she is? It's hard to tell. She has a French look about her, don't you think? It must be the way she wears her hair pulled back into a chignon. But for all her gaiety she has a sad look about her eyes, don't you agree?'

Gordon Conway watched with an amused twinkle in his brown eyes as two women came down the curved staircase leading from the upper floor. They were chattering like magpies, their hair lacquered into beehives, space-age shift dresses showing too much of knobbly knees. Mutton dressed as lamb, in Gordon's opinion.

They didn't grow women like that in Lancashire, he told himself wryly, then flashed them a smile as they walked towards the heavy glass door and out on to the sunlit busy street.

When he turned round Lisa was coming down the stairs. He blinked and drew in his breath. Although he saw her roughly every three months she seemed to grow more lovely every time they met. She was wearing that day a blue dress of fluid silk, as unlike the geometric lines of the current fashion as a dress could be, and yet somehow Lisa had managed to retain the same cut by adapting the severity of the line to her own more feminine taste. Gordon's trained eye took in the detail at a glance, before he stepped forward, holding out his hand.

Lisa shook it warmly, then smiled. 'Gordon.' She wrinkled

her nose. 'It's always so nice to see you. You're a bit of home, I suppose.'

As he followed her up the winding staircase Gordon wondered, not for the first time, why she never made the journey back to the north? She would fly to Paris or Rome at a minute's notice, but never once, since the day she had amazed him by handing him full responsibility for the Lancashire side of the business, had she turned her car on to the new motorway and driven north. Her telephone bill must be astronomical, he told himself, when she would talk to him for an hour at a time, discussing profit margins, approving or otherwise new lines, agreeing with him to mark down prices on slow movers. She would ring him often close on midnight, and he guessed that her days were of eighteen hours at least. Sometimes he wondered if she ever slept. She had told him that the London boutique was her last venture.

'I see no point in making money for the government,' she'd said. Then last spring he had sensed an aching desperation in her voice.

'Peter is going to America,' she'd told him. 'Now that he's got his degree and done a year on computers he feels the States have so much more to offer. Washington, DC, with a firm who evidently think highly of him. It's right,' she'd asserted, before he'd had a chance to comment. 'Young people these days want to stretch their wings. He'll be expected to work harder over there than he would here. A sad reflection on our present society, but true.'

'Have you heard from Peter lately?'

Gordon walked behind Lisa through the large fitting-room and into her inner sanctum beyond, a room with walls of the Lisa Logan violet shade, and a carpet in the palest grey. Here there was evidence of orderly chaos – the large desk in front of the high window was littered with patterns of material and scattered designs. There were pictures, abstract in tones of deep fuchsia whirling to mauve, on the walls, and a velvet chair Victorian-buttoned in pink.

'I used to have a chair like that in my bedroom when I was a young girl,' she had once told him, then her face had closed with its familiar shut-in look.

194

'Peter is fine.' Lisa walked behind her desk and sat down. 'He talks a lot about a girl, would you believe? She's just about to qualify as a doctor, he says. He's already using Americanisms in his letters. He actually started the last one with "Hi, Mom!" I suppose I'll have Yankee-Doodle grandchildren one day.'

She drew a large folder towards her, and as if at an unspoken signal Gordon unbuckled his briefcase and took out a sheaf of papers. For the next two hours they worked steadily until the door opened slightly and a girl with lips painted ice-cream pink and eyes outlined in sooty black poked her head inside.

'We're shutting up now, Miss Logan. Is there anything else?'

Lisa looked up, startled. 'Is it really that time?' She rubbed tired eyes, suddenly young and vulnerable. 'I'd no idea. The rose brocade? Did Mrs Evison approve the alterations?'

The girl smiled. 'She went off with it like Cinderella going to the ball.'

'Well, let's hope she meets her prince.' Lisa put up a hand and tucked a stray wisp of dark hair into the neat chignon. 'Thank you, Fiona. I'll see to the locking up.'

Watching her opening drawers, filing papers away, Gordon Conway suddenly stepped out of line. He had a feeling of *déjà vu*, as if he had always known he was going to do this eventually.

'Will you have dinner with me, Lisa?' he said quickly. 'We can easily get through what's left in the morning, so I'm not talking about a business meal.' He smiled, showing creamy, even teeth. 'The hotel I'm booked into doesn't offer much in the way of evening entertainment, and I don't feel like eating alone.' His grin turned him suddenly into a mischievous boy. 'Come on. Be a devil. Let's go to one of those posh places off St James's Street where you have to take out an extra mortgage if you have a side-salad. I'm feeling in an expansive mood.'

Lisa hesitated. She had always followed Richard's maxim of never getting to know any of her staff too intimately. Poor

195

Richard. She smiled ruefully. Only once had he done just that and look where that stepping out of line had got him . . . . She frowned. But she wasn't Richard and this self-assured man waiting for her reply wasn't a penniless employee in borrowed clothes overwhelmed by his employer's generosity. Besides, her flat in Kensington was suddenly the last place she wanted to be on this early summer evening with the sun touching the stone buildings of London's West End to mellowed beauty.

'I'd have to go home and change,' she said slowly, still not quite sure she was being wise. Then, as Gordon's face relaxed into a broad grin, she swept the last folder into a drawer at the side of her desk and stood up.

'I'll come with you, if I may,' Gordon said. 'Or would you rather I went back to the hotel and picked you up later?'

'We'll take a taxi to the flat,' Lisa said. 'Whilst we're having a drink we can look over some designs I'm working on for the autumn range. Mulberry's the shade, I'm told, and I thought if we used a soft pink with it. . . .'

'But when we go out we forget the business. OK?' Gordon followed her down the winding stairs and out into the street. Holding up a hand, he hailed a cruising taxi, leaving Lisa to follow, already half regretting her impulsive decision.

And later in the small restaurant, as they sat together in the warm gloom, Lisa studied his face as he in turn studied the menu which he had likened to the size of a windbreak.

During the past few years she had been taken out to numerous business lunches and dinners, playing the host herself on many occasions, but this was different. As Gordon Conway had helped her on with the cream silk short coat matching her dress, his hands had lingered on her shoulders. It had been merely a *slight* lingering, but the inference had been there, and Lisa had been startled by her reaction. For a brief moment she had wanted to lean back against him and feel his arms come round her, but she had moved away quickly.

'The lobster thermidor is to be recommended, sir,' the hovering waiter with the face and demeanour of a television

Jeeves whispered, and Gordon raised a questioning eyebrow at her.

'That would be very nice,' Lisa agreed. Then, when they were alone, Gordon told her that it didn't seem all that long ago since his mother could have provided a full-course meal for ten people for what the lobster was going to cost.

'Not that it matters,' he added quickly. 'Tonight only the best is good enough.'

As they ate iced melon, Lisa found herself comparing him with Jonathan Grey. There was the same quizzical lift to his eyebrows, the northern way of mentioning the price of something without embarrassment; but this man was as thick-set as Jonathan was thin – had been thin, she reminded herself. It could be by now that Jonathan had grown fat, maybe a little thin on top, with his father's florid complexion. Perversely, she hoped this was so.

'I think my divorce hit my mother the hardest,' Gordon was saying. 'She adored her grandson, but Claire has remarried and gone to live in South Africa so there isn't much chance of my mother ever seeing the boy again.'

'And you?' Lisa put down her fork, sympathy clouding her eyes.

'I've blocked my mind,' he said simply. 'Claire was given custody, and for the boy's sake I didn't appeal against it. But I'm paying for his education. Naturally.'

'Do you find that easy? Blocking your mind?' Lisa knew the conversation was running away from her, but the atmosphere of the dimly-lit restaurant, with candles gleaming softly in ruby-red wine glasses and couples holding hands at the discreetly placed tables, lulled her into a sense of dreamy contentment.

'It's the only way,' he said simply. 'If life doesn't turn out the way you want it to, you opt out of feeling. It's quite easy once you get the hang of it.'

'But if the feeling persists?' Her eyes were wide in the pale oval of her face.

'Then you're a poor mutt, aren't you?'

Lisa laughed out loud. 'Do you know, I think you could be right!'

The wine waiter came with the wine, and its dryness stung her throat. They were sitting very close on the velvet banquette. She was no longer young, Lisa reminded herself, but equally she was a long, long way from being old, and for the first time in years the close proximity of a more-than-presentable man filled her with longing, so that by the time the wine was finished she did not draw her hand away when Gordon covered it with his own.

They sat very close in the taxi taking them back to her flat, and when he kissed her Lisa knew they were both a little drunk. She giggled and laid her head on his shoulder. If this nice-to-be-with man could block out the memory of his little son in South Africa, then surely she could block out the memory of a tall, dark, thin man living with his wife up in Lancashire, a man who had once told her he was dying of love for her, who would have made her his mistress, keeping her in the secret corners of his life before destroying her as his father had destroyed her mother.

The fact that once again she was thinking along the lines of a confession story in a magazine never occurred to Lisa. She had always thought that way when disturbed. And at that moment she *was* disturbed, gloriously and intoxicatedly disturbed.

But experienced as he was, Gordon was still surprised at the wildness of her abandonment. The swinging sixties it might be, and a long way from home they both might be, but he had never dreamed that his employer needed a man's touch so much.

For a moment the sensible side of his nature asserted itself. Would this mean the end of his job? Would this Lisa he had never dreamed existed be too overcome with embarrassment afterwards to be able to resume their pleasant working relationship? Had she drunk too much wine? Did she love him? Did he love her?

Suddenly the self-questioning was over, and the passion she had unleashed in him swamped all his misgivings. There was a mutual hunger in their mouths and bodies as they clung together. Their clothes seemed to drift away, and all he was aware of was the softness of her skin and the deep pulsating longing inside her. As he took her she gave a gasp of pleasure, then it was all rushing ecstasy and sweetness that went on and on and on. . . .

A long time afterwards Lisa awoke. He was lying still beside her, his lips moving against her neck even as he slept. Her head felt heavy and there was the sour taste of wine in her mouth. She turned her face into the pillow and felt a slow trickle of tears running from the corner of her eye. Stirring, he murmured something, then settled into sleep again. She opened her eyes wide, staring into the darkness of the room, seeing the vague shapes of their clothes scattered like flotsam on the carpet.

Now was the time when they should waken to love. To lie there, face to face, whispering of that love, overcome by what had happened and willing it to happen again. Lisa put a hand over her mouth in a small gesture of comfort, knowing that there was no love, had never been love and never would be. Lust . . . that was what had made it happen, and a liberated woman would recognize that fact and accept it for the truth it happened to be. The tears rolled down – she tasted the sad saltiness of them as they soaked into the pillow. They were both free agents and this sleeping man was, she guessed, as lonely as she felt herself to be.

But men were different. The platitude didn't amuse. It was true. Moving slowly and carefully, she slid from the bed, held her breath as Gordon moaned once, then tiptoed softly through into the bathroom, picking up her discarded clothing as she went.

When Gordon opened his eyes five minutes later and saw her sitting by the window wearing a white towelling robe, he smiled and held out his arms; but as she spoke he sat up in bed, his eyes widening in amazement.

'I'd like you to go, please.' Her voice was as cold and brittle as an icicle. 'It's only one o'clock in the morning. If you turn left as you come out of the flats, then left again, you'll come to the main road where there'll be plenty of taxis at this time.'

'But . . . *what* did you say?' Forgetting he was naked, he

got out of bed. Then, feeling foolish, he pulled a disordered sheet angrily towards him and draped it round his waist.

'I want you to go, Gordon. I want you to forget what's happened, and I never want you to refer to it again.' Lisa stood up, somehow widening the distance between them. 'We'd both had too much to drink, so there's no blame. I want you to forgo our meeting this morning and catch the train back north, and the next time we speak we can be back where we were before . . . before we did what we did.'

'Holy smoke!' Gordon forgot that his very generous monthly salary was paid by the small slim woman regarding him with apparent calm. He sat down heavily on the side of the bed. 'Of all the heartless, unfeeling. . . . Oh, lady, I've met some heartless ones in the past, but you take the biscuit! What are you suggesting? That I took advantage of you?' He ran a hand through his thick brown hair. 'I've heard of one-night stands – I've even experienced a couple – but I've never been thrown out before it's come light. What do you want me to do? Put the money on your dressing-table as I go out?'

'How dare you!' He heard the tears in her voice, but the pride that had been shattered when his wife left him for another man flared his temper, so that he was in two minds whether to dress with as much dignity as he could muster, or walk over to his employer and shake her till her little white teeth rattled.

'So I've just screwed myself out of a job, have I?' The crudity slipped out before he could control his tongue. 'You were asking for it, *Mrs Carr*. What's wrong with you, for Pete's sake? We're not children, either one of us. You're free and so am I.' He reached for his socks. 'So guilt doesn't come into it. What's *wrong* with you?'

'I suppose I've realized I'm too old to join the permissive society.' She was trying to sound flippant but failed miserably. 'I tried, Gordon, but it wasn't any use. I'm sorry.'

'And so am I.' His anger evaporating, the big man reached for his underpants and climbed into them. 'Now I suppose I can consider myself fired?'

'No.' Across the darkened room she stared at him, but he

was unable to read her expression. 'If you can face it, then so can I.'

'Face what?'

All at once he realized she was scared. Of what, he didn't know and he was damned if he'd try to find out at that time in the morning. Not with her watching him struggle into his shirt and tuck the tail flaps into his trousers. She'd emasculated him, that's what she'd done, and if it weren't for the job and his commitments he would tell her where to go. He looked round for his tie and didn't even show surprise when she handed it to him.

'Just go, Gordon,' she was saying brokenly. 'I deserve everything you've said, but I don't want you to give up your job. You've worked hard for me ever since you came in with me. I know your divorce cost you your own business, but we can't work together if we spoil it by . . .'

'Making love?'

'It wasn't love, and you know it.'

'What was it, then?' Gordon slung his jacket over his shoulder and walked towards the door. 'OK, OK. I'm going. I don't understand and maybe I never will. But if you can forget it, then so can I.' He turned and looked straight at her. 'But remember one thing, love. Men are better at forgetting this sort of thing than women. It's a biological truth.'

He looked at her again, hard, with disbelief, as if she were suddenly a totally different person. Then he went out, closing the door with a soft click behind him.

'Oh, God, dear God. . . .' The softly whimpered words were meaningless to Lisa, but she moaned them over and over again as she took off her bathrobe and got into the rumpled bed.

She deserved all Gordon had said to her, and more. It would serve her right if he threw in his job and left her with no choice but to sell the northern side of the business. Turning her head into the pillow she groaned aloud.

But Gordon Conway wouldn't throw in his job, would he? He'd never get one with the same freedom or with such a salary as she paid him, so because of money hers was the power. Hadn't she learned that a long time ago?

The power and the glory. . . . Lisa caught her breath. But, oh, dear God, where was the glory?

Sitting up, she saw Gordon's cigarettes and lighter on the bedside table, but as the smoke curled up from the glowing tip of the cigarette she hadn't really wanted, the supposedly soothing action brought no sudden flash of perception.

Her behaviour was inexplicable, even to herself. The need had been there. Drawing fiercely on the cigarette, she closed her eyes at the recollection of her clinging arms and legs, the passion which had totally overwhelmed her with its intensity. So why had she sent him away, talking to him like a puritanical spinster regretting a moment of unpremeditated folly?

Giving up all attempts to sleep, Lisa stubbed out the cigarette, switched on the light and, reaching down into a cupboard by the side of the bed, took out a bulging folder. There was a lot of work to be got through if the next spring's lines were to be past the drawing-board stage before the end of the summer.

A tear splashed on to the paper, and she brushed it impatiently away. What good did tears do, and what was she crying for, anyway?

In sending Gordon Conway away so abruptly she was punishing her father for deserting her at a time of adolescence when she had had a great need of him. She was also punishing her husband Richard for his deception about Millie Schofield of the devious eyes, for living a lie, and taking her by force one winter's night long ago. But most of all she was punishing Jonathan Grey for offering her a love he had no right to give, and for wanting to turn her into a replica of her mother, sitting by the fire and smoking her days away.

With an outward swing of an arm Lisa knocked the cigarettes and lighter from the little table, and as she did so the folder of drawings slipped from the bed to scatter across the carpet. She made no attempt to pick them up, but just sat there wrapping her arms around herself, swaying backwards and forwards so that her dark hair swung round her pinched and exhausted face.

Her eyes went suddenly vague, dreaming into space.

She was middle-aged, well, almost middle-aged. She was rich, not exactly beyond the dreams of avarice, but wealthy enough never again to wonder where the next meal was coming from.

She was admired because of what she had achieved, but apart from her son, who was three thousand miles away, she wasn't loved. Lisa began to cry. Oh, there were dozens of men like Gordon Conway who would *make* love to her, assuage the deep physical longing that she admitted to, but who would leave her feeling diminished like she was feeling now.

Loneliness swamped her as she gave in to it.

'Oh, Jonathan. . . .' His name was no more than a sigh, as she switched out the light and stared up into the darkness, while the self-pitying tears ran from her eyes and into the pillow which still smelled of Gordon Conway's spicy after-shave lotion.

She couldn't believe the evidence of her own eyes when she saw him the next day.

Lisa was sitting in a taxi, being driven down Regent Street on her way to a meeting with a Jewish manufacturer of expensive accessories, when she saw him striding along, hatless, almost running with the loping stride she remembered so well.

'Stop! Oh, please, stop!' Banging on the glass partition dividing her from the driver, she jumped out of the taxi, thrusting a pound note into his astonished hand. She turned and ran, pushing her way along the pavement crowded with summer tourists, almost knocking an elderly couple over in her haste.

'Jonathan! Oh, Jonathan!' Catching him up, she clutched at his arm.

The man turned round as Lisa's great grey-blue eyes stared at him, dulling with disappointment as she realized her mistake.

She couldn't speak. This stranger was so like Jonathan he might have been his double. The height was the same, the flop of black hair over the forehead the same, but there was no well-remembered humorous tilt to this man's eyes.

'I'm sorry,' she managed to say at last. 'I thought you were someone I knew. Please forgive me.'

'The disappointment is mine, ma'am.' Smiling, the stranger moved on, leaving Lisa standing there on the wide pavement, a cold wind of disillusionment passing over her.

She began to laugh. All alone among the milling summer crowds she found herself laughing silently, even as one side of her mind ordered her to stop. But she couldn't. She knew she was behaving like an hysteric because she had seen it before, years ago, in her mother as Delia had pounded on the wall in a frenzy, all control vanished.

For a moment she wondered if the mirthless agitated laughter that seemed to be bubbling from her was loud enough to be heard, but people were walking past her, talking to each other, window-shopping, enjoying the sunshine, and so she knew the terrible sound was inside her.

'Stop it!' she told herself, struggling for air. Then, as she forced herself to walk back in the direction of Oxford Circus, she remembered the leather zipped briefcase lying on the back seat of the taxi. A briefcase filled with sketches of next spring's designs, as yet the only copies in existence.

Running she knew not where, Lisa stepped off the kerb almost under the wheels of a red London bus.

The man pulling her back to safety opened his mouth wide in astonishment as she twisted away from him.

'Don't touch me!'

As he stared at her he saw tears, thick as glycerine, gliding down her cheeks.

'Can I help you, lassie?' His face was a farmer's face, red and kind, and his vowels were straight from the Lancashire dales, broad, well-defined, tempered with compassion.

'That's a lass in real trouble,' he told his wife, as Lisa stumbled away, shaking her head. 'Proper fashion-plate, too.' He sighed. 'Nay, but I'll be glad to get back home tomorrow, love. The sun might be a bit warmer down here, but that's all what is. You could break your heart here and no one would be the wiser. There's too many folks knowing nowt about each other for my liking.'

At two o'clock the next morning Lisa was working on a fresh set of drawings. All her attempts to get the originals back had been abortive.

'Whip anything, some would,' the kindly voice at the other end of the telephone had told her. 'There's always the chance there'd be money in the case, you see, but leave your telephone number and if it's handed in we'll let you know.'

So she had to start again, while the designs were fresh in her mind. Lisa rubbed her aching eyes. That way the hysteria could be kept under control. Because that's what it had been, and she might as well face it. For the first time in her life she had been on the verge of cracking up, and it was no good pretending it was her age, because she wasn't old enough for menopausal vapours. Besides, she wasn't the type. Everything depended on her. The shop, the girls in her employ, her very existence. If she'd been the type to cry on shoulders, where would she find one? What time had she had to make even one good friend?

Reaching for an eraser Lisa rubbed out a curve and began again.

The ring of the telephone startled her so that she jumped violently. Half-past two in the morning. Who on earth would be ringing her at that time? Picking up the receiver she said a shaky 'Hello?'

'Hi, Mom!'

'Peter!' Her heart was beating so fast she felt it pounding in her throat. 'Are you all right?'

'Did I wake you up?' His voice was so clear he might have been standing there right by her side. 'It's only nine o'clock here, but I had to tell you.' There was singing joy in his voice. 'I've just asked Marianne to marry me and she's said yes. Hold on, Mom, she wants to say hello.'

'Hi, Mrs Carr!' The girl's young voice was filled with the same ringing happiness. 'I hope you'll forgive your son for wanting to talk to you in the middle of your night, but we've just told my parents and he couldn't bear you not to know.'

There was a slight pause. 'I hope you'll come visit us soon. Peter has told me so much about you. I feel I know you already.'

As the bright young voice went on and on Lisa stared with detached contemplation at a moonbeam filtering through the curtains where she hadn't pulled them together closely enough. Peter would never come home again now. She frowned at a pencil which had rolled from the little side-table to the floor. Well, of course he would come home sometimes, for holidays. She had imagined him sleeping on a camp bed in the tiny dining-room, coming into the shop with his smile and the red-gold flame of his hair brightening up her office. But with a wife?

'That's wonderful, darling,' she said automatically, realizing that her son was now at the other end of the line. 'Of course I'll come over to the wedding. Just try to keep me away! Spring? Let me know the date as soon as possible.'

'So you can make sure it doesn't interfere with your business arrangements?'

He was teasing. Lisa gripped the receiver hard. He *had* to be teasing. Peter wasn't given to making sarcastic remarks. He had always known and accepted that the business was her life. Hadn't he?

When the call was over, Lisa sat down on the edge of the bed. Had the fact that she had had to miss his Degree Day ceremony hurt him more than she realized? Hadn't she made it clear enough to him that even as she sat in conference with her banker and a manufacturer who was offering to buy her out, her mind had been with him in his college precincts, standing by his side in her best suit and hat, anticipating proudly his coming glory?

'It's only a rolled-up parchment,' he'd told her. 'Honestly, Mother, it doesn't matter. Pomp and circumstance never bothered me none.'

But it had. That unguarded remark about his wedding day had given him away.

Just as she had given his home away. Lisa's mind went back to the day when she had told her son at the time of his father's funeral that she was going to make a present of

206

the red-bricked house to Irene and the little hairy man Irene was going to marry.

Never for one moment had she considered the fact that it was Peter's home, too. Lisa sighed. How strange that she had never seen it that way. And how sure she had been that he would understand her need to work, when all the time he had nursed a hurt, wanting, really wanting her to be there on his big day, wearing one of her less outlandish creations with maybe a feathered hat on her head.

No wonder he had gone to America. What else could he have done when his own mother had rendered him homeless?

Moving slowly, Lisa sat down at her dressing-table and stared at herself in the mirror. Her tired face looked soggy with self-pity, as for the first time in her life she wallowed in it unashamedly.

'Lisa Logan!' Her reflection stared back at her in total despair. 'You are a success. In your own world you are a great big resounding success. But as a mother? Do you know what you are? A terrible failure.' She watched a tear slide down a cheek. 'You told yourself your son was different; that he could cope because you'd brought him up that way; and now you've got your come-uppance, Lisa Cleverclogs Logan. Because materialistic success can't compensate for unhappiness. Or loneliness. And it's all your fault.'

The sound of her voice in the empty room frightened her, but she knew the silence would have been worse. She knew also that talking to herself was a sign of the hysteria threatening once again, but what had to be said had to be said.

'You are admired, Lisa Logan. Oh, yes, you are very much admired, especially by men. They find you attractive. Gordon Conway found you attractive, and you could sleep around as much as you liked, even at your age.' Leaning forward, she pulled a single silvery strand from her parting. 'But you were born just too soon to be a part of what's going on now. You have a cold puritanical heart, a *northern* puritanical heart, and you're daft enough to try to equate sex with love. Inside you're as unsophisticated as a sixteen-year-old girl. You're a prude. A frustrated, dried-up woman, lacking the courage to do what should be coming naturally. A freak with the mind of a Victorian virgin, pining for a man who would probably not even recognize you if he saw you again.'

Even in her misery, Lisa accepted that she was mouthing a soliloquy that would have sounded better coming from a stage. Like a rerun of a film, she saw herself tearing down Regent Street, calling Jonathan Grey's name, then clutching the arm of a perfect stranger. 'All the world's a stage,' as Angus would undoubtedly have said.

'And now you're going to pour yourself a drink,' she whispered. 'A drink to put you to sleep. The mother and father of all drinks. OK?'

But her hand jittered the bottle of gin against the glass, and as she drank it down she choked, swallowed, then poured some more.

'Damn you to hell, Jonathan Grey!' she yelled. 'Why won't you go away?'

She felt sick; she was trembling so violently that when she lifted a hand and saw it shaking she thrust it behind her. She was mad. Like her mother before her she was going crazy. . . . In another minute she would be pounding on the wall and waking the earnest couple next door. She would be swearing, words which trembled inside her. Filthy, four-letter words waiting inside her head to burst out and echo round the empty room. And when the next-door neighbours saw her there would be horror and disgust mirrored on their faces, the same disgust that had once been mirrored on her own as she looked at Delia.

Setting the glass down, Lisa forced herself to take deep breaths. She walked unsteadily through into the bathroom, dropped her robe down round her ankles, and stepped into the shower.

Raising her face, she let the water cascade over her. Gasping, she turned the control to cold, bowing her head as the water pricked like needles on the back of her neck.

'Count your bloody blessings,' she whispered. 'There are still plenty of them around; and start by forgetting a man who once told you you were the love of his life, because that kind of love doesn't exist. Not even in *books* these days. You're Lisa Logan, not Scarlett O'Hara. OK?'

Her heart was still beating with dull heavy thuds as she towelled her thick dark hair part-dry, but when she climbed into bed and switched off the light she sank almost at once into a sleep nearly as profound as a coma.

And when she walked into the shop the next morning her face was as smooth as glass, with only a light bruised look round her grey-blue eyes denoting the trauma of the night before.

Lisa Logan had found her sense of purpose again; she had come to terms with the way things were and the way they were going to be, and like a true Lancastrian she was accepting the inevitable.

Alone she might be, but defeated – never.

And if Angus Logan, her father, had seen her at that moment he would have smiled at her with his blue, blue eyes and more than likely given his daughter a round of applause.

Twelve

Jonathan Grey sipped his second whisky, neat without ice, and stared at his wife with a kind of detached interest. Amy sat opposite him in the new house with four bedrooms, bathroom 'en suite' off the master bedroom, with a bitter-lemon balanced precariously on the well-upholstered arm of her chair.

Ever since the time she had kicked the drinking habit she had watched him drink with a resigned expression on her face, saying nothing but making it quite clear that she was sure – not that she cared – he was going the way of his father before him.

When he lit a cigarette she wafted the air even before he had taken the first puff, still saying nothing.

'Are you coming out to dinner wearing those things?' Jonathan pointed at the shiny white boots encasing her fat legs like plaster casts. 'I hardly think it's going to snow even in November.'

Once, a long time ago, she would have flared up, taking even the mildest remark as implied criticism, but now nothing her husband said made the slightest difference. It wasn't that Amy actively disliked him, merely that their marriage had deteriorated over the years to a state where he no longer had the power to provoke her into any kind of reaction.

'They're fashionable,' she informed him. 'Fashion boots, not wellingtons.' Holding out a leg she admired their shiny newness. 'Everyone's wearing them now.'

'At your age?' Jonathan wanted to say, but bit back the retort. Amy had made a life of her own, revelling in their undoubted affluence, using her cheque book like a talisman, giving the lie to the supposition that money bought good taste; festooning her neck with gold chains, vulgarizing her fingers with an encrustation of rings, having her auburn hair dyed a fierce carrot shade, and drawing black rings round her pale blue eyes. Proud of her cleavage, she wore dresses which showed it to advantage, belying the fact that for years now she had slept alone, making it more than clear that she found his touch repugnant.

Jonathan had stopped blaming himself, stopped blaming his long-dead father for his wife's defensive, belligerent attitude, stopped telling himself it was her childless state that had turned her against him. Their incompatibility had grown like a fungus, so that all they did now was go through the machinations of a marriage that was one in name only.

The downward slide into cold indifference had begun, he knew, on the day two of Amy's so-called friends had thought she ought to know he had been seen holding hands with Lisa Carr on a windswept platform in Manchester. It was almost as if Amy had been looking for an excuse to start the campaign against him, needing something on which to pin her frustration.

Jonathan stared at the artificial logs glowing red in the ornate electric fire in the hearth. He would have preferred a coal fire, but Amy had wanted to know who would rake the ashes out and cope with the inevitable dust when Mrs Farnworth only obliged three days a week?

What she did with her days puzzled him at times. He knew she had joined a number of societies, vying with the other women in the number of different outfits she could wear in one season, but as far as he could make out she had no hobbies. Pies came from the shop wrapped in cellophane, cakes glistening with lurid pink and green icing came in white boxes from the confectioner's, and Amy would drive three miles to a chip shop she liked rather than grill a plaice from the fish market or bake a river trout in its own juices in the large and expensive oven in the streamlined kitchen.

'Most of *her* models wear boots.' Amy flipped over the pages of a mail-order catalogue lying on the arm of her chair not taken up by her glass of bitter-lemon. 'Not that I would ever want to look like them. Matchsticks with hip bones like coat-hangers wearing dresses like sacks. I suppose *she's* too toffee-nosed for anyone up here now.'

Jonathan knew his wife was referring to Lisa, but passed no comment. It was a long time since Amy had mentioned her name, and somehow the omission had been more ominous than any of her previous snide remarks. Besides, they were going out to dinner at the house of the town's Borough Engineer, and he didn't want to arrive with Amy flushed and ready to put him down whenever he opened his mouth to speak.

His wife stood up, smoothing down the skirt of the emerald-green wild-silk dress over her ample hips. 'There was a piece about her in the paper the other week.'

Jonathan lost his temper. 'Why don't you say who you mean? God damn it, I haven't seen her for years!'

'OK. Lisa Carr – sorry, Lisa Logan. The woman you should have married instead of me.'

Jonathan drained his glass, then immediately jumped up to refill it from the decanter on the massive Swedish-style sideboard. It was strange, but when his wife talked like this with that touch of sadness in her voice, making her suddenly vulnerable, he had the almost forgotten urge to put his arms round her, to try and assuage her obvious sense of deep insecurity. He turned round.

'I married *you*, love.' Walking back to his own chair he sat down heavily. 'I might ask why you married *me*?'

'Because you looked so pretty in your army officer's uniform. Because all my friends were getting married, I suppose.'

Jonathan swilled the whisky round in his glass and stared at it with something akin to distaste. 'We didn't have much of a start, did we?'

Amy twisted the gold chains round her finger. 'You mean the war?'

'That, of course, but not just that. No, I meant my mother dying and us living with my father, his drinking and all those tests you went through at the hospital.'

He didn't mention Amy's years of secret drinking, nor her bitter, frustrated anguish when she was forced to realize she could never have a child. Nor the times he had pleaded with her to adopt a baby, only to be told she wasn't the sort of woman who could love another woman's child.

As if reading his thoughts, Amy said suddenly, '*Her* son got married recently. In America. To a lady doctor. It was in the paper. On account of his mother being a so-called celebrity, I suppose. It said your Lisa Logan had been on television down south being interviewed about her range of evening wear.' Amy sniffed. 'I wouldn't be seen dead in one of her creations. You have to look as if you've just come out of Belsen to wear one of her skimpy frocks.'

'It's time we were going.' Jonathan took a cigarette from an onyx box on the side-table and lit it from a matching lighter. He eyed his wife's ample curves, accentuated by the green dress, sensing again her deep insecurity and doubts about her own appearance.

'You look very nice, love,' he said, holding out her mink stole. 'I like the way you've done your hair.'

Amy treated him to an icy stare. 'You're a bloody liar. You never like the way I look. I see it in your eyes.' Her face went red. 'You compare me with other women, and you always find me wanting. You'd like me to wear plain black dresses like Mrs Borough Engineer will no doubt be wearing tonight, looking like a black crow in need of a good feed.' She snatched a diamanté-encrusted purse from the low table. 'But I won't do it, Jonathan! I'll sit and listen to her talking about her children and how well they're doing at university, and how their Sally is working for Oxfam, an' I'll know all the time she's patronizing me. You will come home with another contract in your pocket and that will be that. The Greys will have shown themselves to be the respectable married couple the business dictates they must be, and all will be well till the next dinner, or the next Masonic Ladies' Night, or the next bridge evening with your business buddies. God, but your self-centredness shocks me rigid. You'd kow-tow to the devil if he bought a plot of land for you to build on.'

'You hate me, don't you, Amy?' Jonathan said, as he turned the car out of the semi-circular drive fringed with standard rose bushes spaced like sentinels.

'Despise would be a better word,' his wife said, checking her hair in the mirror set in the sun-visor in front of the passenger seat.

'Would it worry you if I left you?' Jonathan's expression was grim as he drove along the tree-lined avenue.

'Why should it?' Amy's voice was very cool, very clear. 'I would wave you off, if you really want to know.'

That night, lying alone in the second bedroom of the sprawling ranch-type house, Jonathan allowed his thoughts to take him along paths untrodden for a long, long time. Amy's words had left him drained and sad.

She had enjoyed the dinner; she had been put next to a man Jonathan had never met before. A widower, or a divorcee, Jonathan wasn't sure which, Adam Compton had laughed uproariously throughout the long, calorie-laden meal, swigging his wine like water, accepting second helpings, recounting anecdotes of his inglorious youth in Canada, where he'd served as a flying instructor during the war.

'Never clapped eyes on an enemy aircraft,' he'd bellowed. 'Cushy Compton, that's what they called me. Still do, as a matter of fact.'

And Jonathan had suspected that underneath the table, beneath the spread of his hostess's pink damask tablecloth, his left hand was firmly cupping Amy's knee.

Adam Compton had been asked to make up the numbers, Jonathan was sure of that, but the woman on his right was obviously not Cushy Compton's type. She was a quiet, dark-haired woman in her forties, maybe, though she was so slim it was hard to tell.

She reminded Jonathan of Lisa. . . . He raised himself on an elbow and reached for a cigarette. Why not admit it? Why not admit that *every* small, dark-haired woman reminded him of Lisa? He drew smoke deep into his lungs and coughed. How ridiculous could a man get at his age? Next year he would be fifty. There were silver wings curling over his ears.

He had to wear glasses for reading, and if he didn't cut down on the beer he'd be developing a paunch.

The capacity for romantic love was the prerogative of the young, not the middle-aged. When Lisa had failed to answer his note after her husband had died, he had faced his moment of truth. Lisa wasn't prepared to have an affair, and he wasn't prepared to leave his wife. Stalemate. QED. He was his father's son and Lisa could never forget that. So . . . he had let her walk out of his life.

After all was said and done, he wasn't bloody Rhett Butler in *Gone with the Wind*. He was Jonathan Grey, a Lancashire man born and bred, loyal, dependable, as all northern men were supposed to be. Men from his neck of the woods didn't walk out on their wives because they fancied someone else. Especially when their wives had had a rough deal. He ground out the cigarette with disgust.

There were signs that the new generation would view things differently. Kids born during the war didn't believe that marriages were made in heaven. Already, only halfway through the sixties, the divorce rate was rising dramatically. Fail to make a go of things and get out seemed to be the maxim.

Jonathan crossed his arms over his chest, trying to compose himself for the sleep he craved.

But a long time ago Angus Logan had upped and gone, hadn't he? For a brief moment Jonathan saw himself packing a case and creeping downstairs, leaving his wife sleeping as Captain Logan had done. He shook his head, remembering the trail of sorrow the gallant captain had left behind: his wife dead of misery not two years later, and his daughter marrying the first man who had stretched out a hand to comfort.

And he had let it happen. . . . Blind to his real feelings, filled with hatred of the Logan family, he had pursued his own ends, married a girl who wouldn't sleep with him unless . . . , watched his mother die, and seen his father drink his left-over life away. Because of grief or guilt? He would never know, but the damage done when Angus Logan walked out of his house in the middle of a dark windy night long ago still lingered like the trail of a slimy snail.

Jonathan pulled the sheet over his head as if by doing so his thoughts would be blotted out. Of one thing he was certain. If ever his own marriage ended, it must be Amy who severed the ties. He would never abandon her.

And if that made him a fool, then a fool he was prepared to be.

But in spite of his noble reasonings, his inherent sense of integrity, Jonathan Grey, Master Builder, Rotarian, Mason, sidesman at his local church, whispered a heartfelt prayer: 'Lisa, if ever you do think of me, please, please, remember me with love.'

It was after two o'clock when Jonathan slept at last, but three thousand miles away in Virginia, USA, it was still only nine o'clock.

'I've never seen a racoon,' Lisa was telling the broad-shouldered man sitting by her side on the large couch. 'Oh, my goodness! Do they do a lot of damage in the garden?'

Greg Perry, special correspondent on the *Washington Post*, twinkled at her through heavy-rimmed spectacles. All evening he'd hardly been able to take his eyes off her. She was so pretty, this Englishwoman, so softly spoken, so vulnerable in spite of the fact he'd been told she was a name to be reckoned with in the London scene of *haute couture*. He'd accepted the invitation to Thanksgiving Dinner at the Virginian home of his old friends Jan and Bill Orland with pleasure, knowing that the food would be superb and the company equally so, but never had he dreamed he would be meeting such a honey of an Englishwoman.

The Orlands' daughter Marianne, now qualified as a doctor, was married to this beautiful woman's son, and there they were, glowing with happiness, whispering together at the other side of the room.

Explaining about the racoons, Greg nodded towards the young couple.

'It must be very gratifying to see your son so happy. A pity you couldn't come over for the wedding, but it was so

216

quick and quiet I think even Jan and Bill were taken by surprise.'

'I was in Paris,' Lisa told him, and he saw a shadow cross her lovely face. 'They didn't give me enough notice to make arrangements, but I'm here now and they're as happy as you say, so why worry?'

'That's exactly my motto. Why worry?' He grinned, and Lisa thought suddenly what a nice man he was, even though the placing of them together at table and now in the gracious room for coffee had been a more than obvious ploy at matchmaking.

'He's a great guy, Lisa,' Marianne had said. 'His wife died years ago, but he's been all over the world on assignments. You name a war, and Greg's covered it. You two will have an awful lot to say to each other.'

'The drive out here from Peter and Marianne's apartment in Washington was absolutely breathtaking,' Lisa said. 'The trees must be glorious in your fall, when they're turning red and gold.'

'You just about missed them.' Greg's strong face softened with pride. 'The blossom in the spring and the leaves in the fall. Those are the times to be here. I've recently acquired a lot not far from here – for my old age, you know.' An elongated dimple came and went at the corner of his mouth. 'I have a dock on the lake and a small sailboat plus two canoes. I come out here whenever I can. Did you see the lake as you drove out? No? Well, I'll tell you now, it's man-made, Lisa, 'bout two and a half miles long and half a mile wide, wooded on all shores. Y'know this was once a huge swamp in Civil War days. They fought the Battle of the Wilderness here. Then, at the beginning of this year developers began to dam up the streams, so I can see it turning into a vacation resort when they begin building in earnest. So maybe then I'll just move on again. I don't like being crowded.'

'You'd hate my flat in London then.' Lisa smiled at him. 'It's in a huge block with doors leading into silent corridors. We live like rabbits in a warren, except that rabbits are more sociable.'

'Will you have dinner with me tomorrow evening?'

Startled, Lisa looked round in time to see her son and his wife leaving the room, closely followed by Bill and Jan.

'It's OK.' Greg's eyes crinkled with amusement. 'They've gone down to the games room in the basement to work off some of that turkey and pumpkin pie. I guess they're leaving us alone. Do you mind? And *will* you have dinner with me tomorrow? I'll pick you up around seven if that's OK.'

Lisa hesitated. To refuse would be churlish, but to accept too readily might make him think. . . . And oh, dear God, she was tired of being wined and dined by men who thought she was going to pay for the meal by going to bed with them. Even at her age! She was weary of being told how beautiful she was, how clever, how different from their own wives who did nothing but sit on their bottoms all day.

But this man had never once expressed surprise at her life-style, even when Peter had made her sound like a cross between Coco Chanel and Mary Quant. Maybe it was because women who blazed a trail in their own careers were taken more for granted over here. Greg himself had made them laugh over dinner describing his six a.m. runs before showering and being behind his desk at eight. Even the children started school at a quarter past eight, and Peter's neighbours' kids thought nothing of working at their home-work until nine-thirty every evening. Go . . . go . . . go, that was the way it was, a breathless dashing and striving to achieve. She smiled. 'Thank you. I would like to have dinner with you. At least we'll make the young ones happy.'

'I told you you'd like him, Lisa.' Marianne twisted round in her seat as Peter drove them back to town. 'He's a real nice guy.'

'Pity you can only stay for a week,' Peter said, driving confidently on what to Lisa seemed like the wrong side of the road. 'It doesn't give you all that time to get acquainted.'

'Gordon Conway can only be in London for a short while.' Lisa was glad of the darkness hiding the blush which she could feel warming her cheeks. 'He's a bit out of his depth with the London side of the business. Hem-lines aren't his forté.'

'He sounds like a real nice boy,' Peter said in a mincing voice, and Lisa contradicted him with such vehemence that they both burst out laughing.

'A dark horse my mother.' Peter turned the car out of a long winding lane into the straight wide freeway. 'She's a terrible worry to me. It's her age, of course.'

'And only to be expected,' said his wife. 'Parents can be a problem.'

Alone in her room Lisa struggled to open the window, then gave up in disgust. The apartment was so warm she decided to sleep with only the sheet for covering. Fresh air was not to be tolerated here apparently. It was central-heating in winter and air-conditioning in summer. Along with overheated shops in downtown Washington, a-glitter with Christmas decorations already; 'Have a nice day,' from shop assistants; wide smiles from black lift – no, sorry! – elevator attendants; magnificent white buildings etched against a brilliantly blue sky; shopping malls like indoor fairy grottos, a consumer's paradise; and a general air of such friendliness that already, after two days, Lisa felt relaxed and happy.

Tomorrow morning she was going alone on the Metro bus, which stopped across the road from the apartment, into downtown Washington, to browse round Garfinkel's store, studying the clothes, the accessories, the buttons, the braids. Peter and Marianne were both working and she'd assured them that she'd be perfectly OK. Then, of course, Greg Perry was coming over in the evening to take her to dinner.

Pushing the single sheet aside, Lisa lay on her back listening to the wail of a police siren, followed by another even as the sound of the first died away. Totally contented, so far away from the business that there was nothing she could do about it even if Gordon Conway insulted her very best clients, Lisa breathed in the warm air. She had been cold for a long time, she decided. The storage heaters in the Kensington flat warmed, but didn't cosset. Not like this. You could walk around naked, she thought, leaving all the doors wide open, and still not feel a draught. She was *thawing*, she decided. Slowly and blissfully thawing, bones, muscles, skin. And *spirit*. She smiled into the darkness. She might flirt a little, even fall in love a little. Temporarily, of course. Greg Perry had the most beautiful hands. . . . She shivered at the memory of his hands, then fell suddenly asleep.

Oh, yes, she assured herself, sitting opposite Greg Perry in a candle-lit French restaurant in Georgetown that same evening. This man was perfect for a holiday liaison. He'd been around too much to hurt easily, and the way he was looking at her was giving her a newly-minted feeling of beginning something that wouldn't be spoiled by a serious involvement. In five days she would be flying back in darkness over the Atlantic, and they would never meet again.

'You look happy,' he said.

'I am.'

'Your smile looks as if it wouldn't wash off.'

'Like a cat's.'

'That's right. I like the way you pin your hair up at the back. It's surprising really, because so many women look stern and forbidding like that. Like actresses in a TV soap opera when they go for a job and want to look plain. They succeed, but you don't. Look plain, I mean.' His eyes twinkled at her behind his spectacles. 'Dear Lisa. You're very English, did you know? That's why people are staring at you.'

'Are they? Oh, dear.'

The restaurant was crowded. The menus were almost as big as the tables, which were set disconcertingly close together, but because everyone was talking at once, in fairly loud voices, the sound became diffused so that each small table became like an island.

'The champagne is Dom Pérignon. Would you like some?' he asked her. When it came and she'd drunk a little, he said he could see it sparkling in her eyes.

'You've been working too hard, Lisa,' he told her seriously. 'My guess is you've forgotten how to play. How long is it since your husband died?'

Lisa told him. Then, because she didn't want to talk about

Richard, because the champagne was making her feel light-headed and bubbly inside, she told him about the game she sometimes played.

'See that woman over there? The one in the turquoise silk trouser suit? Well, I saw her come in and she's entirely the wrong shape for trousers. If she wore a more neutral shade, a plain dress with maybe just a string of pearls, and had her hair cut in one of the new geometric shapes, it would show her small features up and she would be a beauty.' She laughed. 'No, I'm not being catty, just professional. It gives me a real kick to be able to redo a woman's appearance like that. I used to do the same with houses, giving a room a completely different look. It's creative, you see, with the same satisfaction that your writing must give you.' Suddenly she blushed. 'Don't get the idea that I think my own image is perfect. It's strange really, but I have difficulty seeing myself objectively. Sometimes I have difficulty seeing myself at all.'

'That's because you're basically too insecure to be self-satisfied.' Greg poured more champagne. 'I guess that some-time, maybe a long way back, perhaps even in your child-hood, you were hurt badly. And when that happens there's a blow to your self-esteem. A man, maybe? A lover who walked out on you?'

'My father,' Lisa said without thinking. 'Oh, my good-ness, Greg. I didn't come out with you to be analysed. What are you, an amateur psychiatrist?'

'A shrink?' He grinned so that the elongated dimples came and went. 'I might well be. There are almost as many shrinks in Washington as in the whole of the rest of the country put together. But Freud did sometimes know what he was talking about, honey.'

'He put every motivation down to sexuality.' Lisa toyed with the fish on her plate. 'And don't you dare tell me I was secretly in love with my own father. I come from the north of England and we don't encourage fanciful ideas like that.' Determined to change the subject, she went on: 'I've always believed that climate, conditions, even the type of industry relevant to one county can formulate a difference in character and outlook. Don't you agree?'

Greg immediately went along with what she'd just said. If this enchantingly lovely woman didn't want to talk about how she was raised, then that was OK. 'I guess I do agree. A New Yorker from the city is a mighty different person from a Californian, a Texan, an Alaskan or, say, a down-easter from Maine. And that's in spite of the fact that hardly anyone in this country is living in the region in which he was raised. There are subtle differences in their choices and judgements. Me now, I'm an amalgam of so many different cultures that I reckon I gave up looking for who I was a long, long time ago.'

'Let's not start looking tonight.' Lisa could feel the champagne warming her voice, flushing her pale cheeks. 'Let's just enjoy this food, this place, these people you say are staring at us.'

'Wondering who the beautiful Englishwoman Greg Perry is with can be.' Greg's eyes were suddenly wise. He would ask no more if that was what she wanted. But how much there was he wished to know.

Before they picked up the car from the parking lot they went for a walk, pacing slowly along the wide pavements in a Georgetown that reminded Lisa so much of Hampstead. They held hands and talked gay, loquacious nonsense. The day had cooled considerably, and the stars had disintegrated into a fine dust powdering the sky.

'I think the snow will come early this year,' Greg said, as they walked more quickly back to the car. 'Any hope of you flying over again for Christmas?'

For the whole of the drive back to Peter and Marianne's apartment Lisa told him how it would be for her at Christmas.

'Orders for party dresses, some of them last-minute, the downstairs shop like a rugby scrum, fitters having hysterics, customers fainting in the crush, Beatles' background music pounding overall, mothers yelling at their daughters, asking them what *do* they think they look like dressed like that, and

222

then on Christmas Eve going back to my flat, flopping down and asking myself is it worth it?'

'And is it, honey?'

'It's my *life*,' Lisa told him. 'The only life I know and the only life I want.'

'I see,' said Greg, seeing more than she ever dreamed. 'Will you let me take you out to Mount Vernon tomorrow to see George Washington's home? I've a few days' leave due and we'll drive along by the Potomac River and eat lunch in a restaurant waited on by serving maids complete with mob caps and tightly-laced bodices.' He turned the car into the drive fronting the wide block of apartments. 'Everything's in a remarkable state of preservation, right down to the slave quarters with tiered bunks.' Switching off the engine, he took Lisa in his arms and kissed her gently.

Just for a moment she was gripped by fear, the terror that had filled her with self-loathing after she had let Gordon Conway make love to her.

Greg put her from him, realizing immediately that for this quiet, lovely woman it was too soon, too early to tell her that already he suspected he was falling in love with her. He touched her nose lightly with his finger, and said, 'Tomorrow, then?'

'He's in love with you,' Lisa's daughter-in-law told her when Greg had gone. 'He couldn't take his eyes off you. What are you going to do?'

'I've heard so many shocking things about him, he must be interesting,' Peter said. 'Malice thrives on nothing, here in Washington. He isn't married and he doesn't live with anyone, so therefore he must be suspect. Perhaps he's . . . .'

'He isn't!' Lisa said without thinking, and they fell about laughing, her son and his pretty wife, leaning on each other till tears came to their eyes.

'What *are* we going to do with you, Mother?' Peter wanted to know. 'Just look at the time! We've been so worried, haven't we, darling?' He looked wickedly knowing. 'English-women have a reputation for going overboard for the first man they meet when they go abroad on holiday. You know, like widows on cruises. It's this new permissive society, they say. A trying to catch up with what they feel they missed.'

'But when it's your own mother!' Marianne's eyebrows arched upwards. 'You feel responsible. I guess you ought to have a serious talk with her.'

'Birds and bees stuff, you mean?'

'Along those lines.'

Lisa watched them happily, thanking God for their happiness, realizing yet again that she wasn't the kind of possessive mother who needed the constant presence of her offspring as long as he was contented. She had brought Peter up to be independent and now that very independence was assuring his contentment. Peter would never go back to England. Already she could see he was totally integrated into American society, part and parcel of the wise-cracking, bustling, striving way of life. Her grandchildren would be born here and, apart from visits, she would have to live her life alone. Exactly as it should be, she told herself firmly, pushing aside the tiny niggle of despair that clouded her present serenity.

'Greg is taking me to Mount Vernon tomorrow,' she said. 'Do you reckon I need a chaperone?'

'Not if you watch your step, Mother,' Peter said, solemn-faced.

And the next five days were sun-filled, even though out of the sun Lisa got an inkling of the cold Washington winter just around the corner. They drove for miles, filling up with petrol, which Greg called gas, at garages where the attendants wore bow ties and told them to 'have a nice day'. They picnicked in pine woods with the Blue Ridge mountains as a back-drop; they drove out to Middleburg and ate at the Red Fox Tavern. 'Established around 1728, would you believe it?' Greg pointed out with pride. On a sunny afternoon they walked the tow path alongside the Chesapeake and Ohio canal.

'In summer,' Greg said, 'the butterflies and dragonflies are really something. You can take a canal trip guided by students dressed in nineteenth-century costumes, the barge pulled along by mules. In those days the children of the bargees started work at the age of eight, dragging the barges when the mules were tired. Can you believe *that*?'

A great surprising tenderness filled Lisa's heart again as she realized this tough man's pride in his heritage. Since that first kiss he had made no attempt to touch her, apart from a friendly arm round her waist or a holding of hands as they walked along. Lisa looked at him, then away as his eyes searched her own. She knew he was seeking a response she could not make, the kind of love she couldn't give. They had begun something of which she already knew the end, and the knowing filled her with a deep sadness.

They drove back in silence that day along a straight wide road with wooded hills on either side. When they got to the huge block of apartments he held both her hands for a moment, jiggling them up and down in the warm comfort of his own. And the question in his eyes asked her what was going to happen to them? What were they going to do next?

'The day after tomorrow I go back home,' Lisa said, giving him her answer.

That night the telephone rang as Lisa and Marianne were in the kitchen frying chicken and simmering rice. Peter and Greg were watching a baseball game on television with a concentration so rapt that it was as if they had staked their entire assets on the results.

'It's for you, Lisa.' Marianne came back into the kitchen, bright blue eyes laughing in her tanned face. 'The man with the plum in his voice again.'

'Hello? Gordon?' Lisa smiled into the receiver. 'You sound as though you're standing right next to me. Everything OK?'

'I'm ringing from the shop, It's a quarter to twelve here on a dark and stormy night.'

'But all's well?' Lisa asked, raising her eyebrows at the two men now watching television with the sound turned off.

'All's very well, I'm glad to say.' Over the thousands of miles Lisa heard the rustle of papers. 'Do you want me to give you the figures? I've got the Lancashire ones here as well. They're down a bit, but we're up.'

'You mean with you away from the north their profit margins drop, but with you down south the London ones rise?'

Lisa felt very happy. Soon they would be sitting down to golden fried chicken, mange-tout peas and mushrooms, finishing off the meal with a slice of Marianne's carrot cake, a towering confection of moist sponge and luscious cream. So she would go back pounds heavier, so what?

But listening obediently to Gordon's figures she was unaware that Greg had turned round in his seat to watch her with an indefinable expression on his craggy face.

She was looking particularly lovely, he was thinking. During the afternoon she had worn her dark hair loose, but now it was upswept in a tiny bun on the top of her head. The style accentuated her delicate features, and the sun had done no more than tinge her cheeks a wild-rose pink. He fingered his own wind-leathered cheeks reflectively. Her cameo-like appearance belied the almost masculine strength of her character. Greg stroked his chin and smiled. Boy, but she was one tough cookie, his little English lady. He was doing OK. Playing it cool, not saying anything to freeze her into that icy silence and stiffened resistance the time he'd kissed her. Just look at her now, teasing the guy back there in London, making it clear that the way she felt right that moment the whole business could go bankrupt and she wouldn't give a damn. Give her another coupla weeks here and she wouldn't *want* to go back. Greg glanced briefly at the television, just to show willing. He wasn't clear in his mind as to what lay ahead for them. He knew that his days of foreign assignments were over, but he reckoned that with Lisa around he wouldn't mind too much being desk-bound during the week, then taking the both of them off to do some fishing, lounging around that old trailer he'd fixed up in Virginia.

She could open up a shop here if that's what she wanted. Somehow he couldn't see Lisa doing the coffee and cookie round. He smiled, watching Lisa again. It would work out fine once he'd gotten her promise to marry him. He wouldn't

226

rush her too much, even so. He could afford to be generous in his understanding, loving her so.

'And that's all, then?' Lisa wrinkled her nose at the two men watching the silent screen. 'I'm almost through,' her expression said, and Greg lifted his shoulders to show there was no need for her to hurry.

Back in London, Gordon Conway glanced at the brief notes he'd made before putting through the call to Washington. He tapped the last item with his forefinger. 'Oh, yes. They did have a bit of a crisis up north – the factory. They've had a lot of rain up there and the women were complaining about the damp coming through the walls. Nellie Smith swore they could have cultivated mushrooms in it.'

'But you were going to get someone to see to it.' Lisa pulled another comical face at the two men: Peter, who in appearance was her father born again, and Greg, next door to being handsome with his brown face and hazel eyes, sitting there holding his pipe gently between two fingers. How easy it would be to love him. . . .

'So we started with the builders,' Gordon was saying. 'After all, they did the restoration work.'

Marianne appeared from the kitchen, looked round as if counting heads, then disappeared again. Peter got up and followed her.

'A good move,' Gordon said. 'The bossman came at once and said he'd have it put right straight away. Free of charge, would you believe it? He must be the last of a dying breed. No one does anything for nothing these days.'

Gordon knew all this could have waited until Lisa was home, but he'd seen the last week's takings with his own two eyes, hadn't he? The London shop was a little gold mine, so a transatlantic call was a mere drop in the ocean, so to speak. Besides, he hadn't figured on having to work such long hours. No wonder Lisa often looked tired halfway to death. Added to which, the sound of her voice still gave him a little frisson of excitement, even though what had been between them was history, dead and past. He squinted at the list, trying to decipher his own spidery scrawl.

'I have the bloke's name here,' he said. 'A Mr Grey. Mr J. Grey.'

'Jonathan!' Lisa closed her eyes against the sudden swell of emotion starting shamefully in her loins, licking its way up into her armpits, throbbing, overwhelming her with intensity. 'Jonathan Grey,' she said again, exulting in the saying of his name.

'You know him, then?' Gordon frowned. 'Apparently he asked for your London address, but Nellie wouldn't give it to him. Per your instructions,' he reminded her. 'You know our Nellie, she'd suspect the Pope of an ulterior motive; but maybe she should have. . . .'

'It doesn't matter.'

But *something* mattered. Greg Perry watched as Lisa replaced the receiver, then smiled at him, not seeing him at all.

During the meal he refused to look at her, knowing for sure she had gone away from him to the secret place in which she dwelled, shutting him and everyone else out as if they didn't exist. And because he prided himself on being essentially masculine, a growing anger against Lisa spread inside him. He recoiled from the sadness this so English woman was forcing him to experience. He'd seen enough of sadness in the wars he'd covered, lugging his portable typewriter round places which had left deep scars on his mind. God damn it, he'd finished with all that! What left-over life he had to live had been deliberately uncomplicated until she'd come along. He told a whopping fisherman's lie and they all laughed.

Except her. At least, her lovely wide mouth laughed, but her eyes . . . . Greg looked away from the dreams slumbering in their depths, then was blazingly angry once again at his own perceptiveness.

He drove back to his apartment later that night, across the bridge over the Potomac River, with clusters of stars grouping together in the moonless sky. He would ask her no more questions, knowing if he did that the answers had roots in her that he must never question. He must let her go, and say nothing.

Two days later, because both Marianne and Peter were working, he drove her out to the airport with the Blue Ridge mountains etched hump-backed against a navy-blue sky.

The passengers crowding the airport lounge were very quiet, sitting on low leather seats hugging their hand-baggage. There was nothing of the daytime noise and bustle, just a sitting there as if already they were suspended in time and space over the Atlantic Ocean.

Greg said, 'It's been nice knowing you, Lisa.'

'Thank you for giving me such a good time. I hope we meet again.' Lisa smiled at him, tucking a strand of dark hair behind an ear. 'Please don't wait till we're called through. I hate goodbyes. I always have done.'

Standing, he pulled her up to face him. His eyes behind the horn-rimmed spectacles were kind, and as his mobile mouth widened to a grin the dimples came and went, adding rather than detracting to his masculinity. Because he was a writer, used to expressing himself truthfully, the words inside his head ran like poetry: 'Goodbye, my love. From tomorrow I will see your face before me every waking minute. Already your voice and your laughter are a part of me. Darling Lisa, I could have been the love of your life. I would have cherished you till death parted us, but I will force myself to forget you, and no other woman will *ever* get so close to me. Never again will I feel this vulnerability. I swear that.'

'Have a good flight,' he said aloud. 'Come back one day.'

Like a fool he sat outside in the parking lot in his car, waiting until the huge plane, with a pounding roar of powerful engines, lifted into the sky.

And he told himself that never would he have dreamed that the sound could fill him with a hurt so deep he almost cried aloud.

Thirteen

'Ee, but tha's never driven all the way from London in this lot, missus?'

The hotel porter's Lancashire accent brought shame-making tears pricking behind Lisa's tired eyes. The little man's legs were bandied from the rickets he'd suffered as a child, but his lined face was as gentle and kind as if in the course of his long life he had never thought or perpetrated anything wrong.

'I just wanted to come home,' Lisa said simply, knowing instinctively that he would understand.

'Aye, well.' The little man swung her case on to the stand by the door. 'Tha looks fair done in.' He smiled, showing an inadequate number of stained brown teeth. 'They've finished with the dining-room, but I can have some tea sent up and mebbe a sandwich. Tha's not thinking of going out again?'

'No.' Lisa smiled back at him. 'And tea would be very welcome, thank you. I'd forgotten how severe the weather can be up here.'

Immediately the porter bridled. 'From what I hear on the wireless it's been none so good down where you come from, neither! But it's been a nasty few days hereabouts. I admit to that.' He stood in the open doorway, eyeing Lisa with frank curiosity. 'There's folks living in some of the steep cobbled streets what haven't been able to get out at all till the ash carts got round to them. There were an ambulance stranded yesterday up Mill Street.'

'I used to live in Mill Street,' Lisa told him.

'Tha never!' Amazement flickered for an instant in the

rheumy eyes. 'So tha's not been back for a while?' He scratched a stubbly chin. 'They're knocking down all them streets, boarding up the houses, tha knows. Moving folks out to what they call better accommodation.' He wrenched his mouth sideways as if to spit. 'Breaking folks' hearts if you ask me.' He took an obviously reluctant backward step. 'Wait till tha sees what they're doing to the town centre. It said in the paper that the town wasn't planned, it were just thrown up, but I'll tell you something for nothing, missus. Them little houses in them little streets made for happiness, even thirty years ago when half the town was on the dole. Now it's all shutting themselves in with the television, and them Beatles shouting along with what's supposed to be music. They knocked the Market House clock down afore Christmas. A hundred-year-old clock that were, and built to last, but down it come.' He widened his mouth into a twinkling grin. 'But would tha believe it? That clock face refused to budge for the best part of an hour. That showed 'em!'

When he went at last, closing the door behind him with a deferential click, Lisa sat down on the edge of the bed and stared round the room.

The long journey had been a living nightmare. As she drove through the outskirts of the town the roads were a skating rink of glistening black ice. Three times she had seen cars abandoned where they had skidded into lamp standards, and she had asked herself over and over again why she had given in to the impulse to get into her car and drive north?

'We will manage,' Fiona had assured her at the shop. 'You worked all through Christmas with a nasty dose of flu. This is our least busy time. Please, Miss Logan. Go away for a few days. Forget work. It will still be here when you come back.'

Anxious faces, soft assurances; herself glimpsed in a mirror, grey of face with dulled, lustreless eyes. A middle-aged woman, stuck on a treadmill of work and more work. Weakly emotional, dreaming in the grey hinterland of the aftermath of a neglected bout of influenza, of a man not free.

A desperate homesickness which would not be denied. And a coming home. At last.

In Washington, DC, a short two months ago, Greg Perry had walked with her along the banks of the Potomac River and told her of his belief that in our lives we grow two-level souls: on the one hand, the level we show to the world, and on the other, dark memories, longings hidden and deep, safely tucked away, never ever surfacing.

But what when they *did* surface? What of a time when behaviour could no longer be rationalized? What then, wise Greg of the weary eyes? Remembering him as clearly as if he sat beside her, Lisa turned her car the next day into the winding road leading to The Laurels.

It was a clear cold morning following a clear cold night, through which Lisa had slept a sleep so profound that it had been more like a coma. But when she got out of the high bed, with its solid interior-sprung mattress, her legs had almost buckled beneath her, and the breakfast of bacon and eggs served in the not quite warm enough dining-room had turned her stomach even before she had picked up her knife and fork.

'It's too cold for snow,' the receptionist had said from her little cubby-hole in the entrance hall. 'Mind how you go, Mrs Carr.'

Lisa stopped the car and got out to stare at the house in which she'd been born. In spite of her high leather boots and the silk square tied round her hair, the icy wind bit treacherously through to her bones, penetrating so that her whole body felt numb, without life. Lisa pulled the collar of her mink three-quarter-length coat up round her face, thrust her hands deep into her pockets and, treading carefully, walked up the laurel-fringed drive.

She had never been back to the house since, as a girl of fifteen, battered by circumstances, mourning the father she knew in her bones she would never see again, she had allowed a young and know-it-all Jonathan Grey to drive her away in one of his father's vans. Lisa shivered, huddled deep into the beautiful coat.

There was the heavy front door her father had closed behind him while she slept in her bedroom at the back of the house, drawing her long hair round her to shut out the memory of her humiliation at the dance, and the sound of voices raised in anger in the sitting-room downstairs.

Now the big windows looked strangely bare, and through the side window of what had once been Angus's study, Lisa saw a dark-haired woman in a white coat writing busily at a desk. The knot of her silk scarf had loosened and, as she fumbled with frozen fingers to tie it tighter, Lisa turned round to see a small stout woman coming up behind her dressed as if for the wilds of Siberia. A woollen scarf was knotted over a bedraggled fur hat, a voluminous tweed coat reached down to the tops of a pair of suede ankle boots, and the face only just revealed was blue and pinched with cold.

'By gum, but it's parky this morning! Cold enough to freeze your bits and pieces solid.' The woman stared with frank curiosity at Lisa. 'Coming in, love? You'll catch your death out here. Did you want to have a word with Matron?'

'Matron?' Lisa frowned. 'I don't understand.'

Agnes Ratcliffe's sharp mind was ticking over swiftly. There was something fishy about this one, standing there in the cold in her posh fur coat with her big eyes staring at nowt as far as she could see. Talked posh too, like some of the ladies she'd once 'done for' before coming to work as an orderly at Evergreen, the private home for old folks who could afford something a bit better than the council provided.

'You got your mother in here, love?' Agnes nodded to herself, making up her own theory as she went along. Another of them guilty ones, shoving their old mother in here to get her out of the way, then coming to visit now and again to tell the poor old dear how lucky she was to be in such a nice place. Empty-handed too. No bag of grapes with pips which would get under the old dear's teeth – that's if they'd remembered to put them in. Agnes made up her mind.

'You look proper clemmed, love. Come inside and I'll see

you have a nice hot cup of tea. Come on, now. You're not going to faint on me, are you?'

Her legs moving without any conscious motivation of their own, Lisa followed the large tweed bottom through the familiar door and into a hall bare of anything but a circular table on which a bunch of russet and gold chrysanthemums were funereally arranged in a fluted white urn.

'In there, love. I'll fetch the tea in a minute. It's time for the trolley. You can have it with them.'

And there was the door against which Lisa had leaned as she listened to her mother pleading on the telephone with Patrick Grey. Then, the whole house had smelled of flowers, wax polish, and Delia's lavishly applied perfume. Lisa felt the blood drain from her cheeks. Now, the smell was of urine thinly disguised by disinfectant, the smell of old, old age.

Five white heads turned as she walked in. Five pairs of eyes blank with senility, dazed by the accumulative effects of the sleeping pills ministered each night, faced her with a momentary and desperate eagerness; saw she did not belong to them and went back to contemplating their own particular void of emptiness.

'They shall not grow old, as we who are left grow old.'

The memories came flooding back. Angus reciting in his wonderful voice, standing by the fireplace over there. Delia striding round the large room, pleated skirts swinging, laughing or shouting in a tantrum, gloriously alive. The freckle-faced child with long plaits watching them carefully, secure in spite of it all. Mrs Parker cooking in the kitchen, Uncle Patrick joking with Angus, casting furtive glances at Delia. . . .

Agnes Ratcliffe, half the size now divested of her many wrappings, came into the hall in time to see the lady in the posh fur coat running towards the front door, heels tapping on the tiled floor. A click of the latch and a slamming of the door and she was gone.

'Couldn't take it,' Agnes muttered to herself. Another one what couldn't accept the fact that it comes to all of us. In time.

Tut-tutting her disapproval, she marched flat-footed into

234

the lounge, tucked a tartan rug more firmly round a pair of bony knees, was rewarded by a quavering toothless smile, and went back to set the trolley for the elevenses which always came at ten.

Shivering with the sweat of utter weakness, Lisa started the car and drove back on to the main road. Strange how Greg's words spoken by the Potomac River on that sunlit day kept coming back to her. 'There is no going back; no good trying to recapture the past,' he had said. 'If you are lost inside, then you are lost wherever you are.'

She ought not to have come. Lisa tried to blink away the sweat running down into her eyes. The fever she had ignored all over Christmas, working at the shop in an aspirin-induced blankness, was catching up with her now. Surely it was a physical condition she was experiencing, not a fanciful desolation of the spirit as Greg would surely have said.

This was her home. Here were her roots. She felt at one with the bleakness of the winter landscape. Affection was here, warmth of friendship; these were her people, their wide-vowelled intonation her own. Never, she thought, would she be able to say barth for bath, and once at a dinner party when she had said, 'Pass the butter, please', the man on her left had laughed and said, 'Lancashire. Not far from Bolton. I'm right, n'est-ce-pas?'

Nursing the car slowly and carefully down the icy road, Lisa admitted to herself that in her present state of weakness she could be halfway to feeling sorry for herself. And if that were so, then she was denying her heritage. She was passing the town hall now and there, emblazoned above the main door, was a huge sign in vivid colours wishing one and all a VERY MERRY CHRISTMAS. She smiled, her spirits lifting. Someone would take it down, maybe before the end of January someone would undoubtedly take it down, but what it was telling her now on almost the last day of the dying year was that she was home.

And somewhere there was someone who would open a door to her knock and widen their eyes in surprised welcome. There had to be. It wasn't possible to live in a town for so

235

long and not have a single friend to hold a hand and draw her inside.

But since leaving school her life had been one of work and more work, making acquaintances by the dozen, but never having the time to find and cherish a real friend.

Within yards of the hotel Lisa suddenly signalled left, turning the car towards the Chorley side of the town, past a cinema showing Elizabeth Bergner in *Escape Me Never*. And in a flash she was back on a rainy afternoon almost thirty years before, coming out into the foyer with Leslie Howard's beautiful voice in her ears, to see Jonathan Grey pinching a brown trilby into shape and teasing her with his wavy smile about going to the dance that night.

The night her father had walked away.... The night everything had changed. For ever.

Instantly Lisa felt a sensation inside her as if she were a stone plummeting down, dropping into a bottomless well.

'I will go and see Irene,' she said aloud.

'Well! Of all the people!' Irene came to the door of the red-bricked house behind the high privet hedge, wiping her hands on a strip of towelling sewn to her apron. One of Millie's innovations, Lisa guessed, and smiled.

'I came up on an impulse,' she said. 'I ought to have rung first, but, well, I thought I'd surprise you.'

Irene seemed to hesitate. The expression in the dolly blue eyes was wary, as lacking in warmth as an empty grate on a rainy winter's day.

'You'd better come in,' she said, after that telling hesitation. 'Close the door quietly. I've just put the baby down for her morning sleep.'

'Baby?' Lisa's eyes gladdened with surprise. 'I didn't know you'd had a baby, Irene. Why didn't you tell me? There was nothing on your Christmas card about a baby.'

In her mind's eye she saw the card, the yearly answer to her own letter. 'From Irene, Edwin and Millie', hastily scrawled in Irene's well-rounded schoolteacher's hand. An acknowledgement, that was all, a politeness in obvious deference to the festive season. A name on a list, to be crossed off with relief if the chain was ever broken.

'She's two months old.' Irene glanced upwards. 'She cries all night then sleeps all morning. It's the only time I have to get anything done.'

And I've interrupted you, Lisa thought, following the wide hips in the baggy tweed skirt down the hall and into the familiar sitting-room at the back of the house. For a moment she had an urge to turn round and walk straight out again.

'It looks just the same.' Swallowing her pride, she walked over to the fireplace. 'But you've had a gas fire put in. That must save a lot of work.'

'It does.' Irene snatched a small clothes-horse away from the tiled hearth. 'Millie didn't like it at first, but she got used to it after a while.'

'How is Millie?' Without being asked, Lisa sat down. The warmth of the room was making her feel sick. She unfastened the large button at the neck of her coat and pushed the silk scarf further back off her head. Irene was folding the nappies now, holding each one against her cheek to make sure it was aired properly.

'Millie?' she said, without turning round. 'Millie's dead. She died three months ago.'

The shock drained what little colour there was from Lisa's pale face. 'But why didn't you let me know? You could have written, or telephoned.'

'Why?' Turning round, Irene looked at Lisa with coldness. 'What would you have done? Sent a wreath? Or come to the funeral and cried in the crematorium?'

Lisa winced. 'But your Christmas card? It was from you, Edwin and Millie.'

'We called the baby Millie.' Irene's cool clear voice shook unexpectedly. 'She never got over my father dying. She was never the same. She mourned him right up to the day she died, and if there's a heaven I hope she's with him now!' She seemed to take a furious control of herself. 'But then, you wouldn't understand that kind of devotion, would you?

237

You went gallivanting off to London before he was cold in his grave.'

'Oh, Irene, Irene. . . .' Lisa felt her heart begin to pound. 'Look at me properly, please. Not with that hate-filled expression in your eyes. I *lived* here once; I tried to love you, oh, dear God, how I tried. I was married to your father and for a long time we loved each other, though I know that's the last thing you want to believe.'

'You stole him from Millie!' Irene's voice was harsh. 'You had nothing! Nothing! Not even a decent roof over your head, so you grabbed what was going, and what was going at that time was my father. You were younger than Millie and prettier than Millie, and so he fell for you. To get you into his bed,' she added crudely. 'Oh, Millie knew that. She had you weighed up right from the start.'

'I'm going.' Lisa stood up, gathering her frayed dignity around her. Inside her head a voice was screaming, but from the closed-in, almost serene expression on her face she might have been utterly devoid of feeling. Hurt always did this to her, froze her into apparent uncaring. In that moment it was as if she looked at Irene through a telescope, seeing her at the end of a tunnel with fair curly hair framing the face of a china doll. She knew then that Irene would always be chained to a way of thinking which no rationalization would change. Hatred could be taught, and Irene had been taught well.

'Close the door quietly, then.'

So Lisa did as she was told, carefully shutting the door of the house to which she had come as a young bride wearing decent navy-blue because of her mother's recent death. Edwin Bates, Irene's husband, was coming up the path carrying a tartan shopping bag with a tin of baby food sticking out, rubber overshoes on his feet, his small face behind the bushy moustache peaked with cold.

'It's all right, Edwin,' Lisa told him before he'd had a chance to speak. 'I'm glad about the baby, really glad.'

Leaving him gawping after her, Lisa slipped and slithered her way to the car. The windscreen had iced over, and she drew on her gloves and rubbed at it, clearing just enough space to see through.

She didn't care. If she said it often enough it would be true. So she said it again, aloud, as she started the car, reversed into a side road and headed back to the town.

In the deserted avenues the trees were bare and black, seemingly bereft of life. The heavy grey sky and the icy ribbon of the wide road seemed to be merged in a deathly scene devoid of colour. Even the grass verges were hoary with frost, a frost without sparkle. Lisa's breathing was laboured, her heart pounding in her chest. The cough that had been with her since her illness shook her body as she drove too quickly, only slowing down when she felt the car's wheels slide dangerously towards the kerb, out of control.

Anger took over. What was she doing anyway, driving around, when on the wireless that very morning motorists had been warned to keep off the roads in the north? Why had she imagined for a single minute that Irene would be glad to see her? Millie Schofield was dead, but from beyond the grave Millie was still working her cross-eyed vengeance. No, that wasn't fair, that was cruel. But Irene had been cruel. The days were long gone when Lisa could charm her way into affection. This year she would be forty-five, but like a child she had run back home. And it served her right, because it was always a mistake to go back. Anyone with any sense would tell you that.

And if she, Lisa Logan, had had any sense she would be three thousand miles away now, held fast in love and affection with Peter and his lovely Marianne. It would be cold there too, but a different kind of cold, a white glittering cold with the Capitol building and the White House etched against a glorious sapphire-blue sky.

She could be walking with Greg Perry, hand in hand along snow-packed sidewalks. She could be *married* to him, lying in bed with him, watching him watching her with his lazy eyes, cocooned in centrally-heated contentment. Lisa glanced at her watch. Almost twelve o'clock. Yes, they would just be waking up over there, and yet here she was, an intruder, a ghost returning to a scene from her past, driving through streets in a cold so damp it froze the very marrow in her bones.

The cough was hurting now, a tearing pain in her chest. Lisa shivered. She knew though, didn't she, why she wasn't married to Greg Perry? She tried to catch her breath. Why not be honest about it? Her one subconscious reason for coming back had been to see him, the one with the uptilted dark eyes and teasing voice, the one who had sworn he was dying of love for her.

She was driving now along a street as familiar as the back of her hand. There was the chip shop where she had queued for two two's and threepennorth of dabs, taking them home in triumph to her mother sitting by the fire and smoking her life away. And to the left and right of her were the steep little streets sloping down to the mills, cobbled streets that had once rung to the sound of clogged feet hurrying through the early morning darkness to the weaving sheds.

Now no one wore clogs, or shawls clutched beneath chins, but foam-back coats instead, at fifty-nine shillings and eleven pence, knee-length against the bitter cold. Lisa glanced at a girl scurrying home for her dinner, back-combed hair above a pointed face blue with cold, a hard-faced girl reminding her suddenly of someone she had known a long time ago.

Signalling left, Lisa drove down a side street, turned right, then left again into Mill Street, coasting down the frozen cobbles.

She had been so intent on keeping the car on the icy street that the scene of utter desolation hadn't registered. The houses on her left had been partially demolished, leaving spaces like gaps in a set of teeth, bare walls open to the lowering sky, windows like sightless eyes showing interiors of front parlours still with patterned wallpapers, dirtied and damp from the erosion of wind and rain. On her right the houses were still standing, with every other window boarded up, waiting for the demolition squad to move in.

Slumped over the wheel, fighting to control the cough shaking her body, Lisa saw with surprise that Number 16, Mrs Ellis's house, had a lived-in look, with lace curtains at the upstairs windows and a potted plant incongruously in place at the front downstairs window.

It was a street of ghosts, a Hollywood set with no spark of life. No children playing hop-scotch on the pavements, no small boys swinging on a rope tied to the evenly spaced standard lamps. No neighbours gossiping on doorsteps, their arms folded over cross-over flowered pinnies, no steps and window bottoms mopped and stoned with a neat edging line in cream. Nothing to show that anyone had ever lived there; a frightening manifestation of the fact that no one would ever live there again.

Getting out of the car, Lisa swayed on legs grown suddenly weak. After she had lifted the iron knocker of Number 16 and heard it bang against the scarred and paint-less door, she stood there staring down at her boots without any expectation that the door would ever open.

'Mrs Ellis?'

The woman Lisa remembered had been as rounded and squat as a beer barrel, with brown hair waved into ridges by steel kirby-grips. Bird-bright eyes had twinkled behind the thick lenses of her spectacles and her cheeks had shone with red-veined colour. This woman's hair was as white as milk. She seemed to have shrunk, but when she smiled the eyes were the same, shrewd and warm, welcoming even as they widened in startled disbelief.

'Nay! It's not young Lisa!' The eyes crinkled round the outer corners with obvious pleasure. 'Well, come in, then. No good standing there catching your death. The kettle's on. Come in, luv, and take that coat off or you won't feel the benefit when you go. Well, I never! This is a surprise. I thought summat nice was going to happen the minute I opened my eyes this morning, but in all my born days I could never have guessed . . . well, well. Sit you down, luv, I'll have the tea brewed in a minute.'

It was too much. Coming after Irene's cold rejection, the warmth in Florence Ellis's Lancashire voice broke Lisa's self-control. Tears came into her eyes, and though she stared into the fire struggling not to blink unless they fell, she wasn't quick enough.

'Nay, luv. Don't upset yourself. I know what it must be like for you coming back to this street after all this time.' A pointed chin jerked towards the dividing wall. 'What you went through as a young lass doesn't bear thinking about. After all this time I still imagine I hear your mother knocking and shouting. Then you finding her dead on the floor like that.' A cup of tea was held out for Lisa to take. 'Get that down you, luv, and there's plenty more where that come from. Strong with plenty of milk, just the way you used to like it.'

'It isn't that, Mrs Ellis.' Lisa took a comforting sip, feeling the hot tea trickle down her aching throat. 'It's seeing you like this. The street all knocked down. It must be terrible for you, living like this with everyone gone.'

Mrs Ellis settled herself in her own chair with her own cup of tea. 'Aye, it's terrible all right, but not as terrible as if I'd done what them buggers – pardon me – at the town hall said I ought to do.' She sniffed. 'Think they know what's best for folks like me when all the time they know next to nowt. Shifting folks out to flats up by the workhouse.'

Lisa looked puzzled. 'Workhouse, Mrs Ellis? You mean the hospital, don't you. It hasn't been a workhouse for donkey's years. There's no such thing as workhouses these days.'

'It'll allus be the workhouse to me. Anyroad, I'm not going, and I've told them so. They're not putting me in a box till I'm dead, and that's what them flats are. Little boxes like what they put eggs in these days. Egg boxes with television aerials sprouting out of them. That's what they are.'

'Joan?' Lisa tried to remember the name of the other daughter. 'And Margaret? It was Margaret, wasn't it?'

The white head nodded. 'Aye, you're right. Our Margaret's gone to Australia. Emigrated four years back with her husband and two little boys. And our Joan, she married one of them GIs and went to live in America. He were stationed at that big camp near Lytham, a nice lad.' She chuckled. 'Always chewing gum, and wore his trousers too tight, but our Joan broke it off with that lad called Jack at the top

242

house to marry him. Always knew which side her bread was buttered did our Joan.'

'And you've never been over to visit either of them?'

The remembered twinkle was back in the short-sighted eyes again. 'Nay, lass. I haven't got the money to go gallivanting all over the world. Besides, they've got their own lives to live now. I fetched them up, and as long as they're happy I'm well content. Nay, the furthest I've ever been was to Morecambe for a week's holiday, and then it rained every day. I've never been one for travel, and neither was my Jimmy. . . .' She nodded towards a framed photograph on the mantelpiece of a soldier in the uniform of a First World War private. 'The one and only time he saw abroad was when they shipped him off to France. It's funny, you know, lass, but while I can't remember what I did yesterday, he seems to have come back to me these past months. I can hear his voice, an' see him coming through from the scullery, wiping his hands on a towel and telling me about his day at the paper mill.' She lifted a brown teapot from the table and held out her hand for Lisa's cup. 'He never wanted to go, but like them all he felt it were his duty. He wouldn't have hurt a fly, but they put a gun in his hand, them war-mad generals did, and sent him over the top to kill Germans he'd never had no truck with. Same as the last time. Men fighting with their feet in the mud and their heads filled with slogans to spur them on.'

She refilled her own cup then sat down, shaking her head at the tragedy of it all. For a while it seemed as if she had almost forgotten that Lisa was there.

'But what are you going to do?' Lisa leaned forward. 'Mrs Ellis? What are you going to do when the bulldozers move in to finish their job? You can't really believe they'll leave you here? Not leave just one house standing on its own.' Her voice was full of compassion, but Lisa knew what she had to say. 'I'm surprised they've let you stay here as it is.'

'*They* haven't let me stop on.' The old face was twisted with loathing for the nameless 'they'. 'Nay, if they'd had their way I would have been out on the street a long time ago. It were that builder chap what stood up for me. Mr

Grey.' A spark of life lit the faded eyes. 'His father used to own the houses on this side, rented them off in the old days. An' now his son is contracting a firm to knock them down. . . .'

'Mr Grey? Jonathan Grey?' Lisa's voice was a whisper.

'Aye, that's him.' Mrs Ellis nodded again. 'He says if I'll be patient he'll find me a place. A house, not a box. He knows how I feel. There's a lot of streets they're leaving alone, and not all that far from here, either. Mr Grey says there's a lot of Pakistanis coming to live in them. Indians, you know. But he says they're good-living and quiet, and he knows I don't mind what colour a face is if there's a kind heart to go with it.' She chuckled. 'I never thought the day would come when I'd have an Indian living next door. Do you remember Gandhi, or was you too young? He came to Darwen in 1931 and stopped in Spring Vale where my mother lived then. He were a funny little man all right. He wore a sheet wrapped round him and walked about in his bare feet, so they say. Then seventeen years later he was shot to death in an ambush. An' that's about all I know about Indians, or Pakistanis, or whatever they want to call them.'

She was talking as the lonely do, rambling from one subject to another, reliving memories and mixing them up even as she remembered. When Lisa got up to go the old woman looked at her strangely for a moment as if she'd forgotten who her visitor was.

'Come again, lass,' she said, as she stood on the step, face as pale as parchment, eyes behind the thick lenses of her spectacles suddenly alert again. 'If there's nobbut a pile of bricks you'll know they've won, but come again.'

When Lisa got back to the hotel she went straight to her room and picked up the telephone. The number was there, engraved on her memory, his *office* number, of course, the number she had sworn never to ring. 2956.

'Is that Grey's, the building contractors?' Surely that wasn't her voice, hoarse with the aftermath of her illness, trembling with nerves? Lisa sat down on the edge of her bed, feeling her face flush and the palms of her hands begin to sweat. 'May I speak to Mr Jonathan Grey, please?'

The new girl who had replaced Sylvia three years before had no need of a swear box. Quiet and efficient, she ran the office with meticulous attention to detail. Invoices were attended to and filed, letters typed as beautifully as if they'd been printed, tenders received and passed through to her boss's office the moment they came in. And telephone messages jotted down and handed over as soon as possible.

'Oh, there was a call for you, Mr Grey.'

Jonathan had rushed into the office at a minute to six o'clock, bringing in with him a rush of cold air, apologizing for his lateness, holding out his hand for the letters to sign, telling his secretary to get herself off home and be careful how she went as the pavements were like glass.

'Important?' He was already halfway to his own office, shrugging off his car coat, prepared, she knew, to spend at least another couple of hours at his desk.

'I don't think so.' His secretary followed him and laid the slip of paper on his desk. 'A Mrs Carr.' She studied her writing. 'Yes, that's right. A Mrs Carr.'

'Lisa?' The paper was snatched from her. 'Where is she? What did she say? God damn it, woman. I can't read your bloody writing! What the hell does this say?'

'It says the White Bull.' There was no reproach in the cool clear voice. 'And the time of the call is also there. Five minutes past one. I told her you were out before she rang off. I assured her you'd get her message.' A slight touch of grievance crept into her tone. 'I didn't know where you were, Mr Grey. You said you had to go and see to some scaffolding reported as unsafe, but you didn't say where. There was no way I could have contacted you, not with the whole town festooned with scaffolding. It might have been on any one of the sites.'

'The number!' Jonathan's face was dark with anger. 'The bloody number, woman!'

'I'll get it. Right away.'

There was no mistaking the grievance now. The straight back was rigid with disapproval as Miss Entwistle, not accustomed to being spoken to like that, walked back to her desk. Tut-tutting to herself, she lifted the telephone directory from a bottom drawer and began to riffle peevishly through its pages.

She knew her boss was overworked. The hours he spent in his office after long days on building sites overseeing his workmen made her wonder if he had a home to go to. Miss Entwistle ran a finger down a page. But tiredness and its consequent irritability was one thing, swearing like that was quite another. Never before had Mr Grey shouted at her like that. It was most uncalled for, and terribly unfair when her going-home time was half-past five. . . .

'Leave it, Miss Entwistle!'

Looking up in astonishment over the turquoise rims of her upswept spectacles, she saw her employer actually running past her desk, dragging on his car coat as he went. The door was wrenched open so violently it was a wonder, Miss Entwistle decided, that it didn't come adrift from its hinges.

She called after him. 'The letters, Mr Grey? You haven't signed the letters!'

'To hell with the letters! Leave them, girl. Go home and leave them. Sign them yourself if needs be, but don't bother me with them now!'

She blinked as the door slammed, shaking the building to its very foundations. Then, muttering to herself, she put the directory tidily away, covered her typewriter, buttoned herself into her sensible tweed knock-about coat, tied a scarf printed with horses' heads over her neatly rolled hair, changed from her flatties into ankle boots trimmed with fur, switched off the lights and went out into the darkened yard, past the piles of timber and through the outer door into the street. Remembering, in spite of her injured feelings, to tread carefully just as Mr Grey had said she must.

The winter's night had closed in, bringing with it a cold so intense that the windscreen iced over as Jonathan switched on the wipers.

Lisa. Lisa. Lisa. A voice in his head said her name over and over again. She was here, in the town, his lovely Lisa. She had been here all day, and he hadn't known. How could that be? Why hadn't he sensed her presence?

It was his fantasy come true, the fantasy he had played out in his mind over and over again – of seeing her walking down a street, skirt swaying round her slim legs, of hearing her voice on the telephone, a wiping out of all the barren years between as she came into his arms and told him that all that had passed was gone and forgotten, that from now on it would be just the two of them unhampered by ghosts intruding on their dreams.

Heedless of the road hardened to glass, he stepped on the accelerator.

Oh, dear God, but he'd played it all wrong up to now. The years he'd wasted showing misplaced loyalty to a wife who had cared less than nothing for him. Integrity. A good old-fashioned doing of what was right. And where had it got him?

Feeling the car wheels slide on the skating rink of a road, he turned a corner too quickly, and had to wrench at the wheel to set it back on course again. An enormous sense of elation possessed him. The fur-lined coat was too hot. Impatiently he pushed it away from his neck.

Amy hadn't deserved all that loyalty. He should have left her long ago. He'd been soft and weak, blaming himself for foisting his father on her early in their marriage, realizing too late that their flimsy so-called love would have died anyway.

He was nearly there. Tension mounted in him like a tightened rope. He felt suddenly young again, the way he'd felt as a twenty-year-old driving his dark green Bentley at maniacal speeds round country roads. A red Ribble bus moved out from the kerb causing him to swerve into the middle of the road to avoid it. The slow-moving cars filled him with a tearing impatience as he cursed them for crawling along like sluggish beetles.

Too late he saw the policeman stepping out into the road, trying to flag him down. Almost standing on the brake pedal to avoid knocking him over, Jonathan felt the car swing powerless and out of control. Frantically he fought the wheel in an attempt to control the steering. He saw the lamp standard looming up in front of him at the same split second that the bonnet of the car rammed into it with a hard grinding crash of metal.

'He was asking for that, the crazy fool,' the policeman muttered, even as he ran to see what, if anything, he could do.

At eight o'clock Lisa gave up staring at the telephone on her bedside table. Jonathan wasn't going to ring.

She had been into the dining-room to toy with the food on her plate, her eyes never leaving the door leading out into the reception area. Surely at any moment she would be summoned to take a call? Surely Jonathan would ring the minute he got back to his office?

It was no use trying to convince herself that her message hadn't been passed on. The coolly efficient voice of his secretary had assured her that Mr Grey would be told when he came in later in the afternoon.

'I never leave before he comes in,' she had said.

But nothing had happened.

Up in her room Lisa took off her shoes, rubbed her cold feet and climbed on to the high bed, piling the pillows against the mahogany headboard. It had been a wasted journey, a desolate homecoming, but it had taught her a lesson. There was no going back. Ever. Forward was the only way.

She knew she ought to ring Gordon Conway. She would have to do just that in the morning, but there was a strange sadness inside her, holding her still, preventing her from making the necessary business call. Gordon would probably insist on coming round to the hotel, and she wasn't in the mood to talk about profit margins, new spring lines. For the time being she just wanted to be, to stay quietly, trying if possible to rationalize this strange and utter desolation.

Lisa picked up a book, the short stories of Katherine Mansfield, a well-thumbed copy she had picked out at random from the shelves in her London flat.

'And after all, the weather was ideal,' she read, and put it down again on the shiny green bedspread.

She would be all right. Well, of *course* she would. Life had been very good to her. She wasn't *consciously* unhappy. It was merely the aftermath of influenza making her feel lethargic, holding her so quietly as if suddenly time itself had ceased to be.

Back in London there were the days in the hustle and bustle of her shop when she felt exhilarated, uplifted, excited by the colours, the scents, the frantic rush to get a new design off the drawing-board and on to the cutting table. Lisa picked up the book again, but the sensitive heart-hurting prose failed to move her, and once more she tossed it aside.

Maybe it was time to do that faintly obnoxious thing and count her blessings. Lisa frowned. Why this sudden feeling of having to reassess, to enumerate her assets? She shrugged. Why not?

OK then. She had some friends, not close and mainly in her own line of business, but they were there none the less. She had money, beautiful clothes, and she could have lovers too if she wanted them. And there was one special man in America who loved her very much. For a moment Greg Perry's craggy features and thick grizzled hair appeared like a colour print before her eyes. There was a man who would have been so easy to love . . . so very easy.

There was her flat with its wildly expensive rent, her books, her records. There was eating in luxurious restaurants, walking in the London parks, the city streets on Sundays; alleyways to be explored, steeped in history, the quietness of St Paul's Cathedral when the tourist season was over, with choirboys rehearsing in the stalls, young pure voices rising to the great high dome.

The list was endless. She could go on and on without mentioning Jonathan Grey once. And all this she had found without him, so she really had no need of him. None at all.

249

Lisa closed her eyes to shut out the sight of the telephone standing black and squat on the locker beside her bed.

Jonathan had loved the girl she had been once; had offered that love and been sent on his way. So why not accept that to him she had been merely a dream, the kind of dream that many a man likes to cherish against the days when they look at their wives and imagine what might have been.

Perhaps it would have been different if their love had been consummated? Lisa's mouth curved upwards into a smile at the way her thoughts were once again emerging as platitudes. But there was more than a grain of truth in her reasoning.

If she and Jonathan had slept together then at least their physical hunger for each other might have been assuaged. Like his father before him, Jonathan could have tired of the chase. Slowly Lisa shook her head so that the dark wings of hair fell across her cheeks.

Love and lust. Some would say there was no difference, but they were wrong, totally misguided. Lust was a momentary thing; *love* was a holding out of hands to the sky.

For a little while Lisa slept, then the silence woke her, a strange eerie silence of winter-cold streets. Through a haze of bewilderment she reminded herself that she was home, back in her birthplace, deep in her grass roots.

And the feeling was terrible. She felt as if she were stranded, completely alone, as if she were on the top of a mountain with dank mist swirling beneath her feet. Shivering, she tried to compose herself into her normal tranquillity.

After tomorrow she must go on alone. Gently she must let the memory of Jonathan Grey slip from her mind, like a dream soon forgotten.

Maybe some day she would love again.

It could be Greg, far away in leafy Virginia, or it could be a man she had still to meet. She could be anywhere in the world. She could afford to travel anywhere she wanted to. To Copenhagen. Yes, why not Copenhagen? Tears misted Lisa's eyes and she blinked them angrily away. Yes, there she'd be dining with a man in the Tivoli Gardens and he would smile at her, making her fall in love with him.

Or Paris? She could be there, following up her idea of branching out, of going into volume business with a bigger sales staff, a second factory. She would walk the boulevards, staring at the clothes, knowing exactly how she was going to adapt them to her own market, and there in a pavement café a man would raise his glass to her. And she would smile back.

As she was smiling now at the idiocy of it all.

It was no use. Lancashire women didn't trade in dreams, and she, Lisa Logan, was a northern woman through and through. She sighed deeply.

All her life she had used Jonathan as her yardstick and, measured against him, no other man had stood a chance. For wasn't he a part of her childhood, a slipping in and out of her life as she grew older, the only one who had known her father and still respected that tall, laughing, dramatic man with hair that blazed red and a fiery gold? Her father. . . . Lisa trembled as the familiar sense of rejection swamped her again.

Still wearing her woollen dress, she had slept the long hours away, and now the room was paling with an approaching freezing dawn. There were tears on her cheeks as the door opened, and all she saw at first was a tall silhouette framed there. Raising herself on an elbow Lisa stared in disbelief.

'Father?' Her voice was a whisper. She was dreaming; she had to be. Sitting up, she stretched out a hand as the figure approached her bed.

'Jonathan? Is it you? Can it possibly . . . ?'

When he came closer she saw that a long scar made ugly with stitch marks ran from his hair-line down his forehead to the corner of an eye. He touched it, smiling his well-remembered wavy smile.

'I had an argument with a lamp post on my way to you last night.' His voice was as teasing as ever. 'They don't bandage these days, just spray something on.' He sat down on the bed beside her. 'I've discharged myself, leaving an

Irish Sister doing her nut, and I've left a little man downstairs doing the same when I insisted on coming up instead of having him phone you.'

Soberly now he reached for her hand. Lisa's heart beat so loudly that she was sure he would hear it. She could feel it in every pulse in her body.

'Oh, Jonathan,' she whispered. 'It's been a long time.'

'Too long, love.' His eyes never left her face, those dark, uptilted eyes she had sworn she was going to forget. 'And now I'm never going to let you go away from me again.'

Suddenly she began to cough, and immediately his arms came round her. 'Sweetheart, you're ill.' Slowly his fingers moved across her back. 'How thin you are. Oh, love, what have they been doing to you?'

'*They*?' The familiar indignation his teasing had always been able to arouse surfaced. 'No one's been doing anything to me! I've had flu, that's all. It's *fashionable* to be thin. Can you imagine a podgy Mary Quant?'

Moving away, Lisa stared into his face. In the half-darkness his eyes seemed almost black. 'You're the one who needs taking care of. You should be at home. In bed.' Her voice faltered. 'Your wife . . . Amy . . . she must be worried sick about you.'

'I doubt if she would be, even if she knew.' His expression hardened and for the first time Lisa noticed the silver wings of hair where once sooty-black sideburns had grown – like the imprint of a tarred thumb, she remembered.

'Amy is living with her boyfriend in Crewe,' Jonathan was saying, his tone dead-pan. 'His name is Cushy Compton. They met at a dinner party given by the Borough Engineer, and that was that.'

'Cushy Compton? In Crewe?' Laughter bubbled in Lisa's throat so that she began to cough again. 'Oh, Jonathan, you're teasing again.'

'Quite true, love, and your laughter is most unseemly.' He winced, putting a hand to his head. 'Oh, Lisa, my darling, I've been the world's biggest fool.' He was serious again. 'You did it, woman, do you know that? You forced your blasted puritanical notions on me so that for years I did what I thought was right. I let you go because you were convinced in that practical mind of yours that we were heading for a replay of our parents' mistakes.'

The pain in his head mingled with the pain of his loss as he thought about the empty years that had divided them. He was tired almost to death, but what he had come to say must be said: 'Lisa. I've loved you since you were a freckle-faced kid with your hair in pigtails. I've dreamed about you at night and ached for you down all the long, lousy years. If I'd been killed last night coming to find you then it would have been a fitting end, wouldn't it? Because that's all my life's been. Endings without beginnings. Longings never satisfied.'

She saw the tears on his cheeks as he struggled to say the words he had wanted to say for a long, long time.

'It's almost too late, Lisa, darling. We're not children any more. We both married the wrong people because of what happened between my father and your mother. Don't you see?' His eyes blazed into hers. 'If you've got someone else then I'll go away. For ever this time. I'm tired, Lisa. I'm so tired of arguments I'll even marry you and be known as Mr Logan, if that will make you happy. I'll come with you to your damned cocktail parties and stand by your side holding a glass of bloody champagne and a biscuit topped with a bloody anchovy's tail if that's what you want. I'll sit like a pansy on a little gold chair and stare at mannequins' legs if that pleases you.' His voice broke. 'But don't leave me again, Lisa. Not again. Never again. Please. I don't think I want to live if you leave me again.'

'Oh, Jonathan.' His name was like a prayer as she whispered it softly. Slowly, as if drugged, she raised a hand and traced the contours of his poor battered face. Gently she lifted the thick, silver-threaded hair away from the stark wound on his forehead. Tenderly she ran a finger down his straight nose, round the long sensitive curve of his mouth, lingering as his lips parted slightly.

It was as sensuous, as deeply erotic as the act of love. Her eyes answered all his unspoken questions, caressing, offering, surrendering joyfully to his adoration.

'I love you,' she murmured at last. 'And I'll never leave you, ever again.'

'Never? Not for a moment?' The teasing was there again, and as they smiled at each other, Jonathan's pain throbbed into a dull ache as if her touch had made him whole again. He held her close.

Here was no clinging vine of a woman. Here in his arms was a woman of great courage and strength, a mixture of beauty and willpower, tempered with compassion.

'I'll put Gordon Conway in charge of the London shop. He'll like that,' she said. Puzzled by his shout of laughter, she drew him down on the bed beside her, and felt his fingers tangle in her hair as they kissed.

'Sweetheart,' he said, the old-fashioned endearment coming easily to his lips. 'When I came in here at first you thought I was your father. You *called* me father.' He held her away from him, tired dark eyes searching her face. 'You know he is dead, don't you? You must have heard?'

The little sound she made gave him her answer. Horrified, he cupped her face in his hands, speaking quietly, gently, as if he would take her pain and make it a part of him.

'It was about six months ago. In Australia. It was just a few lines in the paper. Angus Logan, formerly of The Laurels. No details, merely a mention.'

Sliding his hands down over her shoulders, he drew her close. 'You didn't know, did you, love? And I tell you without preparing you. Oh, God, how stupid can a man be? I never dreamed you wouldn't have heard.'

'It doesn't matter.' Lisa's voice came muffled. 'Don't say anything.' She stirred in his arms. 'For a minute, don't say anything. Please. . . .'

Carefully, calmly, Lisa examined her thoughts, her reaction. So he was dead, her beloved father. Dead and gone. The dream she had sometimes had of him sending for her as he lay dying, of *someone* sending for her, would never materialize. She would never see him again, never hear his voice explaining his rejection of her, wiping out in one glorious moment her bewilderment, her long-held sense of loss. She sighed as Jonathan's arms tightened round her.

Jonathan . . . oh, Jonathan. Her father was dead, but Jonathan was here. Lisa lifted her head, no trace of tears on her face.

'It doesn't matter,' she said again. 'Darling, it honestly doesn't matter. If I cry now it will be because I feel you are expecting me to cry.' Her lips curved into a faint smile. 'I'm still a Logan you know, and passing up a chance of high drama doesn't come easily. But I feel *nothing*. Only a fleeting sadness that I'll never talk to my father again.'

In the half-light her eyes were very clear. 'It's taken me a long time to accept the truth of what he did, but now I am able to. My father died for me the day he walked away. My mourning has been over for a long time, and now I know he's never going to come back I can let him go properly.' She smiled a twisted smile. 'I think that's how he would want it to be. Don't you?'

The sadness in her voice almost broke his heart. 'But my father would have been so proud of me, so very pleased for me. The Logan name, you see. I lifted it out of the mud for him, Jonathan. I wish he'd known I'd made it, almost to the top. Is that a conceited way to think?'

'Maybe he *did* know, love. Why not believe that?'

Jonathan answered her tenderly, all teasing gone from his voice.

For a brief moment, the tall shadow of the man with red-gold hair was between them, his memory holding them still. Like a blessing, Lisa thought, letting him go from her, willingly, without reproach or bitter condemnation.

'I'm grateful to you for telling me. It's better that I know,' she whispered.

And that was all. As he held her close, Jonathan's eyes misted over with the tears that should have been hers.

'*I'm* here now,' he whispered.

When the cold northern light crept into the room they were sleeping, the past over and done with, their future promising contentment unhampered at long last by what had gone before.

A Selection of Arrow Books

Prices and other details are liable to change

ARROW BOOKS, BOOKSERVICE BY POST, PO BOX 29, DOUGLAS, ISLE OF MAN, BRITISH ISLES

NAME...

ADDRESS ....

....

....

Please enclose a cheque or postal order made out to Arrow Books Ltd. for the amount due and allow the following for postage and packing.

U.K. CUSTOMERS: Please allow 22p per book to a maximum of £3.00.

B.F.P.O. & EIRE: Please allow 22p per book to a maximum of £3.00.

OVERSEAS CUSTOMERS: Please allow 22p per book.

Whilst every effort is made to keep prices low it is sometimes necessary to increase cover prices at short notice. Arrow Books reserve the right to show new retail prices on covers which may differ from those previously advertised in the text or elsewhere.